THE SIN-EATER

AND OTHER TALES

THE SIN-EATER

THE
WASHER OF THE FORD

AND

OTHER LEGENDARY MORALITIES

BY

"FIONA MACLEOD"
(WILLIAM SHARP)

Fredonia Books
Amsterdam, The Netherlands

The Sin Eater, The Washer of the Ford and Other
Legendary Moralities

by
Fiona Macleod
(William Sharp)

ISBN: 1-4101-0612-8

Reprinted from the 1927 edition

Fredonia Books
Amsterdam, The Netherlands
http://www.fredoniabooks.com

In order to make original editions of historical works
available to scholars at an economical price, this
facsimile of the original edition of 1927 is
reproduced from the best available copy and has
been digitally enhanced to improve legibility, but the
text remains unaltered to retain historical
authenticity.

TO
GEORGE MEREDITH
IN GRATITUDE AND HOMAGE
AND BECAUSE HE IS
PRINCE OF CELTDOM

CONTENTS

The Tales marked * were not included in the original editions of
THE SIN-EATER or of THE WASHER OF THE FORD

THE SIN-EATER

THE WASHER OF THE FORD

vii

Contents

THE SIN-EATER

AND OTHER TALES

"Here are told the stories of these pictures of the imagination, of magic and romance. Yet they were gravely chosen withal and for reasons manifold. . . . What if they be but dreams? 'We are such stuff as dreams are made of.' What if they be but magic and romance? These things are not ancient and dead, but modern and increasing. For wherever a man learns power over Nature, there is Magic: wherever he carries out an ideal into Life, there is Romance."

PATRICK GEDDES,
"The Interpreter."

FROM IONA.

To George Meredith.

Here, where the sound of the falling wave is faintly to be heard, and rather as in the spiral chamber of a shell than in the windy open, I write these few dedicatory words. I am alone here, betwixt sea and sky, for there is no other living thing for the seeing on this bouldered height of Dûn-I except a single blue shadow that dreams slowly athwart the hillside. The bleating of lambs and ewes, the lowing of kine, these come up from the Machar *that lies between the west slopes and the shoreless sea to the west; these ascend as the very smoke of sound. All round the island there is a continuous breathing: deeper and more prolonged on the west, where the sea-heart is; but audible everywhere. This moment, the seals on Soa are putting their breasts against the running tide: for I see a flashing of fins here and there in patches at the north end of the Sound, and already from the ruddy granite shores of the Ross there* is a congregation of seafowl—gannets and guillemots, skuas and herring-gulls, the long-necked northern-diver, the tern, the cormorant. In this sunflood, the waters of the Sound dance their blue bodies and swirl their flashing white hair o' foam; and, as I look, they seem to me like children of the wind and the sunshine, leaping and running in these sungold pastures, with a laughter as sweet against the ears as the voices of children at play.

The joy of life vibrates everywhere. Yet the Weaver doth not sleep, but only dreams. He loves the sun-drowned shadows. They are invisible thus, but they are there, in the sunlight itself. Sure, they may be heard: as, an hour ago, when on my way hither by the Stairway of the Kings—for so sometimes they call here the ancient stones of the mouldered princes of long ago—I heard a mother moaning because of the son that had had to go over-sea and leave her in her old age; and heard also a child sobbing, because of the sorrow of childhood—that sorrow so mysterious, so unfathomable, so for ever incommunicable.

To the little one I spoke. But all she would say, looking up through dark, tear-wet eyes, already filled with the shadow of the burden of woman, was: " Ha mee dūvăchŭs."

"Tha mi Dubhachas !—*I have the gloom*."

4

Ah, that saying! How often I have heard it in the remote Isles! "The Gloom." It is not grief, nor any common sorrow, nor that deep despondency of weariness that comes of accomplished things, too soon, too literally fulfilled. But it is akin to each of these, and involves each. It is, rather, the unconscious knowledge of the lamentation of a race, the unknowing surety of an inheritance of woe.

On the lips of the children of what people, save in the last despoiled sanctuaries of the Gael, could be heard these all too significant sayings: "Tha mi Dubhachas—*I have the gloom*"; "Ma tha sin an Dàn—*If that be ordained, If it be Destiny*"? *Never shall I forget the lisping of this phrase—common from The Seven Hunters, that are the extreme of the Hebrid Isles, to the Rhinns of Islay, and from the Ord of Sutherland to the Mull of Cantyre—never shall I forget the lisping of this phrase in the mouth of a little birdikin of a lass, not more than three years old—a phrase caught, no doubt, as the jay catches the storm-note of the missel-thrush, but not the less significant, not the less piteous ·* "Ma tha sin an Dàn—*If it be Destiny!*"

This is so. And yet not a stone's throw from where I lie, half hidden beneath an over-

5   B

hanging rock, is a Pool of Healing. To this small, black-brown tarn, pilgrims of every generation, for hundreds upon hundreds of years, have come. Solitary, these: not only because the pilgrim to the Fount of Eternal Youth—which, as all Gaeldom knows, is beneath this tarn on Dûn-I of Iona—must fare hither alone, and at dawn, so as to touch the healing water the moment the first sunray quickens it—but solitary, also, because those who go in quest of this Fount of Youth are the dreamers and the Children of Dreams, and these are not many, and few come to this lonely place. Yet, an Isle of Dream, Iona is, indeed. Here the last sun-worshippers bowed before the Rising of God; here Columba and his hymning priests laboured and brooded; and here Oran dreamed beneath the monkish cowl that pagan dream of his. Here, too, the eyes of Fionn and Oisìn, and of many another of the heroic men and women of the Fiànna, lingered often: here the Pict and the Celt bowed beneath the yoke of the Norse pirate, who, too, left his dreams, or rather his strangely beautiful soul-rainbows, as a heritage to the stricken; here, for century after century, the Gael has lived, suffered, joyed, dreamed his impossible, beautiful dream; as here, now, he still lives, still suffers patiently, still dreams, and through all and over all, broods deep against the mystery of things. He is an elemental, among the elemental forces. They have the voices of wind and sea; he has these words of the soul of the Celtic race: "Tha mi Dubhachas—Ma tha sin an Dàn." It is because the Fount of Youth that is upon Dûn-I of Iona is not the only Wellspring of Peace, that the Gael can front "an Dàn" as he does, and can endure his "Dubhachas." Who knows where its tributaries are? They may be in your heart, or in mine, and in a myriad others.

I would that the birds of Angus Ogue might, for once, be changed, not into the kisses of love, but into doves of peace; that they might fly forth into the green world, and be nesled there awhile, crooning their incommunicable song that would yet bring joy and hope.

Why, you may think, do I write these things? It is because I wish to say to you, and to all who may read this book, that in what I have said lies the secret of the Gael. The beauty of the World, the pathos of Life, the gloom, the fatalism, the spiritual glamour—it is out of these, the inheritance of the Gael, that I have wrought these tales.

Well I know that they do not give "a

rounded and complete portrait of the Celt." It is more than likely that I could not do so if I tried, but I have not tried; not even to give " a rounded and complete portrait" of the Gael, who is to the Celtic race what the Franco-Breton is to the French, a creature not with-out blitheness and humour, laughter-loving, indolent, steadfast, gentle, fierce, but above all attuned to elemental passions, to the poetry of nature, and wrought in every nerve and fibre by the gloom and mystery of his environment.

Elsewhere I may give such delineation as I can, and is within my own knowledge, of the manysidedness of the Celt, and even of the in-sular Gael. But in this book, as in Pharais *and* The Mountain Lovers, *I give the life of the Gael in what is, to me, in accord with my own observation and experience, its most poignant characteristics—that is, of course, in certain circumstances, in a particular environ-ment. Almost needless to say, I do not pre-sent such mere sport of Destiny as Neil Ross, the Sin-Eater, or Neil MacCodrum. ("The Dàn-nan-Ròn") as typical Gaels, any more than I would have Gloom Achanna, whose sombre personality colours three of the tales of* Under the Dark Star, *accepted as typical of the perverted Celt. They are true in their degree ; that is all. But I do aver that Alasdair*

*Achanna, the Anointed man; and the fisher-
men of Iona of whom I speak; and Ian Mòr
of the Hills; and others akin to these—are
typical. This, obviously, may be said without
affirming that they are "rounded and complete" types of the Gaelic Celt. Of course
they are nothing of the kind. This, also, may
be said: that they are not typical to the exclu-
sion of other types. Could Ian Mòr be common anywhere? Are there so many poet-
dreamers? Could Ethlenn Stuart or Eilidh
McIan be met with in each strath, on every
hillside? Is the beautiful and one inevitable
phrase to be found on any lips? All men
speak of love; but only you have said the supreme thing of the passion of love; namely,
that Passion is noble strength on fire. You
only have said this. It is individually characteristic; it is racially typical; and yet a thousand poets have come and gone, a million million hearts have beat to this chord, and the
phrase has waited, isolate, for you. Is it
therefore not indicative? Whether with
phrase, or the lilt of a free music, or with man
—there should be no saying that he or it does
not exist because invisible through the dust of
the common highway.*

*It must not be forgotten that "the Celtic
Fringe" is of divers colours. The Armorican,*

9

the Cymric, the Gael of Ireland, and the Scottish Gael are of the same stock, but are not the same people. Even the crofter of Donegal or the fisherman of Clare is no more than an older or younger brother of the Hebridean or the Highlander; certainly they are not twins, of an indistinguishable likeness. Some of my critics, heedless of the complex conditions which differentiate the Irish and the Scottish Celt, complain of the Celtic gloom that dusks the life of the men and women I have tried to draw. That may be just. I wish merely to say that I have not striven to depict the blither Irish Celt. I have sought mainly to express something of what I have seen as paramount, something of " the Celtic Gloom" which, to many Gaels, if not to all, is so distinctive in the remote life of a doomed and passing race. Possibly, though of course it is unlikely they should write save out of fullness of knowledge, those of my critics to whom I allude have dwelt for years among these distant isles, intimate with the speech and mind and daily life and veiled, secretive inner nature of the men and women who inhabit them. I cannot judge, for I do not profess to know every glen in the Highlands, or to have set foot on every one of the Thousand Isles.

A doomed and passing race. Yes, but not wholly so. The Celt has at last reached his horizon. There is no shore beyond. He knows it. This has been the burden of his song since Malvina led the blind Oisìn to his grave by the sea. "Even the Children of Light must go down into darkness." But this apparition of a passing race is no more than the fulfilment of a glorious resurrection before our very eyes. For the genius of the Celtic race stands out now with averted torch, and the light of it is a glory before the eyes, and the flame of it is blown into the hearts of the mightier conquering people. The Celt falls, but his spirit rises in the heart and the brain of the Anglo-Celtic peoples, with whom are the destinies of the generations to come.

Well, this is a far cry, from one small voice on the hill-slope of Dûn-I of Iona, to the clarion-call of the future! But, sure, even in this Isle of Joy, as it seems to-day in this dazzle of golden light and splashing wave, there is all the gloom and all the mystery which lived in the minds of the old seers and bards. Yonder, where that thin spray quivers against the thyme-set cliff, is the Spouting Cave, where to this day the Mar-Tarbh, dread crea-ture of the sea, swims at the full of the tide.

Beyond, out of sight behind these heights, is Port-na-Churaich, where a thousand years ago, Columba landed in his coracle. Here, eastward, is the landing-place for the dead of old, brought hence, out of Christendom, for sacred burial in the Isle of the Saints. All the story of Albyn is here. Iona is the microcosm of Gaeldom.

Last night, about the hour of the sun's going, I lay upon the heights near the Cave, overlooking the Machar—*the sandy, rock-frontiered plain of duneland on the west side of Iona, exposed to the Atlantic. There was neither man nor beast, no living thing to see, save one solitary human creature. This brown, bent, aged man toiled at kelp-burning. I watched the smoke till it merged into the sea-mist that came creeping swiftly out of the north, and down from Dûn-I eastward. At last nothing was visible. The mist shrouded everything. I could hear the dull, rhythmic beat of the waves. That was all. No sound, nothing visible.*

It was, or seemed, a long while before a rapid-thud-thud trampled the heavy air. Then I heard the rush, the stamping and neighing of some young mares, pasturing there, as they raced to and fro, bewildered or mayhap only in play. A glimpse I caught of three, with flying manes and tails ; the others were blurred shadows only. A swirl, and the mist disclosed them : a swirl, and the mist enfolded them again. Then, silence once more.

All at once, though not for a long time thereafter, the mist rose and drifted seaward.

All was as before. The Kelp-Burner still stood, straking the smouldering seaweed. Above him a column ascended, bluely spiral, dusked with gloom of shadow.

The Kelp-Burner : who is he but the Gael of the Isles ? Who but the Celt in his sorrow ? The mist falls and the mist rises. He is there all the same, behind it, part of it : and the column of smoke is the incense out of his longing heart that desires Heaven and Earth, and is dowered only with poverty and pain, hunger and weariness, a little isle of the seas, a great hope, and the love of love.

In that mist I had dreamed a dream. When I woke, these strange, unfamiliar words were upon my lips : Am Dia beo, an Domhan basacha,' an Diomhair Cinne'-Daonna.

Am Dia beo, an Domhan basacha, an Diomhair Cinne'-Daonna : "*The Living God, the dying World, and the mysterious Race of Men.*"

13

I know not what obscure and remote ancestral memory rose, there, to the surface; but I imagined for a moment that the Spirit of the race, and not a solitary human being, found utterance in this so typical saying. It is the sense of an abiding spiritual Presence, of a waning, a perishing World, and of the mystery and incommunicable destiny of Man, which distinguishes the ethical life of the Celt.

"The Three Powers," I murmured, as I rose to leave the place where I was. "These are the three powers: the Living God, the evanescent World, and Man. And somewhere in the darkness—an Dàn, Destiny."

Yes, Ma tha sìn an Dàn; that is where we come to again. It is Destiny, then, that is the Protagonist in the Celtic Drama—the most moving, the most poignant of all that make up the too tragic Tragi-Comedy of human life. And it is Destiny, that sombre Demogorgon of the Gael, whose boding breath, whose menace, whose shadow, glooms so much of the remote life I know, and hence glooms also this book of interpretations—for pages of life must either be interpretative or merely documentary, and these following pages have for the most part been written as by one who repeats, with curious insistence, a haunting, fa-

*miliar, yet ever wild and remote air, whose
obscure meanings he would fain reiterate, in-
terpret.*

*You, of all living writers, can best under-
stand this; for in you the Celtic genius burns
a pure flame. True, the Cymric blood that is
in you moves to a more lightsome measure
than that of the Scottish Gael, and the acci-
dents of temperament and life have combined
to make you a writer for great peoples rather
than for a people. But though England ap-
propriate you as her son, and all the Anglo-
Celtic peoples are the heritors of your genius,
we claim your brain. Now, we are a scattered
band. The Breton's eyes are slowly turning
from the sea, and slowly his ears are forgetting the whisper of the wind around Menhir
and Dolmen. The Cornishman has lost his
language, and there is now no bond between
him and his ancient kin The Manxman has
ever been the mere yeoman of the Celtic chivalry; but even his rude dialect perishes year by
year. In Wales, a great tradition survives; in
Ireland, a supreme tradition fades through
sunset-hued horizons to the edge o' dark; in
Celtic Scotland, a passionate regret, a despairing love and longing, narrows yearly before a
bastard utilitarianism which is almost as great*

*a curse to our despoiled land as Calvinistic
theology has been and is.*

*But with you, and others not less enthusi-
astic if less brilliant, we need not despair.
"The Englishman may trample down the
heather," say the shepherds of Argyle, "but
he cannot trample down the wind."*

The Sin-Eater

SIN.

*Taste this bread, this substance; tell me
Is it bread or flesh?*

[*The* SENSES *approach.*]

THE SMELL.

*Its smell
Is the smell of bread.*

SIN.

*Touch, come. Why tremble?
Say what's this thou touchest?*

THE TOUCH.

Bread.

SIN.

*Sight, declare what thou discernest
In this object.*

THE SIGHT.

Bread alone.

[CALDERON : *Los Encantos de la Culpa.*

A wet wind out of the south mazed and
moaned through the sea-mist that hung over
the Ross. In all the bays and creeks was a
continuous weary lapping of water. There
was no other sound anywhere.

17

Thus was it at daybreak; it was thus at noon; thus was it now in the darkening of the day. A confused thrusting and falling of sounds through the silence betokened the hour of the setting. Curlews wailed in the mist; on the seething limpet-covered rocks the skuas and terns screamed, or uttered hoarse rasping cries. Ever and again the prolonged note of the oyster-catcher shrilled against the air, as an echo flying blindly along a blank wall of cliff. Out of weedy places, wherein the tide sobbed with long gurgling moans, came at intervals the barking of a seal.

Inland by the hamlet of Contullich, there is a reedy tarn called the Loch-a-chaoruinn.[1] By the shores of this mournful water a man moved. It was a slow, weary walk that of the man Neil Ross. He had come from Duninch, thirty miles to the eastward, and had not rested foot, nor eaten, nor had word of man or woman since his going west an hour after dawn.

At the bend of the loch nearest the clachan he came upon an old woman carrying peat. To his reiterated question as to where he was, and if the tarn were Feur-Lochan above

---

[1] *Contullich* *i.e.*, Ceann-nan-tulaich, "the end of the hillocks." *Loch-a-chaoruinn* means the loch of the rowan-trees.

Fionnaphort, that is, on the straight of Iona on the west side of the Ross of Mull, she did not at first make any answer. The rain trickled down her withered brown face, over which the thin grey locks hung limply. It was only in the deep-set eyes that the flame of life still glimmered, though that dimly.

The man had used the English when first he spoke, but as though mechanically. Supposing that he had not been understood, he repeated his question in the Gaelic.

After a minute's silence the old woman answered in the native tongue, but only to put a question in return.

"I am thinking it is a long time since you have been in Iona?"

The man stirred uneasily.

"And why is that, mother?" he asked, in a weak voice hoarse with damp and fatigue; "how is it you will be knowing that I have been in Iona at all?"

"Because I knew your kith and kin there, Neil Ross."

"I have not been hearing that name, mother, for many a long year. And as for the old face o' you, it is unbeknown to me."

"I was at the naming of you, for all that. Well do I remember the day that Silis Macallum gave you birth; and I was at the house on the croft of Ballyrona when Murtagh Ross, that was your father, laughed. It was an ill-laughing, that."

"I am knowing it. The curse of God on him!"

"'Tis not the first, nor the last, though the grass is on his head three years agone now."

"You that know who I am will be knowing that I have no kith or kin now on Iona?"

"Ay, they are all under grey stone or running wave. Donald your brother, and Murtagh your next brother, and little Silis, and your mother Silis herself and your two brothers of your father, Angus and Ian Macullum, and your father Murtagh Ross, and his lawful childless wife Dionaid, and his sister Anna, one and all they lie beneath the green wave or in the brown mould. It is said there is a curse upon all who live at Ballyrona. The owl builds now in the rafters, and it is the big sea-rat that runs across the fireless hearth."

"It is there I am going."

"The foolishness is on you, Neil Ross."

"Now it is that I am knowing who you are. It is old Sheen Macarthur I am speaking to."

"*Tha mise*—it is I."

"And you will be alone now, too, I am thinking, Sheen ? "

"I am alone. God took my three boys at the one fishing ten years ago, and before there was moonrise in the blackness of my heart my man went. It was after the drowning of Anndra that my croft was taken from me. Then I crossed the Sound, and shared with my widow sister, Elsie McVurie, till *she* went ; and then the two cows had to go ; and I had no rent ; and was old."

In the silence that followed, the rain dribbled from the sodden bracken and dripping loneroid. Big tears rolled slowly down the deep lines on the face of Sheen. Once there was a sob in her throat, but she put her shaking hand to it, and it was still.

Neil Ross shifted from foot to foot. The ooze in that marshy place squelched with each restless movement he made. Beyond them a plover wheeled a blurred splatch in the mist, crying its mournful cry over and over and over.

It was a pitiful thing to hear ; ah, bitter loneliness, bitter patience of poor old women. That he knew well. But he was too weary, and his heart was nigh full of its own burthen. The words could not come to his lips. But at last he spoke.

"*Tha mo chridhe goirt*," he said with tears in his voice, as he put his hand on her bent shoulder; "my heart is sore."

She put up her old face against his.

"'*S tha e ruidhinn mo chridhe*," she whispered—"It is touching my heart you are."

After that they walked on slowly through the dripping mist, each dumb and brooding deep.

"Where will you be staying this night?" asked Sheen suddenly, when they had traversed a wide boggy stretch of land; adding, as by an afterthought—"ah, it is asking you were if the tarn there was Feur-Lochan. No; it is Loch-a-chaoruinn, and the clachan that is near is Contullich."

"Which way?"

"Yonder; to the right."

"And you are not going there?"

"No. I am going to the steading of Andrew Blair. Maybe you are for knowing it? It is called the Baile-na-Chlais-nambuid-heag."[1]

"I do not remember. But it is remembering a Blair I am. He was Adam the son of Adam the son of Robert. He and my father did many an ill deed together.

"Ay, to the Stones be it said. Sure, now, there was even till this weary day no man or

[1] The farm in the hollow of the yellow flowers.

woman who had a good word for Adam Blair."

"And why that—why till this day?"

"It is not yet the third hour since he went into the silence."

Neil Ross uttered a sound like a stifled curse. For a time he trudged wearily on.

"Then I am too late," he said at last, but as though speaking to himself. "I had hoped to see him face to face again, and curse him between the eyes. It was he who made Murtagh Ross break his troth to my mother, and marry that other woman, barren at that, God be praised! And they say ill of him, do they?"

"Ay, it is evil that is upon him. This crime and that, God knows: and the shadow of murder on his brow and in his eyes. Well, well, 'tis ill to be speaking of a man in corpse, and that near by. 'Tis Himself only that knows, Neil Ross."

"Maybe ay, and maybe no. But where is it that I can be sleeping this night, Sheen Macarthur?"

"They will not be taking a stranger at the farm this night of the nights, I am thinking. There is no place else, for seven miles yet, when there is the clachan before you will be coming to Fionnaphort. There is the warm byre, Neil my man, or if you can bide by my peats you may rest and welcome, though there is no bed for you, and no food either save some of the porridge that is over."

"And that will do well enough for me, Sheen, and Himself bless you for it."

And so it was.

After old Sheen Macarthur had given the wayfarer food—poor food at that, but welcome to one nigh starved, and for the heartsome way it was given, and because of the thanks to God that was upon it before even spoon was lifted—she told him a lie. It was the good lie of tender love.

"Sure now, after all, Neil my man," she said, "it is sleeping at the farm I ought to be, for Maisie Macdonald, the wise-woman, will be sitting by the corpse, and there will be none to keep her company. It is there I must be going, and if I am weary, there is a good bed for me just beyond the dead-board, which I am not minding at all. So if it is tired you are sitting by the peats, lie down on my bed there, and have the sleep, and God be with you."

With that she went, and soundlessly, for Neil Ross was already asleep, where he sat on an upturned *claar* with his elbows on his knees and his flame-lit face in his hands.

The rain had ceased ; but the mist still hung over the land, though in thin veils now, and these slowly drifting seaward. Sheen stepped wearily along the stony path that led from her bothy to the farm-house. She stood still once, the fear upon her, for she saw three or four blurred yellow gleams moving beyond her eastward along the dyke. She knew what they were—the corpse-lights that on the night of death go between the bier and the place of burial. More than once she had seen them before the last hour, and by that token had known the end to be near.

Good Catholic that she was, she crossed herself and took heart. Then, muttering—

> "*Crois nan nooi aingeal leam*
> *'O mhullach mo chinn*
> *Gu craican mo bhonn,*'

> "The cross of the nine angels be about me,
> From the top of my head
> To the soles of my feet,"

she went on her way fearlessly.

When she came to the White House she entered by the milk-shed that was between the byre and the kitchen. At the end of it was a paved place, with washing-tubs. At one of these stood a girl that served in the house ; an ignorant lass called Jessie McFall, out of Oban. She was ignorant, indeed, not to know that to wash clothes with a newly dead body near by was an ill thing to do. Was it not a matter for the knowing that the corpse could hear, and might rise up in the night and clothe itself in a clean white shroud ?

She was still speaking to the lassie when Maisie Macdonald, the deid-watcher, opened the door of the room behind the kitchen, to see who it was that was come. The two old women nodded silently. It was not till Sheen was in the closed room, midway in which something covered with a sheet lay on a board, that any word was spoken.

" *Duit sìth mòr*, Beann Macdonald."

" And deep peace to you, too, Sheen ; and to him that is there."

" *Och, ochone, mise 'n diugh;* 'tis a dark hour this."

" Ay, it is bad. Will you have been hearing or seeing anything ? "

" Well, as for that, I am thinking I saw lights moving betwixt here and the green place over there."

" The corpse-lights ? "

" Well, it is calling them that they are,"

" I *thought* they would be out. And I have been hearing the noise of the planks—the cracking of the boards, you know, that will be used for the coffin to-morrow."

A long silence followed. The old women had seated themselves by the corpse, their cloaks over their heads. The room was fireless, and it was lit only by a tall wax death-candle, kept against the hour of the going.

At last Sheen began swaying slowly to and fro, crooning low the while. "I would not be for doing that, Sheen Macarthur," said the deid-watcher, in a low voice, but meaningly; adding, after a moment's pause, "*the mice have all left the house.*"

Sheen sat upright, a look half of terror, half of awe in her eyes.

"God save the sinful soul that is hiding," she whispered.

Well she knew what Maisie meant. If the soul of the dead be a lost soul it knows its doom. The house of death is the house of sanctuary. But before the dawn that follows the death-night the soul must go forth, whosoever or whatsoever wait for it in the homeless, shelterless plains of air around and beyond. If it be well with the soul, it need have no fear; if it be not ill with the soul, it may fare forth with surety; but if it be ill with the soul, ill will the going be. Thus is it that the spirit of an evil man cannot stay and yet dare not go ; and so it strives to hide itself in secret places anywhere, in dark channels and blind walls. And the wise creatures that live near man smell the terror, and flee. Maisie repeated the saying of Sheen ; then, after a silence, added :

"Adam Blair will not lie in his grave for a year and a day, because of the sins that are upon him. And it is knowing that, they are, here. He will be the Watcher of the Dead for a year and a day."

"Ay, sure, there will be dark prints in the dawn-dew over yonder."

Once more the old women relapsed into silence. Through the night there was a sighing sound. It was not the sea, which was too far off to be heard save in a day of storm. The wind it was, that was dragging itself across the sodden moors like a wounded thing, moaning and sighing.

Out of sheer weariness, Sheen twice rocked forward from her stool, heavy with sleep. At last Maisie led her over to the niche-bed opposite, and laid her down there, and waited till the deep furrows in the face relaxed somewhat, and the thin breath laboured slow across the fallen jaw.

"Poor old woman," she muttered, heedless of her own grey hairs and greyer years ; "a bitter bad thing it is to be old, old and weary. 'Tis the sorrow that ; God keep the pain of it."

As for herself she did not sleep at all that night, but sat between the living and the dead, with her plaid shrouding her. Once, when Sheen gave a low, terrified scream in her sleep, she rose, and in a loud voice cried "*Sheeach-ad!* Away with you!" And with that she lifted the shroud from the dead man, and took the pennies off the eyelids, and lifted each lid ; then, staring into these filmed wells, muttered an ancient incantation that would compel the soul of Adam Blair to leave the spirit of Sheen alone, and return to the cold corpse that was its coffin till the wood was ready.

The dawn came at last. Sheen slept, and Adam Blair slept a deeper sleep, and Maisie stared out of her wan weary eyes against the red and stormy flares of light that came into the sky.

When, an hour after sunrise, Sheen Mac-arthur reached her bothy, she found Neil Ross, heavy with slumber, upon her bed. The fire was not out, though no flame or spark was visible but she stooped and blew at the heart of the peats till the redness came, and once it came it grew. Having done this, she kneeled and said a rune of the morning, and after that a prayer, and then a prayer for the poor man Neil. She could pray no more because of the tears. She rose and put the meal and water into the pot, for the porridge to be ready against his awaking. One of the hens that was there came and pecked at her ragged skirt. "Poor beastie," she said, "sure, that will just be the way I am pulling at the white robe of the Mother o' God. 'Tis a bit meal for you, cluckie, and for me a healing hand upon my tears—O, och, ochone, the tears, the tears!"

It was not till the third hour after sunrise of that bleak day in the winter of the winters that Neil Ross stirred and arose. He ate in silence. Once he said that he smelled the snow coming out of the north. Sheen said no word at all.

After the porridge, he took his pipe, but there was no tobacco. All that Sheen had was the pipeful she kept against the gloom of the Sabbath. It was her one solace in the long weary week. She gave him this, and held a burning peat to his mouth, and hungered over the thin, rank smoke that curled upward.

It was within half an hour of noon that, after an absence, she returned.

"Not between you and me, Neil Ross," she began abruptly, "but just for the asking, and

30

what is beyond.   Is it any money you are having upon you?"

"No."

"Nothing?"

"Nothing."

"Then how will you be getting across to Iona? It is seven long miles to Fionnaphort, and bitter cold at that, and you will be needing food, and then the ferry, the ferry across the Sound, you know."

"Ay, I know."

"What would you do for a silver piece, Neil my man?"

"You have none to give me, Sheen Macarthur, and if you had, it would not be taking it I would."

"Would you kiss a dead man for a crown-piece—a crown-piece of five good shillings?"

Neil Ross stared.   Then he sprang to his feet.

"It is Adam Blair you are meaning, woman! God curse him in death now that he is no longer in life!"

Then, shaking and trembling, he sat down again, and brooded against the dull red glow of the peats.

But, when he rose, in the last quarter before noon, his face was white.

"The dead are dead, Sheen Macarthur.

They can know or do nothing. I will do it. It is willed. Yes, I am going up to the house there. And now I am going from here. God Himself has my thanks to you, and my blessing too. They will come back to you. It is not forgetting you I will be. Good-bye."

"Good-bye, Neil, son of the woman that was my friend. A south wind to you! Go up by the farm. In the front of the house you will see what you will be seeing. Maisie Macdonald will be there. She will tell you what's for the telling. There is no harm in it, sure; sure, the dead are dead. It is praying for you I will be, Neil Ross. Peace to you!"

"And to you, Sheen."

And with that the man went.

When Neil Ross reached the byres of the farm in the wide hollow, he saw two figures standing as though awaiting him, but each alone and unseen of the other. In front of the house was a man he knew to be Andrew Blair; behind the milk-shed was a woman he guessed to be Maisie Macdonald.

It was the woman he came upon first.

"Are you the friend of Sheen Macarthur?" she asked in a whisper, as she beckoned him to the doorway

"I am."

32

" I am knowing no names, or anything. And no one here will know you, I am thinking. So do the thing, and begone."

"There is no harm to it ? "

" None."

" It will be a thing often done, is it not ? "

" Ay, sure."

" And the evil does not abide ? "

" No. The—the—person—the person takes them away, and—"

" *Them?* "

" For sure, man ! Them—the sins of the corpse. He takes them away, and are you for thinking God would let the innocent suffer for the guilty ? No—the person—the Sin-Eater, you know—takes them away on himself, and one by one the air of heaven washes them away till he, the Sin-Eater, is clean and whole as before."

" But if it is a man you hate—if it is a corpse that is the corpse of one who has been a curse and a foe—if—"

" *Sst !* Be still now with your foolishness. It is only an idle saying, I am thinking. Do it, and take the money, and go. It will be hell enough for Adam Blair, miser as he was, if he is for knowing that five good shillings of his money are to go to a passing tramp, because of an old ancient silly tale."

Neil Ross laughed low at that. It was for pleasure to him.

"Hush wi' ye! Andrew Blair is waiting round there. Say that I have sent you round, as I have neither bite nor bit to give."

Turning on his heel Neil walked slowly round to the front of the house. A tall man was there, gaunt and brown, with hairless face and lank brown hair, but with eyes cold and grey as the sea.

"Good day to you an' good faring. Will you be passing this way to anywhere?"

"Health to you. I am a stranger here. It is on my way to Iona I am. But I have the hunger upon me. There is not a brown bit in my pocket. I asked at the door there, near the byres. The woman told me she could give me nothing—not a penny even, worse luck—nor, for that, a drink of warm milk. 'Tis a sore land this."

"You have the Gaelic of the Isles. Is it from Iona you are?"

"It is from the Isles of the West I come."

"From Tiree?—from Coll?"

"No."

"From the Long Island—or from Uist— or maybe from Benbecula?"

"No."

34

" Oh well, sure it is no matter to me. But may I be asking your name ? "

" Macallum."

" Do you know there is a death here, Macallum ? "

" If I didn't, I would know it now, because of what lies yonder."

Mechanically, Andrew Blair looked round. As he knew, a rough bier was there, that was made of a dead-board laid upon three milking-stools. Beside it was a *claar*, a small tub to hold potatoes. On the bier was a corpse, covered with a canvas sheeting that looked like a sail.

" He was a worthy man, my father," began the son of the dead man, slowly ; " but he had his faults, like all of us. I might even be saying that he had his sins, to the Stones be it said. You will be knowing, Macallum, what is thought among the folk—that a stranger, passing by, may take away the sins of the dead, and that too without any hurt whatever —any hurt whatever."

" Ay, sure."

" And you will be knowing what is done ? "

" Ay."

" With the Bread—and the Water——"

" Ay."

" It is a small thing to do. It is a Christian

35

thing. I would be doing it myself, and that gladly ; but the—the—passer-by who——"

" It is talking of the Sin-Eater you are ? "

" Yes, yes, for sure. The Sin-Eater as he is called—and a good Christian act it is, for all that the ministers and the priests make a frowning at it—the Sin-Eater must be a stranger. He must be a stranger, and should know nothing of the dead man, above all bear him no grudge."

At that, Neil Ross's eyes lightened for a moment.

" And why that ? "

" Who knows ? I have heard this, and I have heard that. If the Sin-Eater was having the dead man he could take the sins and fling them into the sea and they would be changed into demons of the air that would harry the flying soul till Judgment-Day."

" And how would that thing be done ? "

The man spake with flashing eyes and parted lips, the breath coming swift. Andrew Blair looked at him suspiciously, and hesitated, before in a cold voice he spoke again.

" That is all folly, I am thinking, Macallum. Maybe it is all folly, the whole of it. But see here, I have no time to be talking with you. If you will take the bread and the water

you shall have a good meal if you want it, and
—and—yes, look you, my man, I will be giving
you a shilling too, for luck."

"I will have no meal in this house, Anndra
mhic Adam ; nor will I do this thing unless
you will be giving me two silver half-crowns.
That is the sum I must have, or no other."

"Two half-crowns ! Why, man, for one
half-crown——"

"Then be eating the sins o' your father
yourself, Andrew Blair ! It is going I am."

"Stop, man ! Stop, Macallum. See here :
I will be giving you what you ask."

"So be it. Is the—are you ready ? "

"Ay, come this way."

With that the two men turned, and moved
slowly toward the bier.

In the doorway of the house stood a man
and two women ; farther in, a woman ; and
at the window to the left the serving-wench,
Jessie McFall, and two men of the farm. Of
those in the doorway, the man was Peter, the
half-witted youngest brother of Andrew Blair ;
the taller and older woman was Catreen, the
widow of Adam the second brother ; and the
thin slight woman, with staring eyes and
drooping mouth, was Muireall, the wife of
Andrew. The old woman, behind these, was
Maisie Macdonald.

Andrew Blair stooped and took a saucer out of the *claar*. This he put upon the covered breast of the corpse. He stooped again, and brought forth a thick square piece of new-made bread. That also he placed upon the breast of the corpse. Then he stooped again, and with that he emptied a spoonful of salt alongside the bread.

" I must see the corpse," said Neil Ross, simply.

" It is not needful, Macallum."

" I must be seeing the corpse, I tell you—and for that, too, the bread and the water should be on the naked breast."

" No, no, man, it—"

But here a voice, that of Maisie the wise-woman, came upon them, saying that the man was right, and that the eating of the sins should be done in that way and no other.

With an ill grace the son of the dead man drew back the sheeting. Beneath it the corpse was in a clean white shirt, a death-gown long ago prepared, that covered him from his neck to his feet, and left only the dusky, yellowish face exposed.

While Andrew Blair unfastened the shirt, and placed the saucer and the bread and the salt on the breast, the man beside him stood staring fixedly on the frozen features of the corpse. The new laird had to speak to him twice before he heard.

"I am ready. And you, now? What is it you are muttering over against the lips of the dead?"

"It is giving him a message I am. There is no harm in that, sure?"

"Keep to your own folk, Macallum. You are from the West you say, and we are from the North. There can be no messages between you and a Blair of Strathmore, no messages for *you* to be giving."

"He that lies here knows well the man to whom I am sending a message—" and at this response Andrew Blair scowled darkly. He would fain have sent the man about his business, but he feared he might get no other.

"It is thinking I am that you are not a Macallum at all. I know all of that name in Mull, Iona, Skye, and the near isles. What will the name of your naming be, and of your father, and of his place?"

Whether he really wanted an answer, or whether he sought only to divert the man from his procrastination, his question had a satisfactory result.

"Well, now, it's ready I am, Anndra mhic Adam."

With that, Adam Blair stooped once more,

and from the *claar* brought a small jug of water. From this he filled the saucer.

"You know what to say and what to do, Macallum."

There was not one there who did not have a shortened breath because of the mystery that was now before them, and the fearfulness of it. Neil Ross drew himself up, erect, stiff, with white, drawn face. All who waited, save Adam Blair, thought that the moving of his lips was because of the prayer that was slipping upon them, like the last lapsing of the ebb-tide. But Blair was watching him closely, and knew that it was no prayer which stole out against the blank air that was around the dead.

Slowly Neil Ross extended his right arm. He took a pinch of the salt and put it in the saucer, then took another pinch and sprinkled it upon the bread. His hand shook for a moment as he touched the saucer. But there was no shaking as he raised it toward his lips, or when he held it before him when he spoke.

"With this water that has salt in it, and has lain on thy corpse, O Adam mhic Anndra mhic Adam Mòr, I drink away all the evil that is upon thee." There was throbbing silence while he paused—"and may it be upon me, and not upon thee, if with this water it cannot flow away."

Thereupon he raised the saucer and passed it thrice round the head of the corpse sunways, and having done this, lifted it to his lips and drank as much as his mouth would hold. Thereafter he poured the remnant over his left hand, and let it trickle to the ground. Then he took the piece of bread. Thrice, too, he passed it round the head of the corpse sunways.

He turned and looked at the man by his side, then at the others who watched him with beating hearts.

With a loud clear voice he took the sins.

"*Thoir dhomh do ciontachd, O Adam mhic Anndra mhic Adam Mòr!* Give me thy sins *to* take away from thee! Lo, now, as I stand here, I break this bread that has lain on thee in corpse, and I am eating it, I am, and in that eating I take upon me the sins of thee, O man that was alive and is now white with the stillness!"

Thereupon Neil Ross broke the bread and ate of it, and took upon himself the sins of Adam Blair that was dead. It was a bitter swallowing, that. The remainder of the bread he crumbled in his hand, and threw it on the ground, and trod upon it. Andrew Blair gave a sigh of relief. His cold eyes lightened with malice.

41

"Be off with you, now, Macullam. We are wanting no tramps at the farm here, and perhaps you had better not be trying to get work this side Iona, for it is known as the Sin-Eater you will be, and that won't be for the helping, I am thinking! There: there are the two half-crowns for you—and may they bring you no harm, you that are *Scapegoat* now!"

The Sin-Eater turned at that, and stared like a hill-bull. *Scapegoat!* Ay, that's what he was. Sin-Eater, scapegoat! Was he not, too, another Judas, to have sold for silver that which was not for the selling? No, no, for sure Maisie Macdonald could tell him the rune that would serve for the easing of this burden. He would soon be quit of it.

Slowly he took the money, turned it over, and put it in his pocket.

"I am going, Andrew Blair," he said quietly; "I am going now. I will not say to him that is there in the silence, *A chuid do Pharas da!*—nor will I say to you, *Gu'n gleidheadh Dia thu*—nor will I say to this dwelling that is the home of thee and thine, *Gu'n beannaicheadh Dia an tigh!*" [1]

[1] (1) *A chuid do Pharas da!* "His share of heaven be his." (2) *Gu'n gleidheadh Dia thu!* "May God preserve you." (3) *Gu'n beannaicheadh Dia an tigh!* "God's blessing on this house."

Here there was a pause. All listeneᴅ. Andrew Blair shifted uneasily, the furtive eyes of him going this way and that like a ferret in the grass.

"But, Andrew Blair, I will say this ; when you fare abroad, *Droch caoidh ort !* and when you go upon the water, *Gaoth gun direadh ort!* Ay, ay, Anndra mhic Adam, *Dia ad aghaidh 's ad aodann—agus bas dunach ort! Dhonas's dholas ort, agus leat-sa !*" [1]

The bitterness of these words was like snow in June upon all there. They stood amazed. None spoke. No one moved.

Neil Ross turned upon his heel, and with a bright light in his eyes walked away from the dead and the living. He went by the byres, whence he had come. Andrew Blair remained where he was, now glooming at the corpse, now biting his nails and staring at the damp sods at his feet.

When Neil reached the end of the milk-shed he saw Maisie Macdonald there, waiting.

"These were ill sayings of yours, Neil

[1] (1) *Droch caoidh ort!* "May a fatal accident happen to you" (lit. "Bad moan on you"), (2) *Gaoth gun direadh ort!* "May you drift to your drowning" (lit. "Wind without direction on you"). (3) *Dia ad aghaidh, etc!* "God against thee and in thy face—and may a death of woe be yours. Evil and sorrow to thee and thine!"

Ross," she said in a low voice, so that she might not be overheard from the house.

"So, it is knowing me you are."

"Sheen Macarthur told me."

"I have good cause."

"That is a true word. I know it."

"Tell me this thing. What is the rune that is said for the throwing into the sea of the sins of the dead? See here, Maisie Macdonald. There is no money of that man that I would carry a mile with me. Here it is. It is yours, if you will tell me that rune."

Maisie took the money hesitatingly. Then, stooping, she said slowly the few lines of the old, old rune.

"Will you be remembering that?"

"It is not forgetting it I will be, Maisie."

"Wait a moment. There is some warm milk here."

With that she went, and then, from within, beckoned to him to enter.

"There is no one here, Neil Ross. Drink the milk."

He drank: and while he did so she drew a leather pouch from some hidden place in her dress.

"And now I have this to give you."

She counted out ten pennies and two farthings.

44

"It is all the coppers I have. You are welcome to them. Take them, friend of my friend. They will give you the food you need, and the ferry across the Sound."

"I will do that, Maisie Macdonald, and thanks to you. It is not forgetting it I will be, nor you, good woman. And now, tell me: Is it safe that I am? He called me a 'scape-goat,' he, Andrew Blair! Can evil touch me between this and the sea?"

"You must go to the place where the evil was done to you and yours; and that, I know, is on the west side of Iona. Go, and God preserve you. But here, too, is a *sian* that will be for the safety."

Thereupon with swift mutterings she said this charm: an old, familiar *sian* against Sudden Harm:

"*Sian a chuir Moire air Mac ort,*
  Sian ro' marbhadh, sian ro' lot ort,
  Sian eadar a' chlioch 's a' ghlun,
  Sian nan Tri ann an aon ort,
  O mhullach do chinn gu bonn do chois ort:
  Sian seachd eadar a h-aon ort,,
  Sian seachd eadar a dha ort,
  Sian seaehd eadar a tri ort,
  Sian seachd eadar a ceithir ort,
  Sian seachd eadar a coig ort,
  Sian seachd eadar a sia ort,
  Sian seachd paidir nan seach paidir dol deiseil ri
diugh narach ort, ga do ghleidheadh bho bheud 's bho
mhi-thapadh !"

45

Scarcely had she finished before she heard heavy steps approaching.

"Away with you," she whispered ; repeating in a loud angry tone, "Away with you ! *Seachad ! Seachad !* "

And with that Neil Ross slipped from the milk-shed and crossed the yard, and was behind the byres, before Andrew Blair, with sullen mien and swift wild eyes, strode from the house.

It was with a grim smile on his face that Neil tramped down the wet heather till he reached the high road, and fared thence as through a marsh because of the rains there had been.

For the first mile he thought of the angry mind of the dead man, bitter at paying of the silver. For the second mile he thought of the evil that had been wrought for him and his. For the third mile he pondered over all that he had heard, and done, and taken upon him that day.

Then he sat down upon a broken granite-heap by the way, and brooded deep, till one hour went, and then another, and the third was upon him.

A man driving two calves came toward him out of the west. He did not hear or see. The man stopped, spoke again. Neil gave no answer. The drover shrugged his shoulders, hesitated, and walked slowly on, often looking back.

An hour later a shepherd came by the way he himself had tramped. He was a tall, gaunt man with a squint. The small pale-blue eyes glittered out of a mass of red hair that almost covered his face. He stood still opposite Neil, and leaned on his *cromak*.

"*Latha math leat*," he said at last, "I wish you good day."

Neil glanced at him, but did not speak.

"What is your name, for I seem to know you?"

But Neil had already forgotten him. The shepherd took out his snuff-mull, helped himself, and handed the mull to the lonely wayfarer. Neil mechanically helped himself.

"*Am bheil thu 'dol do Fhionphort?*" cried the shepherd again, "are you going to Fionnaphort?"

"*Tha mise 'dol a dh' I-challum-chille*," Neil answered in a low, weary voice, and as a man adream, "I am on my way to Iona."

"I am thinking I know now who you are. You are the man Macallum."

Neil looked, but did not speak. His eyes dreamed against what the other could not see or know. The shepherd called angrily to his

47

dogs to keep the sheep from straying ; then, with a resentful air, turned to his victim.

"You are a silent man for sure, you are. I'm hoping it is not the curse upon you already."

"What curse ?"

"Ah, *that* has brought the wind against the mist ! I was thinking so ! "

"What curse ?"

"You are the man that was the Sin-Eater over there ?"

"Ay."

"The man Macallum ?"

"Ay."

"Strange it is, but three days ago I saw you in Tobermory, and heard you give your name as Neil Ross, to an Iona man that was there."

"Well ?"

"Oh, sure, it is nothing to me. But they say the Sin-Eater should not be a man with a hidden lump in his pack." [1]

"Why ?"

"For the dead know, and are content. There is no shaking off my sins, then : for that man."

"It is a lie."

[1] *i.e.* with a criminal secret, or an undiscovered crime.

"Maybe ay, and maybe no."

"Well, have you more to be saying to me? I am obliged to you for your company, but it is not needing it I am, though no offence."

"Och, man, there's no offence between you and me. Sure, there's Iona in me, too, for the father of my father married a woman that was the granddaughter of Tomais Macdonald, who was a fisherman there. No, no, it is rather warning you I would be."

"And for what?"

"Well, well, just because of that laugh I heard about."

"What laugh?"

"The laugh of Adam Blair that is dead."

Neil Ross stared, his eyes large and wild. He leaned a little forward. No word came from him. The look that was on his face was the question.

"Yes: it was this way. Sure, the telling of it is just as I heard it. After you ate the sins of Adam Blair, the people there brought out the coffin. When they were putting him into it, he was as stiff as a sheep dead in the snow—and just like that, too, with his eyes wide open. Well, some one saw you trampling the heather down the slope that is in front of the house, and said, 'It is the Sin-Eater!' With that, Andrew Blair sneered, and said,

'Ay, 'tis the scapegoat he is!' Then, after a while, he went on: 'The Sin-Eater they call him; ay, just so; and a bitter good bargain it is, too, if all's true that's thought true!'—and with that he laughed, and then his wife that was behind him laughed, and then—"

"Weel, what then?"

"Well, 'tis Himself that hears and knows if it is true! But this is the thing I was told: After that laughing there was a stillness, and a dread. For all there saw that the corpse had turned its head and was looking after you as you went down the heather. Then, Neil Ross, if that be your true name, Adam Blair that was dead put up his white face against the sky, and laughed."

At this, Ross sprang to his feet with a gasping sob.

"It is a lie, that thing," he cried, shaking his fist at the shepherd, "It is a lie."

"It is no lie. And by the same token, Andrew Blair shrank back white and shaking, and his woman had the swoon upon her, and who knows but the corpse might have come to life again had it not been for Maisie Macdonald, the deid watcher, who clapped a handful of salt on his eyes, and tilted the coffin so that the bottom of it slid forward and so let the whole fall flat on the ground, with Adam

Blair in it sideways, and as likely as not cursing and groaning, as his wont was, for the
hurt both to his old bones and his old ancient
dignity."

Ross glared at the man as though the madness was upon him. Fear, and horror, and
fierce rage, swung him now this way and now
that.

" What will the name of you be, shepherd ? "
he stuttered huskily.

" It is Eachainn Gilleasbuig I am to our-
selves, and the English of that for those who
have no Gaelic is Hector Gillespie ; and I am
Eachainn mac Ian mac Alasdair, of Srath-
sheean, that is where Sutherland lies against
Ross."

" Then take this thing, and that is, the curse
of the Sin-Eater ! And a bitter bad thing may
it be upon you and yours ! "

And with that Neil the Sin-Eater flung his
hand up into the air, and then leaped past the
shepherd, and a minute later was running
through the frightened sheep, with his head
low, and a white foam on his lips, and his eyes
red with blood as a seal's that has the death-
wound on it.

On the third day of the seventh month from
that day, Aulay Macneil, coming into Ballie-

more of Iona from the west side of the island,
said to old Ronald MacCormick, that was the
father of his wife, that he had seen Neil Ross
again, and that he was "absent"—for though
he had spoken to him, Neil would not answer,
but only gloomed at him from the wet weedy
rock where he sat.

The going back of the man had loosed every
tongue that was in Iona. When, too, it was
known that he was wrought in some terrible
way, if not actually mad, the islanders whispered that it was because of the sins of Adam
Blair. Seldom or never now did they speak
of him by his name, but simply as "The Sin-
Eater." The thing was not so rare as to cause
this strangeness, nor did many (and perhaps
none did) think that the sins of the dead ever
might or could abide with the living who had
merely done a good Christian, charitable
thing. But there was a reason.

Not long after Neil Ross had come again
to Iona, and had settled down in the ruined
roofless house on the croft of Ballyrona, just
like a fox or a wild-cat, as the saying was,
he was given fishing-work to do by Aulay
Macneil, who lived at Ard-an-teine, at the
rocky north end of the *Màchar* or plain that
is on the west Atlantic coast of the island.

One moonlit night, either the seventh or

the ninth after the earthing of Adam Blair at his own place in the Ross, Aulay Macneil saw Neil Ross steal out of the shadow of Bally-rona and make for the sea. Macneil was there, by the rocks, mending a lobster-creel. He had gone there because of the sadness. Well, when he saw the Sin-Eater he watched.

Neil crept from rock to rock till he reached the last fang that churns the sea into yeast when the tide sucks the land, just opposite.

Then he called out something that Aulay Macneil could not catch. With that he springs up, and throws his arms above him.

"Then," says Aulay, when he tells the tale, "it was like a ghost he was. The moonshine was on his face like the curl o' a wave. White! there is no whiteness like that of the human face. It was whiter than the foam about the skerry it was, whiter than the moon-shining, whiter than—well, as white as the painted letters on the black boards of the fishing-cobles. There he stood, for all that the sea was about him, the slip-slop waves leapin' wild, and the tide making too at that. He was shaking like a sail two points off the wind. It was then that all of a sudden he called in a womany screamin' voice :

"'I am throwing the sins of Adam Blair into the midst of ye, white dogs o' the sea !

Drown them, tear them, drag them away out into the black deeps ! Ay, ay, ay, ye dancin' wild waves, this is the third time I am doing it ; and now there is none left, no, not a sin, not a sin.

'O-hi, O-ri, dark tide o' the sea,
I am giving the sins of a dead man to thee !
By the Stones, by the Wind, by the Fire, by the Tree,
From the dead man's sins set me free, set me free !
Adam mhic Anndra mhic Adam and me,
Set us free ! Set us free !

" Ay, sure, the Sin-Eater sang that over and over ; and after the third singing he swung his arms and screamed :

'And listen to me, black waters an' running tide,
That rune is the good rune told me by Maisie the wise,
And I am Neil, the son of Silis Macallum,
By the black-hearted evil man Murtagh Ross,
That was the friend of Adam Mac Anndra, God against him ! '

" And with that he scrambled and fell into the sea. But, as I am Aulay Mac Luais and no other, he was up in a moment, an' swimmin' like a seal, and then over the rocks again, an' away back to that lonely roofless place once more, laughing wild at times, an' muttering an' whispering."

The Sin-Eater

It was this tale of Aulay Macneil's that
stood between Neil Ross and the islefolk.
There was something behind all that, they
whispered one to another.

So it was always the Sin-Eater he was
called at last. None sought him. The few
children who came upon him, now and again,
fled at his approach, or at the very sight of
him. Only Aulay Macneil saw him at times,
and had word of him.

After a month had gone by, all knew that
the Sin-Eater was wrought to madness, because of this awful thing; the burden of Adam
Blair's sins would not go from him! Night
and day he could hear them laughing low, it
was said.

But it was the quiet madness. He went to
and fro like a shadow in the grass, and almost
as soundless as that, and as voiceless. More
and more the name of him grew as a terror.
There were few folk on that wild west coast
of Iona, and these few avoided him when the
word ran that he had knowledge of strange
things, and converse, too, with the secrets of
the sea.

One day Aulay Macneil, in his boat, but
dumb with amaze and terror for him, saw
him at high tide swimming on a long rolling
wave right into the hollow of the Spouting

55

Cave. In the memory of man, no one had done this and escaped one of three things : a snatching away into oblivion, a strangled death, or madness. The islanders know that there swims into the cave at full tide a Mar-Tarbh, a dreadful creature of the sea that some call a kelpie; only it is not a kelpie, which is like a woman, but rather is a sea-bull, offspring of the cattle that are never seen. Ill indeed for any sheep or goat, ay or even dog or child, if any happen to be leaning over the edge of the Spouting Cave when the Mar-Tarbh roars ; for, of a surety, it will fall in and straightway be devoured.

With awe and trembling Aulay listened for the screaming of the doomed man. It was full tide, and the sea-beast would be there.

The minutes passed, and no sign. Only the hollow booming of the sea, as it moved like a baffled blind giant round the cavern-bases ; only the rush and spray of the water flung up the narrow shaft high into the windy air above the cliff it penetrates.

At last he saw what looked like a mass of sea-weed swirled out on the surge. It was the Sin-Eater. With a leap, Aulay was at his oars. The boat swung through the sea. Just before Neil Ross was about to sink for the

second time, he caught him, and dragged him
into the boat.

But then, as ever after, nothing was to be
got out of the Sin-Eater save a single saying :
"*Tha e lamhan fuar!   Tha e lamhan fuar !*"
" It has a cold, cold hand ! "

The telling of this and other tales left none
free upon the island to look upon the " scapegoat " save as one accursed.

It was in the third month that a new phase
of his madness came upon Neil Ross.

The horror of the sea and the passion for
the sea came over him at the same happening.
Oftentimes he would race along the shore,
screaming wild names to it, now hot with hate
and loathing, now as the pleading of a man
with the woman of his love. And strange
chants to it, too, were upon his lips. Old, old
lines of forgotten runes were overheard by
Aulay Macneil, and not Aulay only—lines
wherein the ancient sea-name of the island,
Iona, that was given to it long before it was
called Iona, or any other of the nine names
that are said to belong to it, occurred again
and again.

The flowing tide it was that wrought him
thus. At the ebb he would wander across
the weedy slabs or among the rocks, silent,
and more like a lost *duinshee* than a man.

57

Then again after three months a change in his madness came. None knew what it was, though Aulay said that the man moaned and moaned because of the awful burden he bore. No drowning seas for the sins that could not be washed away, no grave for the live sins that would be quick till the Day of the Judgment.

For weeks thereafter he disappeared. As to where he was, it is not for the knowing.

Then at last came that third day of the seventh month when, as I have said, Aulay Macneil told old Ronald MacCormick that he had seen the Sin-Eater again.

It was only a half-truth that he told, though. For after he had seen Neil Ross upon the rock, he had followed him when he rose and wandered back to the roofless place which he haunted now as of yore. Less wretched a shelter now it was, because of the summer that was come, though a cold, wet summer at that.

" Is that you, Neil Ross ?" he had asked, as he peered into the shadows among the ruins of the house.

" That's not my name," said the Sin-Eater ; and he seemed as strange then and there as though he were a castaway from a foreign ship.

"And what will it be then, you that are my friend, and sure knowing me as Aulay Mac Luais—Aulay Macneil that never grudges you bit or sup?"

"*I am Judas.*"

"And at that word," says Aulay Macneil, when he tells the tale, "at that word the pulse in my heart was like a bat in a shut room. But after a bit I took up the talk.

"'Indeed,' I said, 'and I was not for knowing that. May I be so bold as to ask whose son, and of what place?"

"But all he said to me was, '*I am Judas.*'"

"Well, I said, to comfort him, 'Sure, it's not such a bad name in itself, though I am knowing some which have a more homelike sound.' But no, it was no good.

"'I am Judas. And because I sold the Son of God for five pieces of silver—' But here I interrupted him and said, 'Sure now, Neil,—I mean, Judas—it was eight times five.' Yet the simpleness of his sorrow prevailed, and I listened with the wet in my eyes.

"'I am Judas. And because I sold the Son of God for five silver shillings, He laid upon me all the nameless black sins of the world. And that is why I am bearing them till the Day of Days.'"

59

And this was the end of the Sin-Eater—for
I will not tell the long story of Aulay Macneil, that gets longer and longer every winter, but only the unchanging close of it.

I will tell it in the words of Aulay.

"A bitter wild day it was, that day I saw
him to see him no more. It was late. The
sea was red with the flamin' light that burned
up the air betwixt Iona and all that is west of
West. I was on the shore, looking at the
sea. The big green waves came in like the
chariots in the Holy Book. Well, it was on
the black shoulder of one of them, just short
of the ton o' foam that swept above it, that I
saw a spar surgin' by.

"'What is that?' I said to myself. And
the reason of my wondering was this. I saw
that a smaller spar was swung across it. And
while I was watching that thing another great
billow came in with a roar, and hurled the
double-spar back, and not so far from me but
I might have gripped it. But who would have
gripped that thing if he were for seeing what
I saw?

"It is Himself knows that what I say is a
true thing.

"On that spar was Neil Ross, the Sin-
Eater. Naked he was as the day he was born.

60

And he was lashed, too, ay, sure he was lashed
to it by ropes round and round his legs and
his waist and his left arm. It was the Cross
he was on. I saw that thing with the fear
upon me. Ah, poor drifting wreck that he
was ! *Judas on the Cross !* It was his *eric !*

"But even as I watched, shaking in my
limbs, I saw that there was life in him still.
The lips were moving, and his right arm was
ever for swinging this way and that. 'Twas
like an oar working him off a lee shore ; ay,
that was what I thought.

"Then all at once he caught sight of me.
Well, he knew me, poor man, that has his
share of Heaven now, I am thinking !

"He waved, and called, but the hearing
could not be, because of a big surge o' water
that came tumbling down upon him. In the
stroke of an oar he was swept close by the
rocks where I was standing. In that floun-
derin', seethin' whirlpool I saw the white face
of him for a moment, an', as he went out on
the resurge like a hauled net, I heard these
words fallin' against my ears :

"'*An eirig m'anama !*—In ransom for my
soul !'

"And with that I saw the double-spar turn
over and slide down the back-sweep of a
drowning big wave. Ay, sure, it went out to

61

the deep sea swift enough then. It was in
the big eddy that rushes between Skerry-Mòr
and Skerry-Beag. I did not see it again, no,
not for the quarter of an hour, I am thinking. Then I saw just the whirling top of it
rising out of the flying yeast of a great black,
blustering wave that was rushing northward
before the current that is called the Black-
Eddy.

" With that you have the end of Neil Ross :
ay, sure, him that was called the Sin-Eater.
And that is a true thing, and may God save
us the sorrow of sorrows !

" And that is all."

THE NINTH WAVE

The wind fell as we crossed the Sound.
There was only one oar in the boat, and
we lay idly adrift. The tide was still on the
ebb, and so we made way for Soa, though well
before the island could be reached the tide
would turn, and the sea-wind would stir, and
we be up the Sound, and at Balliemore again
almost as quick as the laying of a net.

As we—and by "us" I am meaning Pàdruig Macrae and Ivor McLean, fishermen of
Iona, and myself beside Ivor at the helm—
as we slid slowly passed the ragged islet known
as Eilean-na-h'Aon-Chaorach, torn and rent
by the tides and surges of a thousand years,
I saw a school of seals basking in the sun.
One by one slithered into the water, and I
could note the dark forms, like moving patches
of sea-weed, drifting in the green under-
glooms.

Then after a time we bore down upon
Sgeir-na-Oir, a barren rock. Three great
cormorants stood watching us. Their necks
shone in the sunlight like snakes mailed in

blue and green. On the upper ledges were
eight or ten northern divers. They did not
seem to see us, though I knew that their fierce
light-blue eyes noted every motion we made.
The small sea-ducks bobbed up and down,
first one flirt of a little black-feathered rump,
then another, then a third, till a score or so
were under water, and half a hundred more
were ready at a moment's notice to follow suit.
A skua hopped among the sputtering weed,
and screamed disconsolately at intervals.
Among the myriad colonies of close-set mus-
sels, which gave a blue bloom, like that of the
sloe, to the weed-covered boulders, a few
kitti-wakes and dotterels flitted to and fro.
High over head, white against the blue as a
cloudlet, a gannet hung motionless, seemingly
frozen to the sky.

Below the lapse of the boat the water was
pale green. I could see the liath and saithe
fanning their fins in slow flight, and sometimes a little scurrying cloud of tiny fluckles
and inch-long codling. For two or three
fathoms beyond the boat the waters were blue.
If blueness can be alive, and have its own life
and movement, it must be happy on these
western seas, where it dreams into shadowy
Lethes of amethyst and deep, dark oblivions
of violet.

Suddenly a streak of silver ran for a moment along the sea to starboard. It was like an arrow of moonlight shot along the surface of the blue and gold. Almost immediately afterward, a stertorous sigh was audible. A black knife cut the flow of the water: the shoulder of a pollack.

"The mackerel are coming in from the sea," said Macrae. He leaned forward, wet the palm of his hand, and held it seaward. "Ay, the tide has turned—

Ohrone—achree—an—Srùth-màra !
Ohrone—achree—an—Lionadh !"

he droned monotonously, over and over with few variations.

"An' it's Oh an' Oh for the tides o' the sea,
An' it's Oh for the flowing tide,"

I sang at last in mockery.

"Come, Pàdruig," I cried, "you are as bad as Peter McAlpin's lassie, Elsie, with the pipes !"

Both men laughed lightly. On the last Sabbath, old McAlpin had held a prayer-meeting in his little house in the "street," in Balliemore of Iona. At the end of his discourse he told his hearers that the voice of God was

terrible only to the evil-doer but beautiful to
the righteous man, and that this voice was
even now among them, speaking in a thousand ways and yet in one way. And at this
moment, that elfin granddaughter of his, who
was in the byre close by, let go upon the pipes
with so long and weary a whine that the collies by the fire whimpered, and would have
howled outright but for the Word of God that
still lay open on the big stool in front of old
Peter. For it was in this way that the dogs
knew when the Sabbath readings were over ;
and there was not one that would dare to bark
or howl, much less rise and go out, till the
Book was closed with a loud, solemn bang.
Well, again and again that weary quavering
moan went up and down the room, till even
old McAlpin smiled, though he was fair angry
with Elsie. But he made the sign of silence,
and began : My brethren, even in this trial it
may be the Almighty has a message for us "
—when at that moment Elsie was kicked by a
cow, and fell against the board with the pipes,
and squeezed out so wild a wail that McAlpin
started up and cried, in the Lowland way that
he had won out of his wife, "*Hoots, havers,
an' a' ! coom oot o' that, ye Deil's spunkie !*"

So it was this memory that made Pàdruig
and Ivor smile. Suddenly Ivor began with

a long rising and falling cadence, an old Gaelic
rune of the Faring of the Tide.

Athair, A mhic, A Spioraid Naoimh,
Biodh an Tri-aon leinn, a la's a dh' oidhche ;
S'air chul nan tonn, no air thaobh nam beann !

O Father, Son, and Holy Spirit,
Be the Three-in-one with us day and night,
On the crested wave, when waves run high !

And out of the place in the West
Where Tir-nan-Og, the Land of Youth
Is, the Land of Youth everlasting,
Send the great Tide that carries the sea-weed
And brings the birds, out of the North :
And bid it wind as a snake through the bracken,
As a great snake through the heather of the sea,
The fair blooming heather of the sunlit sea.

And may it bring the fish to our nets,
And the great fish to our lines :
And may it sweep away the sea-hounds
That devour the herring :
And may it drown the heavy pollack
That respect not our nets
But fall into and tear them and ruin them wholly.

And may I, or any that is of my blood,
Behold not the Wave-Haunter who comes in with the
            Tide,
Or the Maighdeann-màra who broods in the shallows,
Where the sea-caves are, in the ebb :
And fair may my fishing be, and the fishing of those
            near to me,

67

And good may this Tide be, and good may it bring:
And may there be no calling in the Flow, this Sruth-
  màra,
And may there be no burden in the Ebb! *Ochone!*

An ainm an Athar, s' an Mhic, s' an Spioraid Naoimh,
Biodh an Tri-aon leinn, a la's a dh' oidhche,
S' air chul nan tonn, no air thaobh nam beann!
                                Ochone! arone!

Both men sang the closing lines with loudly
swelling voices and with a wailing fervour
which no words of mine could convey.

Runes of this kind prevail all over the isles,
from the Butt of Lewis to the Rhinns of Islay:
identical in spirit, though varying in lines and
phrases, according to the mood and temperament of the *rannaiche* or singer, the local or
peculiar physiognomy of nature, the instinct-
ive yielding to hereditary wonder-words, and
other compelling circumstances of the outer
and inner life. Almost needless to say, the
sea-maid or sea-witch and the Wave-Haunter
occur in many of those wild runes, particu-
larly in those that are impromptu. In the
Outer Hebrides, the runes are wild natural
hymns rather than Pagan chants; though
marked distinctions prevail there also—for in
Harris and the Lews the folk are Protestant
almost to a man, while in Benbecula and the
Southern Hebrides the Catholics are in a like

ascendancy. But all are at one in the common Brotherhood of Sorrow.

The only lines in Ivor McLean's wailing song which puzzled me were the two last which came before "the good words," "in the name of the Father, the Son, and the Spirit," etc.

"Tell me, in English, Ivor," I said, after a silence, wherein I pondered the Gaelic words, "what is the meaning of—

'And may there be no calling in the Flow, this Strùth-mára,
And may there be no burden in the Ebb?'"

"Yes, I will be telling you what is the meaning of that. When the great tide that wells out of the hollow of the sea, and sweeps toward all the coasts of the world, first stirs, when she will be knowing that the Ebb is not any more moving at all, she sends out nine long waves. And I will be forgetting what these waves are : but one will be to shepherd the sea-wead that is for the blessing of man, and another is for to wake the fish that sleep in the deeps, and another is for this, and another will be for that, and the seventh is to rouse the Wave-Haunter and all the creatures of the water that fear and hate man, and the eighth no man knows, though the priests

69

D

say it is to carry the Whisper of Mary, and
the ninth—"

"And the ninth, Ivor?"

"May it be far from us, from you and from
me and from those of us! An' I will be sayin' nothing against it, not I; nor against anything that is in the sea! An' you will be not-
ing that!

"Well, this ninth wave goes through the
water on the forehead of the tide. An' wherever it will be going it *calls*. An' the call of
it is, '*Come away, come away, the sea waits!
Follow! . . . Come away, come away, the sea
waits! Follow!*'[1] An' whoever hears that
must arise and go, whether he be fish or pollack, or seal or otter, or great skua or small
tern, or bird or beast of the shore, or bird or
beast of the sea, or whether it be man or
woman or child, or any of the others."

"*Any of the others, Ivor?*"

"I will not be saying anything about that,"
replied McLean, gravely; "you will be knowing well what I mean, and if you do not
it is not for me to talk of that which is not to
be talked about.

"Well, as I was for saying: that calling of

[1] Ivor, of course, gave these words in the Gaelic,
the sound of which has the strange wail of the sea
in it.

the ninth wave of the Tide is what Ian-Mòr
of the hill speaks of as 'the whisper of the
snow that falls on the hair, the whisper of the
frost that lies on the cold face of him that
will never be waking again.'"

" *Death?* "

" It is *you* that will be saying it."

"Well," he resumed after a moment's hush,
"a man may live by the sea for five score
years and never hear that ninth wave call in
any *Srùth-màra*, but soon or late he will hear
it. An' many is the Flood that will be silent
for all of us: but there will be one Flood for
each of us that will be a dreadful Voice, a
voice of terror and of dreadfulness. And
whoever hears that Voice, he for sure will be
the burden in the Ebb."

" Has any heard that Voice, and lived ? "

McLean looked at me, but said nothing.
Pàdruig Macrae rose, tautened a rope, and
made a sign to me to put the helm alee. Then,
looking into the green water slipping by—
for the tide was feeling our keel, and a
stronger breath from the sea lay against the
hollow that was growing in the sail—he said to
Ivor :

"You should be telling her of Ivor Mac-
Ivor mhic Niall."

"Who was Ivor MacNeil ? " I said.

71

" He was the father of my mother," answered McLean, "and was known throughout the north isles as Ivor Carminish, for he had a farm on the eastern lands of Carminish which lie between the hills called Strondeval and Rondeval, that are in the far south of the northern Hebrides, and near what will be known to you as the Obb of Harris.

" And I will now be telling you about him in the Gaelic, for it is more easy to me, and more pleasant for us all.

" When Ivor MacEachainn Carminish, that was Ivor's father, died, he left the farm to his elder son and to his second son, Seumas. By this time, Ivor was married, and had the daughter who is my mother. But he was a lonely man, and an islesman to the heart's core. So . . . but you will be knowing the isles that lay off the Obb of Harris — the Saghay, and Ensay, and Killegray, and farther west, Berneray and, north-west, Pabaidh, and beyond that again, Shillaidh ? "

For the moment I was confused, for these names are so common: and I was thinking of the big isle of Berneray that lies in huge Loch Roag that has swallowed so great a mouthful of Western Lewis, to the seaward of which also are the two Pabbays, Pabaidh Mòr and Pabaidh Beag. But when McLean added, "and other isles of the Caolas Harrish" (the Sound of Harris), I remembered aright ; and indeed I knew both, though the nor' isles better, for I had lived near Callernish on the inner waters of Roag.

"Well, Carminish had sheep-runs upon some of these. One summer the gloom came upon him, and he left Seumas to take care of the farm and of Morag his wife, and of Sìne their daughter ; and he went to live upon Pabbay, near the old castle that is by the Rua Dune on the south-east of the isle. There he stayed for three months. But on the last night of each month he heard the sea calling in his sleep ; and what he heard was like '*Come away, come away, the sea waits! Follow . . . Come away, come away, the sea waits! Follow!*' And he knew the voice of the ninth wave ; and that it would not be there in the darkness of sleep if it were not already moving toward him through the dark ways of *An Dàn* (Destiny). So, thinking to pass away from a place doomed for him, and that he might be safe elsewhere, he sailed north to a kinsman's croft on Aird-Vanish in the island of Taransay. But at the end of that month he heard in his sleep the noise of tidal waters, and at the gathering of the ebb he heard '*Come away, come away, the sea waits!*

Follow !' Then once more, when the November heat-spell had come, he sailed farther northward still. He stopped a while at Eilean Mhealastaidh, which is under the morning shadow of high Griomabhal on the mainland, and at other places, till he settled, in the third week, at his cousin Eachainn MacEachainn's bothy, near Callernish, where the Great Stones of old stand by the sea, and hear nothing forever but the noise of the waves of the North Sea and the cry of the sea-wind.

" And when the last night of November had come and gone, and he had heard in his sleep no calling of the ninth wave of the Flowing Tide, he took heart of grace. All through that next day he went in peace. Eachainn wondered often with slant eyes when he saw the morose man smile, and heard his silence give way now and again to a short, mirthless laugh.

"The two were at the porridge, and Eachainn was muttering his *Bui'cheas dha'n Ti*, the Thanks to the Being, when Carminish suddenly leaped to his feet, and, with white face, stood shaking like a rope in the wind.

" In the name of the Son, what is it, Ivor mhic Ivor ? What is it, Carminish ?' cried Eachainn.

" But the stricken man could scarce speak. At last, with a long sigh, he turned and

74

looked at his kinsman, and that look went
down into the shivering heart like the polar
wind into a crofter's hut.

" ' *What will be that ?* ' said Carminish, in
a hoarse whisper.

" Eachainn listened, but he could hear no
wailing *beann-sith*, no unwonted sound.

" ' Sure, I hear nothing but the wind moaning through the Great Stones, an' beyond
them the noise of the Flowin' Tide.'

" ' The Flowing Tide !   The Flowing Tide ! '
cried Carminish, and no longer with the hush
in the voice.   ' An' what is it you hear in the
Flowing Tide ? '

" Eachainn looked in silence. What was
the thing he could say ? For now he knew.

" Ah, och, och, ochone, you may well sigh,
Eachainn mhic Eachainn ! For the ninth wave
o' the Flowing Tide is coming out o' the
North Sea upon this shore, an' already I can
hear it calling, ' *Come away, come away, the
sea waits ! Follow !* . . . *Come away, come
away, the sea waits ! Follow !* '

" And with that Carminish dashed out the
light that was upon the table, and leaped upon
Eachainn, and dinged him to the floor and
would have killed him but for the growing
noise of the sea beyond the Stannin' Stones o'
Callanish, and the woe-weary sough o' the

wind, an' the calling, calling, '*Come, come away! Come, come away!*'

"And so he rose and staggered to the door, and flung himself out into the night, while Eachainn lay upon the floor and gasped for breath, and then crawled to his knees, an' took the Book from the shelf by his fern-straw mattress, an' put his cheek against it, an' moaned to God, an' cried like a child for the doom that was upon Ivor MacIvor mhic Niall, who was of his own blood, and his own foster-brother at that.

"And while he moaned, Carminish was stalking through the great, gaunt, looming Stones of the Druids, that were here before St. Colum and his *Shona* came, and laughing wild. And all the time the tide was coming in, and the tide and the deep sea and the waves of the shore and the wind in the salt grass and the weary reeds and the black-pool gale made a noise of a dreadful hymn, that was the death-hymn, the going-rune, of Ivor the son of Ivor of the kindred of Niall.

"And it was there that they found his body in the grey dawn, wet and stiff with the salt ooze. For the soul that was in him had heard the call of the ninth wave that was for him. So, and may the Being keep back that hour for us, there was a burden upon that Ebb on the morning of that day.

"Also, there is this thing for the hearing. In the dim dark before the curlew cried at dawn, Eachainn heard a voice about the house, a voice going like a thing blind and baffled,

> "'*Cha till, cha till, cha till mi tuille !*'
> I return, I return, I return never more!"

THE JUDGMENT O' GOD

The wind that blows on the feet of the dead came calling loud across the Ross, as we put about the boat off the Rudhe Callachain in the Sound of Iona. The ebb sucked at the keel, while, like a cork, we were swung lightly by the swell. For we were in the strait between Eilean Dubh and the Isle of the Swine; and that is where the current has a bad pull, the current that is made of the inflow and the outflow. I have heard that a weary woman of the olden days broods down there in a cave, and that day and night she weaves a web of water, which a fierce spirit in the sea tears this way and that as soon as woven.

So we put about, and went before the east wind ; and below the dip of the sail alee I watched Soa grow bigger and gaunter and blacker against the white wave. As we came so near that it was as though the wash of the sea among the hollows bubbled in our ears, I saw a large bull-seal lying half-in, half-out of the water, and staring at us with an angry, fearless look. Pàdruig and Ivor caught sight of it almost at the same moment.

To my surprise Pàdruig suddenly rose and put a spell upon it. I could hear the wind through his clothes as he stood by the mast.

The *rosad* or spell was, of course, in the Gaelic, but its meaning was something like this:

> *Ho, ro, O Ron dubh, O Ron dubh !*
> *An ainm an Athar, O Ron !*
> *'S an mhic, O Ron !*
> *'S an Spioraid Naoimh,*
> *O Ron-à-mhàra, O Ron dubh !*

> Ho, ro, O black Seal, O black Seal !
> In the name of the Father,
> And of the Son,
> And of the Holy Ghost,
> O Seal of the deep sea, O black Seal

> Hearken the thing that I say to thee,
> I, Phadric MacAlastair MhicCrae,
> Who dwell in a house on the Island
> That you look on night and day from Soa !
> For I put *rosad* upon thee,

> And upon the woman-seal that won thee,
> And the women-seal that are thine,
> And the young that thou hast,
> Ay, upon thee and all thy kin
> I put *rosad*, O Ron dubh, O Ron-à-mhàra !

And may no harm come to me or mine,
Or to any fishing or snaring that is of me,
Or to any sailing by storm or dusk,
Or when the moonshine fills the blind eyes of the dead,
No harm to me or mine
From thee or thine!

With a slow, swinging motion of his head Pàdruig broke out again into the first words of the incantation, and now Ivor joined him; and with the call of the wind and the leaping and the splashing of the waves was blent the chant of the two fishermen:

Ho, ro, O Ron dubh! O Ron dubh!
An ainm an Athar, 's an Mhic, 's an Spioraid Naoimh,
O Ron-à'mhàra, O Ron dubh!

Then the men sat back, with that dazed look in the eyes I have so often seen in those of men or women of the Isles who are wrought. No word was spoken till we came almost straight upon Eilean-na-h' Aon-Chao-rach. Then at the rocks we tacked and went splashing up the Sound, like a pollack on a Sabbath noon.[1]

[1] The Iona fishermen, and indeed the Gaelic and Scottish fishermen generally, believe that the pollack (porpoise) knows when it is the Sabbath; and on that day will come closer to the land, and be more wanton in its gambols on the sun-warmed surface of the sea, than on the days when the herring-boats are abroad.

"What was wrong with the old man of the sea?" I asked Pàdruig.

At first he would say nothing. He looked vaguely at a coiled rope; then, with hand-shaded gaze across to the red rocks at Fionnaphort. I repeated my question. He took refuge in English.

"It wass ferry likely the *Clansman* would be pringing ta new minister-body. Did you pe knowing him, or his people, or where he came from?"

But I was not to be put off thus; and at last, while Ivor stared down the green shelving lawns of the sea below us, Pàdruig told me this thing. His reluctance was partly due to the shyness which with the Gael almost invariably follows strong emotion; and partly to that strange, obscure, secretive instinct which is also so characteristically Celtic, and often even prevents Gaels of far apart isles, or of different clans, from communicating to each other stories or legends of a peculiarly intimate kind.

"I will tell you what my father told me, and what, if you like, you may hear again from the sister of my father, who is the wife of Ian Finlay, who has the farm on the north side of Dùn I.

"You will have heard of old Robert Ach-

anna of Eilanmore, off the Ord o' Sutherland ?
To be sure, for have you not stayed there.
Well, I need not tell you how he came there
out of the south ; but it will be news to you to
learn that my elder brother Murdoch was had
by him as a shepherd, and to help on the farm.
And the way of that thing was this : Murdoch
had gone to the fishing north of Skye, with
Angus and William Macdonald, and in the
great gale that broke up their boat, among so
many others, he found himself stranded on
Eilanmore. Achanna told him that as he was
ruined, and so far from home, he would give
him employment, and though Murdoch had
never thought to serve under a Galloway man,
he agreed.

" For a year he worked on the upper farm,
Ardoch-beag, as it was called. There the
gloom came upon him. Turn which way he
would, the beauty that is in the day was no
more. In vain, when he came out into the
air in the morning, did he cry *Deasiul !* and
keep by the sunway. At night he heard the
sea calling in his sleep. So, when the lambing
was over, he told Achanna that he must go,
for he hungered for the sea. True, the wave
ran all around Eilanmore, but the farm was
between bare hills and among high moors,
and the house was in a hollow place. But it

was needful for him to go. Even then, though he did not know it, the madness of the sea was upon him.

"But the Galloway man did not wish to lose my brother, who was a quiet man, and worked for a small wage. Murdoch was a silent lad, but he had often the light in his eyes, and none knew of what he was thinking ; maybe it was of a lass, or a friend, or of the ingle-neuk where his old mother sang o' nights, or of the sight and sound of Iona that was his own land ; but I'm considerin' it was the sea he was dreamin' of—how the waves ran laughin' an' dancin' against the tide like lambkins comin' to meet the shep herd, or how the big green billows went sweepin' white an' ghostly through the moonless nights.

"So the troth that was come to between them was this : that Murdoch should abide for a year longer, that is, till Lammastide ; then that he should no longer live at Ardoch-beag, but instead should go and keep the sheep on Bac-Mòr."

"On Bac-Mòr, Pàdruig," I interrupted, "for sure, you do not mean *our* Bac-Mòr ? "

"For sure I mean no other : Bac-Mòr, of the Treshnish Isles, that is eleven miles north

of Iona and a long four north-west of Staffa ;
an' just Bac-Mòr an' no other."

"Murdoch would be near home, there."

"Ay, near, an' farther away ; for 'tis to be
farther off to be near that your heart loves
but ye canna get."

"Well, Murdoch agreed to this, but he did
not know there was no boat on the island. It
was all very well in the summer. The her-
rin' smacks lay off Bac-Mòr or Bac-Beag
many a time ; and he could see them mornin',
noon, an' night ; an' nigh every day he could
watch the big steamer comin' southward down
the Mornish and Treshnish coasts of Mull
and stand by for an hour off Staffa, or else
come northward out of the Sound of Iona
round the Eilean Rabach ; and once or twice
a week he saw the *Clansman* coming or going
from Bunessan in the Ross to Scarnish in the
Isle of Tiree. Maybe, too, now and again a
foreign sloop or a coasting schooner would
sail by ; and twice, at least, a yacht lay off the
wild shore, and put a boat in at the landing-
place, and let some laughing folk loose upon
that quiet place. The first time, it was a
steam-yacht, owned by a rich foreigner, either
an Englishman or an American, I misremem-
ber now : an' he spoke to Murdoch as though

he were a savage, and he and his gay folk
laughed when my brother spoke in the only
English he had (an' sober good English it
was), an' then he shoved some money into his
hand, as though both were evil-doers and were
ashamed to be seen doing what they did.

"'An' what is this for?' said my brother.

"'O it's for yourself, my man, to drink our
health with,' answered the English lord, or
whatever he was, rudely.

"Then Murdoch looked at him and his
quietly; an' he said, 'God has your health an'
my health in the hollow of His hand. But I
wish you well. Only I am not being your man
any more than I am for calling *you my* man;
an' I will ask you to take back this money to
drink with; nor have I any need for money,
but only for that which is free to all—but that
only God can give.' And with that the foreign people went away, and laughed less. But
when the second yacht came, though it was a
yawl owned by a Glasgow man who had folk
in the west, Murdoch would not come down
to the shore, but lay under the shadow of a
rock amid his sheep, and kept his eyes upon
the sun that was moving west out of the south.

"Well, all through the fine months Murdoch stayed on Bac-Mòr, and thereafter
through the early winter. The last time I

saw him was at the New Year. On Hogmanay night my father was drinking hard,
and nothing would serve him but he must bor-
row Alec Macarthur's boat, and that he and
our mother and myself, and Ian Finlay and
his wife, my sister, should go out before the
quiet south wind that was blowing, and see
Murdoch where he lay sleeping or sat dreaming in his lonely bothy. And truth, we went.
It was a white sailing, that I remember. The
moonshinings ran in and out of the wavelets
like herrings through salmon nets. The fire-
flauchts, too, went speeding about. I was but
a laddie then, an' I noted it all; an' the sheet-
lightning that played behind the cloudy lift
in the nor'-west.

"But when we got to Bac-Mòr there was
no sign of Murdoch at the bothy; no, not
though we called high and low. Then my
father and Ian Finlay went to look, and we
stayed by the peats. When they came back,
an hour later, I saw that my father was no
more in drink. He had the same look in his
eyes as Ronald McLean had that day last winter when they told him his bit girlie had been
caught by the smallpox in Glasgow.

"I could not hear, or I could not make out
what was said; but I know that we all got
into the boat again, all except my father. And

he stayed. And next day, Ian Finlay and Alec Macarthur went out to Bac-Mòr and brought him back.

"And from him and from Ian I knew all there was to be known. It was a hard New Year for all, and since that day till a night of which I will tell you, my father brooded and drank, drank and brooded, and my mother wept through the winter gloamings and spent the night starin' into the peats wi' her knittin' lyin' on her lap.

"For when they had gone to seek Murdoch that Hogmanay night, they came upon him away from his sheep. But this was what they saw. There was a black rock that stood out in the moonshine, with the water all about it. And on this rock Murdoch lay naked, and laughin' wild. An' every now and then he would lean forward, and stretch his arms out, an' call to his dearie. An' at last, just as the watchers, shiverin' wi' fear an' awe, were going to close in upon him, they saw a—a—thing —come out o' the water. It was long an' dark, an' Ian said its eyes were like clots o' blood; but as to that no man can say yea or nay, for Ian himself admits it was a seal.

"An' this thing is true, *an ainm an Athar!* they saw the dark beast o' the sea creep on to the rock beside Murdoch, an' lie down beside

him, and let him clasp an' kiss it. An' then
he stood up, and laughed till the skin crept
on those who heard, and cried out on his
dearie and on a' the dumb things o' the sea,
an' the Wave-Hunter an' the grey shadow ;
an' he raised his hands, an' cursed the world
o' men, and cried out to God, ' *Turn your face
to your own airidh, O God, an' may rain an'
storm an' snow be between us !* '

"An' wi' that Deirg, his collie, could bide
no more, but loupit across the water, and was
on the rock beside him, wi' his fell bristling
like a hedge-rat. For both the naked man an'
the wet gleamin' beast, a great sea-seal out
o' the north, turned upon Deirg, an' he fought
for his life. But what could the puir thing
do ? The seal buried her fangs in his shoulder, at last, an' pinned him to the ground.
Then Murdoch stooped, an' dragged her off,
an' bent down an' tore at the throat of Deirg
wi' his own teeth. Ay, God's truth it is ! An'
when the collie was stark, he took him up by
the hind legs an' the tail, an' swung him round
an' round his head, an' whirled him into the
sea, where he fell black in a white splatch o'
the moon.

"An' wi' that, Murdoch slipped, and reeled
backward into the sea, his hands gripping at
the whirling stars. An' the thing beside him

louped after him, an' my father an' Ian heard
a cry an' a cryin' that made their hearts sob.
But when they got down to the rock they
saw nothing, except the floating body o'
Deirg.

"Sure it was a weary night for the old man,
there on Bac-Mòr by himself, with that awful
thing that had happened. He stayed there to
see and hear what might be seen and heard.
But nothing he heard, nothing saw. It was
afterwards that he heard how Donncha Mac-
Donald had been on Bac-Mòr three days before this, and how Murdoch had told him he
was in love wi' a *maigdeannhmara*, a sea-
maid.

"But this thing has to be known. It was a
month later, on the night o' the full moon, that
Ian Finlay and Ian MacArthur and Seumas
Macallum were upset in the calm water inside
the Sound, just off Port-na-Frang, and were
nigh drowned, but that they called upon God
and the Son, and so escaped and heard no
more the laughter of Murdoch from the sea.

"And at midnight my father heard the
voice of his eldest son at the door; but ho
would not let him in; but in the morning he
found his boat broken and shred in splinters,
and his one net all torn. An' that day was
the Sabbath; so being a holy day he took the

Scripture with him, an' he and Neil Morrison
the minister, having had the Bread an' Wine,
went along the Sound in a boat, following a
shadow in the water, till they came to Soa.
An' there Neil Morrison read the Word o'
God to the seals that lay baskin' in the sun ;
and one, a female, snarled and showed her
fangs ; and another, a black one, lifted its
head, and made a noise that was not like the
barking of any seal, but was as the laughter
of Murdoch when he swung the dead body
of Deirg.

"And that is all that is to be said. And
silence is best now between you and any other.
And no man knows the judgments o' God.

"And that is all."

THE HARPING OF CRAVETHEEN

When Cormac, that was known throughout all Northern Eiré as Cormac Conlingas, Cormac the son of Concobar the son of Nessa, was one of the ten hostages to Conairy Mòr for the lealty of the Ultonians, he was loved by men and women because of his strength, his valour, and his comeliness.

He was taller than the tallest of his nine comrades by an inch, and broader by two inches than the broadest; though that fellowship of nine was of the tallest and broadest men among the Ultonians, who were the greatest warriors that green Banba, as Eiré or Erin was called by the bards who loved her, has ever seen.

The shenachies sang of him as a proud champion, with eyes full of light and fire, his countenance broad above and narrow below, ruddy-faced, with hair as of the gold of the September moon.

The commonalty spoke of his mighty spear-thrust, of his deft sword-swing, the terror of his wrath, of the fury of his battle-lust, of his laughter and light joy, and the singing that was on his lips when his sword had the silence upon it. No man dared touch " Blue-Green," as Cormac Conlingas called it—the "Whispering Sword," as it was named among his fellows. "Blue-Green," for in its sweep it gleamed blue-green as the leaping levin, whispered whenever it was athirst, and a red draught it was that would quench that thirst, and no other draught for the drinking ; and it whispered when there was a ferment of the red blood among men who hated while they feared the Ultonians ; and it whispered whenever a shadow dogged the shadow of Cormac, the son of Concobar the son of Nessa. Therefore it was that of all who desired his death, there was none that did not fear the doom-whisper of the sword that had been forged by Lên, the Smith, where he sits and works forever amid his mist of rainbows. Women spoke of his strength as though it were their proud beauty. He had the way of the sunlight with him, they said. And of the sunfire, added ever one, below her breath ; and that was Eilidh,[1] the daughter of

[1] The name Eilidh (pronounced *Eill'ik*, or *Isle-ee* with a long accent on the first syllable) is also ancient, but lingers in the Isles still, and indeed throughout the Western Highlands, as also, I understand, in Connaught and Connemara. Somhairle (Somerled) is pronounced *So-irl-ū̄.*

Conn Mac Art and of Dearduil, the daughter
of Somhairle, the Prince of the Isles—Eilidh,
the daughter of Dearduil the daughter of
Morna, the three queens of beauty in the
three generations of the generations.

She was not of the Ultonians, this fair
Eilidh ; but of the people who were subject
to Conairy Mòr. It was when the ten hostages abode with the Red Prince that she grew
faint and wan with the love-sickness. Her
mother, Dearduil, knew who the man was.
She put a mirror of polished steel against the
mouth of the girl while she slept, and then
it was that she saw the flames of love burning a red heart on which was written in white
fire—" I am the heart of Cormac, the son of
Concobar." Gladness was hers, as well as
fear. Sure, there was no greater hero than
Cormac Conlingas ; but then he was an Ultonian, and would soon be for going away ;
and ill-pleased would Conairy Mòr be that
the beautiful Eilidh, who was his ward since
the death of Conn, should be the wife of one
of the men of Concobar Mac Nessa whom in
his heart he hated.

There was a warrior there called Art Mac
Art Mòr. Conairy Mòr favoured him, and
had promised him Eilidh. One day this man
came to the overlord, and said this thing :

"Is she, Eilidh, to be hearing the lowing of the kine that are upon my hills?"

"That is so, Art Mac Art."

"I have spoken to the girl. She is like the wind in the grass."

"It is the way of women. Follow, and trace, and you shall not find. But say 'Come,' and they will come; and say 'Do,' and they will obey."

"I have put the word upon her, and she has laughed at me. I have said 'Come,' and she asked me if the running wave heard the voice of yesterday's wind. I have said 'Do,' and she called to me, 'Do the hills nod when the fox barks?'"

"What is the thing that is behind your lips, Art Mac Art Mòr?"

"This. That you send the man away who is the cause of the mischief that is upon Eilidh."

"Who is the man?"

"He is of the Hostages."

Conairy Mòr brooded awhile. Then he stroked his beard, brown-black as burn-water in shadow; and laughed.

"Why is there laughter upon you, my king?"

"Sure, I laugh to think of the blood of a white maid. They say it is of milk, but I am

94

thinking it must be the milk of the hero-women of old that was red and warm as the stream the White Hound that courses through the night swims in. And that blood that is in Eilidh leads to the blood of heroes. She would have the weight of Cormac, the Yellow-haired, on her breast!"

"His blood or mine!"

The king kept silence for a time. Then he smiled, and that boded ill. Then, after a while, he frowned, and that was not so ill."

"Not thine, Art."

"And if not mine, what of Cormac Mac Concobar?"

"He shall go."

"Alone?"

"Alone."

And, sure, it was on the eve of that day that Dearduil went to warn Cormac Conlingas, and to beg him to leave the whiteness of the snow without a red stain.

But, when she entered his sleeping-place, Eilidh was there, upon the deer-skins.

Dearduil looked for long before she spoke.

"By what is in your eyes, Eilidh my daughter, this is not the first time you have come to Cormac Conlingas?"

The girl laughed low. The white arms of her moved through the sheen of her hair like

95

sickles among the corn. She looked at Cormac. The flame that was in her eyes was bright in his. The wife of Conn turned to him.

"No," he said gravely. "it is not the first time."

"Has the seed been sown, O husbandman ?"

"The seed has been sown."

"It is death."

"The tide flows, the tide ebbs."

"Cormac, there will be two dead this night if Conary Mòr hears this thing. And even now his word moves against you. Do you love Eilidh ?"

Cormac smiled slightly, but made no answer.

"If you love her, you would not see her slain."

"There is no great evil in being slain, Dearduil-nic-Somhairle."

"She is a woman, and she has your child below her heart."

"That is a true thing."

"Will you save her ?"

"If she will."

"Speak, Eilidh."

Then the terror that was in the girl's heart arose and moved about like a white bewil-

dered bird in the dark. She knew that Dearduil had spoken out of her heart. She knew
that Art Mac Art Mòr was in this evil. She
knew that death was near for Cormac, and
near for her. The limbs that had trembled
with love, trembled now with the breath ot the
fear. Suddenly she drew a long sobbing sigh.

"Speak, Eilidh."

She turned her face to the wall.

"Speak Eilidh."

"I will speak. Go, Cormac Conlingas."

The chief of the Ultonians started. This
doom to life was worse to him than the death-
doom. An angry flame burned in his eyes.
His lip curled.

"May it not be a man-child you will have,
Eilidh of the gold-brown hair," he said scornfully, "for it would be an ill thing for a son
of Cormac Mac Concobar to be a coward, as
his mother was, and to fear death as she did,
though never before her any of her race."

And with that he turned upon his heel, and
went out.

Cormac Conlingas had not gone far when
he met Art Mac Art Mòr, with the others.

"It is the king's word," said Art, simply.

"I am ready," answered Cormac. "Is it
death?"

"Come; the king shall tell you."

But there was to be no blood that night. Only, on the morrow the hostages were nine. The tenth man rode slowly north-eastward, against the greying of the dawn.

If, in the heart of Cormac Conlingas, there was sorrow and a bitter pain, because of Eilidh, whom he loved, and from whom he would fain have taken the harshness of his word, there was, in the heart of Eilidh, the sound as of trodden sods.

That day it was worse for her.

Conairy Mòr came to her himself. Art was at his right hand. The king asked her if she would give her troth to the son of Art-Mòr, and, that being given, if she would be his wife.

"That cannot be," she said. The fear that had been in the girl's heart was dead now. The saying of Cormac had killed it. She knew that, like her ancestor, the mother of Somhairle, she could, if need be, have a log of burning wood against her breast and face the torture as though she were no more than holding a dead child there.

"And for why cannot it be?" asked Conairy Mòr.

"For it is not Art's child that I carry in my womb," answered Eilidh, simply.

The king gloomed. Art Mac Art put his

right hand to the dagger at his silver-bossed leathern belt.

" Is it a wanton that you are ? "

" No : by my mother's truth, and the mother of my mother. I love another man than Art Mac Art Mòr, and that man loves me, and I am his."

" Who is this man ? "

" His name is in my heart only."

" I will ask you three things, Eilidh, daughter of Dearduil. Is the man one of your race ? is he of noble blood ? is he fit to wed the king's ward ? "

" He is more fit to wed the king's ward than any man in Eiré. He is of noble blood, and himself the son of a king. But he is an Ultonian."

" Thou hast said. It is Cormac Mac Concobar Mac Nessa.

" It is Cormac Conlingas."

With a loud laugh Art Mac Art strode forward. He raised his hand and flung it across the face of the girl.

" Art thou his tenth or his hundredth ? Well, I would not have you now as a servingwench."

Once more the king gloomed. It went ill with him, that sight of a man striking a woman, howsoever lightly.

99

"Art, I have slain a better man than you, for a thing less worthy than that. Take heed."

The man frowned, with the red light in his eyes.

"Will you do as you said, O king?"

"No, not now. Eilidh, that blow has saved you. I was going to let Art have his way of you, and then do with you what he willed, servitude or death. But now you are free of him. Only this thing I say; no Ultonian shall ever take you in his arms. You shall wed Cravetheen, the step-brother of Art."

"Cravetheen the Harper?"

"Even so."

"He is old, and is neither comely nor gracious."

"There is no age upon him that a maid need mock at; and he is gracious enough to those who do not cross him; and he has the mouth of honey, he has, and, if not as comely as Cormac Conlingas, is yet fair to see."

"But—"

"I have said."

And so it was. Cravetheen took Eilidh to wife. But he left the great Dûn of Conairy Mòr and went to live in his own dûn in the

forest that clothed the frontiers of the land
of the Ultonians

He took his harp that night when for the
first time she lay upon the deerskins in his
dûn, and he played a wild air. Eilidh listened.
The tears came into her eyes. Then deep
shadows darkened them. Then she clenched
her hands till her nails drew blood. At last
she lay with her face to the wall, trembling.

For Cravetheen was a harper that had been
taught by a Green Hunter on the slopes of
Sliav-Sheean. He could say that in music that
the Druids themselves could not say aright in
words.

And when he had ended he went over to his
wife, and said this only :

"No, Eilidh, for all you are so white and
soft, and for all the sweet ways of you, I shall
not be laying my heart upon yours this night,
nor for many nights But a day shall come
when I will be playing you a marriage song.
But before that day I will play to you twice."
"And beware the third playing" said, when
he had gone, his old mother, who sat before
the smouldering logs, crooning and muttering.

As for the second playing ; that was not till
months later. It was on the set of the sun that
had shone on the birthing of the child of
Eilidh and Cormac Conlingas.

All through the soundless labour of the woman, for she had the pride of pride, Cravetheen the Harper played. What he played was that the child might be born dead. Eilidh knew this, and gave it the breath straight from her heart. " My pulse to you," she whispered between her smothered sobs. Then Cravetheen played that it might be born blind and deaf and dumb. But Eilidh knew this, and she whispered to the soul that was behind her eyes, *Give it light ;* and to the soul that was listening behind her ears, *Give it hearing* : and to the soul whose silence was beneath her silence, *Give it speech*.

And so the child was born ; and it was a man-child, and fair to see.

When the swoon was upon Eilidh, Cravetheen ceased from his harping. He rose, and looked upon the woman, Then he lifted the child, and laid it on a doeskin in the sunlight, on a green place, that was the meeting-place of the moonshine dancers, With that he took up his harp again, and again played.

At the first playing, the birds ceased from singing : there was silence amid the boughs. At the second, the leaves ceased from rustling : there was silence on the branches. At the third, the hare leaped no more, the fox blinked with sleep, the wolf lay down. At the fourth, and fifth, aud sixth, the wind folded its wings like a great bird, the wood-breeze crept beneath the bracken and fell asleep, the earth sighed and was still. There was silence there —for sure, silence everywhere, as of sleep.

At the seventh playing, the quiet people came out upon the green place. They were small and dainty, clad in green with small, white faces; just like lilies-of-the-valley they were.

They laughed low among themselves, and some clapped their hands. One climbed a thistle, and swung round and round till he fell on his back with a thud, like the fall of a dewdrop, and cried pitifully. There was no peace till a *duinshee* took him by a green leg, and shoved him down a hole in the grass and stopped it with a dandelion.

Then one among them, with a scarlet robe and a green cap with a thread of thistledown waving from it like a plume, and with his wee, wee eyes aflame, stepped forward and began to play on a little harp made of a bird-bone with three gossamer-films for strings. And the wild air that he played and the songs that he sang were those *fonnsheen* that few hear now, but that those who do hear know to be sweeter than the sorrow of joy.

Suddenly Cravetheen ceased playing, and then there was silence with the Green Harper also.

All of the hillside-folk stood still. When an eddy of air moved along the grass they wavered to and fro like reeds with the coolness at their feet.

Then the Green Harper threw aside his scarlet cloak and his green cap, and the hair of him was white and flowing as the *canna*. He broke the three threads of gossamer, and flung away the bird-bone harp. Then he drew a wee bit reed from his waist-band that was made of beaten gold, and put it to his lips, and began to play. And what he played was so passing sweet that Cravetheen went into a dream, and played the same wild air, and he not knowing it, nor any man.

It was with that that the soul of the child heard the elfin-music, and came free. Sure, it is a hard thing for the naked spirit to steal away from its warm home of the flesh, with the blood coming and going forever like a mother's hand, warm and soft. But to the playing of Cravetheen and the Green Harper there was no denying. The soul came forth, and stood with great frightened eyes.

"*Shrink! Shrink! Shrink!*" cried all the

quiet people, and, as they cried, the human spirit shrank so as to be at one with them.

Then, as it seemed, two shining white flowers—for they were bonnie, bonnie—stepped forward and took the human by the hand, and led it away. And as they went, the others followed, all singing a glad song, that fell strange and faint upon the ear of Cravetheen. All passed into the hillside, save the Green Harper, who stopped awhile, playing and playing and playing, till Cravetheen dreamed he was Alldai, the God of Gods, and that the sun was his bride, and the moon his paramour, and the stars his children and the joys that were before him. Then he, too, passed.

With that, Cravetheen came out of his trance, and rubbed his eyes as a man startled from sleep.

He looked at the child. It would be a changeling now, he knew. But when he looked again he saw that it was dead.

So he called to Gealcas, that was his mother, and gave her the body.

"Take that to Eilidh," he said, "and tell her that this is the second playing; and that I will be playing once again, before it's breast to breast with us."

And these were the words that Gealcas said

to Eilidh, who in her heart cursed Cravetheen, and mocked his cruel patience, and
longed for Cormac of the Yellow Hair, and
cared not for all the harping that Cravetheen
could do now.

It was the Month of the White Flowers
that Cormac Conlingas came again.

He was in the southland when news reached
him that his father, Concobar Mac Nessa, was
dead. He knew that if he were not speedily
in Ulster, the Ultonians might not grant him
the Ard-Righship. He, surely, and no other,
should be Ard-Righ after Concobar ; yet there
was one other who might well become over-
lord of the Ultonians in his place, were he not
swift with word and act.

So swift was he that he mounted and rode
away from his fellows without taking with
him the famous Spear of Pisarr, which was a
terror in battle. This was that fiery, living
spear, wrought by the son of Turenn, and won
out of Eiré by the god Lu Lam-fáda. In battle it flew hither and thither, a live thing.

He rode from noon to within an hour of
the setting of the sun. Then he saw a long,
green hill rise like a pine-cone out of the
wood, bossed with still-standing stones of an
ancient ruined dûn. Against it a blue column

of smoke trailed. Cormac knew now where he was. Word had come to him recently from Eilidh herself.

He drew rein, and stared awhile. Then he smiled ; then once more he gloomed, and his eyes were heavy with the shadow of that gloom.

It was then that he drew " Blue-Green " from its sheath, and listened. There was a faint murmur along the blade, as of gnats above a pool ; but there was no whispering.

Once more he smiled.

" It will be for the happening," he murmured. Then, leaning back, he sang this Rune to Eilidh.

Oimé, Oimé, Woman of the white breasts, Eilidh ;
Woman of the gold-brown hair, and lips of the red
    red rowan !

           Oimé, O-rì, Oimé !

Where is the swan that is whiter, with breast more
    soft,
Or the wave on the sea that moves as thou movest
    Eilidh—

           Oimé, a-rò ; Oime, a-rò !

It is the marrow in my bones that is aching, aching,
    Eilidh ;
It is the blood in my body that is a bitter, wild tide
    Oimé !

           O-rì, O-hion, O-rì, aròne !

Is it the heart of thee calling that I am hearing,
   Eilidh,
Or the wind in the wood, or the beating of the sea,
   Eilidh,
          Or the beating of the sea?

Shule, shule agràh, shule agràh, shule agràh, Shule!
Heart of me, move to me! move to me! heart of me,
   Eilidh, Eilidh,
          Move to me!

Ah, let the wild hawk take it, the name of me, Cormac
   Conlingas,
Take it and tear at thy heart with it, heart that of old
   was so hot with it,
          Eilidh, Eilidh, o-rì, Eilidh, Eilidh!

And the last words of that song were so
loud and clear—loud and clear as the voice of
the war-horn—that Eilidh heard. The heart
of her leaped, the breast of her heaved, the
pulses danced in the surge of the blood. Once
more it was with her as though she were with
child by Cormac Conlingas. She bade the old
mother of Cravetheen and all who abode in
the Dûn to remain within, and not one to put
the gaze upon the grianan, her own place
there, or upon whom she should lead to it.
Then she went forth to meet Cormac, glad to
think of Cravetheen far thence on the hunting, and not to be back again till the third day.

It was a meeting of two waves, that. Each
was lost in the other. Then, after long look-

ing in the eyes, and with the words aswoon
on the lips, they moved hand in hand toward
the Dûn.

And as they moved, the Whispering of the
Sword made a sound like the going of wind
through grass.

"What is that?" said Eilidh, her eyes large.

"It is the wind in the grass," Cormac answered.

And as they entered the Dûn the Whispering of the Sword made a confused murmur
as of the wind among swaying pines.

"What is that?" Eilidh asked, fear in her
eyes.

"It is the wind in the forest," said Cormac.

But when, after he had eaten and drunken,
they went up to the Grianan, and lay down
upon the deer-skins, the Whispering of the
Sword was so loud that it was as the surf of
the sea in a wild wind.

"What is that?" cried Eilidh, with a sob in
her throat.

"It is the wind on the sea," Cormac said,
his voice hoarse and low.

"There is no sea within three days' march,"
whispered Eilidh, as she clasped her hands.

But Cormac said nothing. And, now, the
Sword was silent also.

It was starshine when Cravetheen returned. He was playing one of the *fonnsheen* he knew, as he came through the wood in the moonlight; for in the hunting of a stag he had made a great circle and was now near Dunchraig again, Dunchraig that was his Dûn. But he had left his horse with his kindred in the valley, and had come afoot through the wood.

He stopped as he was nigh upon the rocks against which the Dûn was built. He saw the blackness of the shadow of a living thing.

"Who is that?" he cried.

"It is I, Murtagh Làm-Rossa,"—and with that a man out of the Dûn came forward slowly and hesitatingly. He was a man who hated Eilidh, because she had put him to shame.

Cravetheen looked at him.

"I am waiting," he said.

Still the man hesitated.

"I am waiting, Murtagh Làm-Rossa."

"This is a bitter thing I have to say. I was on my way for the telling."

"It is of Eilidh that is my wife?"

"You have said it."

"Speak."

"She does not sleep alone in the Grianan,

and there is no one of the Dûn who is there
with her."

"Who is there?"

"A man."

"Cravetheen drew a long breath. His hand
went to the wolf-knife at his belt.

"What man?"

"Cormac mac Concobar, that is called Cormac Conlingas."

Again Cravetheen drew a deep breath, and
the blood was on his lip.

"You are knowing this thing for sure?"

"I am knowing it."

"That is what no other man shall do—"
and with that Cravetheen flashed the wolf-
knife in the moonshine, and thrust it with a
sucking sound into the heart of Murtagh
Làm-Rossa.

With a groan the man sank. His white
hands wandered among the fibrous dust of
the pine-needles : his face was as a livid wave
with the foam of death on it.

Cravetheen looked at the froth on his lips ;
it was like that of the sped deer. He looked
at the bubbles about the hilt of the knife ; they
were as the yeast of cranberries.

"That is the sure way of silence," he said ;
and he moved on, and thought no more of the
man.

In the shadow of the Dûn he stood a long while in thought. He could not reach the Grianan, he knew. Swords and spears for Eilidh, before then, mayhap ; and, if not, there was Cormac Conlingas—and not Cormac only, but the Sword " Blue-Green," and the Spear " Pisarr."

But a thought drove into his mind as a wind into a corrie. He put back his sword, and took his harp again. " It is the third playing," he muttered and smiled grimly, knowing that he smiled. Then once more he stood on the green rath of the quiet people, and played the *fonnsheen*, till they heard. And when the old elfin harper was come, Cravetheen played the Tune of the Asking.

" What will you be wanting, Cravetheena Mac Roury," asked the Green Harper.

" The Tune of the Trancing Sleep, green prince of the hill."

" Sure, you shall have it . . ." and with that the Green Harper gave the magic melody, so that not a leaf stirred, not a bird moved, and even the dew ceased to fall.

Then Cravetheen took his harp and played.

The dogs in the Dûn rose, but none howled. Then all lay down nosing their outstretched paws. Thrice the stallions in the rear of the Dûn put back their ears, but no neighing was

on their curled lips. The mares whimpered,
and then stood with heads low, asleep. The
armed men did not awake, but slumbered
deep. The women dreamed into the darkness
where no dream is. The old mother of Cravetheen stirred, crooned wearily, bowed her grey
head and was in Tir-na'n-òg again, walking
with Roury mac Roury that loved her, him
that was slain with a spear and a sword long,
long ago.

Only Eilidh and Cormac Conlingas were
waking. Sweet was that wild harping against
their ears.

"It will be the Green Harper himself,"
whispered Cormac, drowsy with the sleep that
was upon him.

"It will be the harping of Cravetheen I am
thinking," said Eilidh, with a low sigh, yet as
though that thing were nothing to her. But
Cormac did not hear, for he was asleep.

"I see nine shadows leaping upon the
wall," murmured Eilidh, while her heart beat
and her limbs lay in chains.

"'. . . *move to me, heart of me, Eilidh, Eilidh,*
Move to me!'"

murmured Cormac in his dream.

"I see nine hounds leaping into the Dûn,"
Eilidh cried, though none heard.

Cormac smiled in his sleep.

"Ah, ah, I see nine red phantoms leaping into the room!" screamed Eilidh; but none heard.

Cormac smiled in his sleep.

And then it was that the nine red flames grew ninefold, and the whole dûn was wrapped in flame.

For this was the doing of Cravetheen the Harper. All there died in the flame. That was the end of Eilidh, that was so fair. She laughed the pain away, and died. And Cormac smiled, and as the flame leaped on his breast he muttered, "*Ah, hot heart of Eilidh! —heart to me—move to me!*" And he died.

There was no dûn, and there were no folk, and no stallions and mares, and no baying hounds, when Cravetheen ceased from the playing—but only ashes.

He looked at them till dawn. Then he rose, and he broke his harp. Northward he went, to tell the Ultonians that thing, and to die the death.

And this was the end of Cormac the Hero, Cormac the son of Concobar the son of Nessa, that was called Cormac Conlingas.

SILK O' THE KINE [1]

"What I shall now be telling you," said Ian Mòr to me once—and indeed, I should remember the time of it well, for it was in the last year of his life, when rarely any other than myself saw aught of Ian of the Hills. "What I shall now be telling you is an ancient forgotten tale of a man and woman of the old heroic days. The name of the man was Isla, and the name of the woman was Eilidh."

"Ah yes, for sure," Ian added, as I interrupted him; "I knew you would be saying that; but it is not of Eilidh that loved Cormac that I am now speaking. Nor am I taking the hidden way with Isla, that was my friend, nor with Eilidh that is my name-child, [2] whom you know. Let the Birdeen be, bless her bonnie heart! No, what I am for telling you is all as new to you as the green grass to a lambkin; and no one has heard it from these

---

[1] *Silk o' the Kine*, one of the poetic "secret" names of conquered Erin, was in ancient days, there and in the Scottish Isles, a designation for a woman of rare beauty.

[2] See Vol. III., *The Dominion of Dreams.*

tired lips o' mine since I was a boy, and learned it off the mouth of old Barabol Mac-Aodh, that was my foster-mother."

Of all the many tales of the olden time that Ian Mòr told me, and are to be found in no book, this was the last. That is why I give it here, where I have spoken much of him.

Ian told me this thing one winter night, while we sat before the peats, where the ingle was full of warm shadows. We were in the croft of the small hill-farm of Glenivore, which was held by my cousin, Silis Macfarlane. But we were alone then, for Silis was over at the far end of the Strath, because of the baffling against death of her dearest friend, Giorsal MacDiarmid.

It was warm there, before the peats, with a thick wedge of spruce driven into the heart of them. The resin crackled and sent blue sparks of flame up through the red and yellow tongues that licked the sooty chimney-slopes, in which, as in a shell, we could hear an endless soughing of the wind.

Outside, the snow lay deep. It was so hard on the surface that the white hares, leaping across it, went soundless as shadows, and as trackless.

In the far-off days, when Somhairle was Maormor of the Isles, the most beautiful woman of her time was named Eilidh.

The king had sworn that whosoever was his best man in battle, when next the Fomorian pirates out of the north came down upon the isles, should have Eilidh to wife.

Eilidh, who, because of her soft, white beauty, for all the burning brown of her by the sun and wind, was also called Silk o' the Kine, laughed low when she heard this. For she loved the one man in all the world for her, and that was Isla, the son of Isla Mòr the blind chief of Islay. He, too, loved her even as she loved him. He was a poet as well as a warrior, and scarce she knew whether she loved best the fire in his eyes when, girt with his gleaming weapons and with his fair hair unbound, he went forth to battle ; or the shine in his eyes when, harp in hand, he chanted of the great deeds of old, or made a sweet song to her, Eilidh, his queen of women ; or the flame in his eyes when, meeting her at the setting of the sun, he stood speechless, wrought to silence because of his worshipping love of her.

One day she bade him go to the Isle of the Swans to fetch her enough of the breast-down of the wild cygnets for her to make a white cloak of. While he was still absent—and the going there, and the faring thereupon, and the returning took three days—the Fomorians came down upon the Long Island.

It was a hard fight that was fought, but at last the Norlanders were driven back with slaughter. Somhairle, the Maormor, was all but slain in that fight, and the corbies would have had his eyes had it not been for Osra Mac Osra, who with his javelin slew the spearman who had waylaid the king while he slipped in the Fomorian blood he had spilt.

While the ale was being drunk out of the great horns that night, Somhairle called for Eilidh.

The girl came to the rath where the king and his warriors feasted, white and beautiful as moonlight among turbulent, black waves.

A murmur went up from many bearded lips. The king scowled. Then there was silence.

"I am here, O King," said Eilidh. The sweet voice of her was like soft rain in the woods at the time of the greening.

Somhairle looked at her. Sure, she was fair to see. No wonder men called her Silk o' the Kine. His pulse beat against the stormy tide in his veins. Then, suddenly, his gaze fell upon Osra. The heart of his kins-

man that had saved him was his own ; and he
smiled, and lusted after Eilidh no more.

"Eilidh, that are called Silk o' the Kine,
dost thou see this man here before me ? "

" I see the man."

" Let the name of him, then, be upon your
lips."

" It is Osra Mac Osra."

" It is this Osra and no other man that is to
wind thee, fair Silk o' the Kine. And by the
same token, I have sworn to him that he shall
lie breast to breast with thee this night. So
go hence to where Osra has his sleeping-
place, and await him there upon the deerskins.
From this hour thou art his wife. It is
said."

Then a silence fell again upon all there,
when, after a loud surf of babbling laughter
and talk, they saw that Eilidh stood where she
was, heedless of the king's word.

Somhairle gloomed. The great black eyes
under his cloudy mass of hair flamed upon
her.

" Is it dumb you are, Eilidh," he said at
last, in a cold, hard voice. " Or do you wait
for Osra to take you hence ? "

" I am listening," she answered, and that
whisper was heard by all there. It was as the
wind in the heather, low and sweet.

Then all listened.

The playing of a harp was heard. None played like that save Isla Mac Isla Mòr.

Then the deerskins were drawn aside, and Isla came among those who feasted there.

"Welcome, O thou who wast afar off when the foe came," began Somhairle, with bitter mocking.

But Isla took no note of that. He went forward till he was nigh upon the Maormor. Then he waited.

"Well, Isla that is called Isla-Aluinn, Isla fair-to-see, what is the thing you want of me, that you stand there, close-kin to death I am warning you?"

"I want Eilidh that is called Silk o' the Kine."

"Eilidh is the wife of another man."

"There is no other man, O King."

"A brave word that! And who says it, O Isla my over-lord!"

"I say it."

Somhairle, the great Maormor, laughed, and his laugh was like a black bird of omen let loose against a night of storm.

"And what of Eilidh?"

"Let her speak."

With that the Maormor turned to the girl, who did not quail.

"Speak, Silk o' the Kine!"

"There is no other man, O King."

"Fool, I have this moment wedded you and Osra Mac Osra."

"I am wife to Isla-Aluinn."

"Thou canst not be wife to two men!"

"That may be, O King. I know not. But I am wife to Isla-Aluinn.

The king scowled darkly. None at the board whispered even. Osra shifted uneasily, clasping his sword-hilt. Isla stood, his eyes ashine as they rested on Eilidh. He knew nothing in life or death could come between them.

"Art thou not still a maid, Eilidh?" Somhairle asked at last.

"No."

"Shame to thee, wanton."

The girl smiled. But in her eyes, darkened now, there shone a flame.

"Is Isla-Aluinn the man?"

"He is the man."

With that the king laughed a bitter laugh.

"Seize him!" he cried.

But Isla made no movement. So those who were about to bind him stood by, ready with naked swords.

"Take up your harp," said Somhairle.

Isla stooped, and lifted the harp.

" Play now the wedding song of Osra Mac Osra and Eilidh Silk o' the Kine."

Isla smiled, but it was a grim smile that, and only Eilidh understood. Then he struck the harp, and he sang thus far this song out of his heart to the woman he loved better than life.

Eilidh, Eilidh, heart of my life, my pulse, my flame,
There are two men loving thee, and two who are
    calling thee wife!

But only one husband to thee, Eilidh, that art my
    wife and my joy;
Ay, sure thy womb knows me and the child thou
    bearest is mine.

Thou to me, I to thee, there is nought else in the
    world, Eilidh, Silk o' the Kine,—
Nought else in the world, no, no other man for thee,
    no woman for me!

But with that Somhairle rose, and dashed the hilt of his great spear upon the ground.

" Let the twain go," he shouted.

Then all stood or leaned back, as Isla and Eilidh slowly moved through their midst, hand in hand. Not one there but knew they went to their death.

" This night shall be theirs," cried the king with mocking wrath. " Then, Osra, you can

have your will of Silk o' the Kine that is your
wife, and have Isla-Aluinn to be your slave—
and this for the rising and setting of three
moons from to-night. Then they shall each
be blinded and made dumb, and that for the
same space of time. And at the end of that
time they shall be thrown upon the snow to
the wolves."

Nevertheless Osra groaned in his heart because of that night of Isla with Eilidh. Not
all the years of the years could give him a joy
like unto that.

In the silence of the mid-dark he went
stealthily to where the twain lay.

It was there he was found in the morning,
where he had died soundlessly, with Eilidh's
dagger up to the hilt in his heart.

But none saw them go, save one; and that
was Sorch the brother of Isla, Sorch who in
later days was called Sorch Mouth o' Honey
because of his sweet songs. Of all songs
that he sang none was so sweet against the
ears as that of the love of Eilidh and
Isla. Two lovers these that loved as few
love; and deathless, too, because of that
great love.

And what Sorch saw was this. Just before
the rising of the sun, Isla and Eilidh came
hand in hand from out of the rath, where they

123

had lain awake all night because of their deep joy.

Silently, but unhasting, fearless still as of yore, they moved across the low dunes that withheld the sea from the land.

The waves were just frothed, so low were they. The loud glad singing of them filled the morning. Eilidh and Isla stopped when the first waves met their feet. They cast their raiment from them. Eilidh flung the gold fillet of her dusky hair far into the sea. Isla broke his sword, and saw the two halves shelve through the moving greenness. Then they turned, and kissed each other upon the lips.

And the end of the song of Sorch is this : that neither he nor any man knows whether they went to life or to death ; but that Isla and Eilidh swam out together against the sun, and were seen never again by any of their kin or race. Two strong swimmers were these, who swam out together into the sunlight ; Eilidh and Isla.

ULA AND URLA[1]

Ula and Urla were under vow to meet by the Stone of Sorrow. But Ula, dying first, stumbled blindfold when he passed the Shadowy Gate ; and till Urla's hour was upon her, she remembered not.

These were the names that had been given to them in the north isles, when the birlinn that ran down the war-galley of the vikings brought them before the Maormor.

No word had they spoken that day, and no name. They were of the Gael, though Ula's hair was yellow, and though his eyes were blue as the heart of a wave. They would ask nothing, for both were in love with death. The Maormor of Siol Tormaid looked at Urla, and his desire gnawed at his heart. But he knew what was in her mind, because he saw into it through her eyes, and he feared the sudden slaying in the dark.

[1] The first part of the story of Ula and Urla, as Isla and Eilidh, is told in " Silk o' the Kine." [The name Eilidh is pronounced Eily (*liq.*) or Isle-ih.]

Nevertheless, he brooded night and day upon her beauty. Her skin was more white than the foam of the moon : her eyes were as a star-lit dewy dusk. When she moved, he saw her like a doe in the fern : when she stooped, it was as the fall of wind-swayed water. In his eyes there was a shimmer as of the sun-flood in a calm sea. In that dazzle he was led astray.

"Go," he said to Ula, on a day of the days. "Go: the men of Siol Torquil will take you to the south isles, and so you can hale to your own place, be it Eirèann or Manannan, or wherever the south wind puts its hand upon your home."

It was on that day Ula spoke for the first time.

"I will go, Coll mac Torcall; but I go not alone. Urla that I love goes whither I go."

"She is my spoil. But, man out of Eirèann —for so I know you to be, because of the manner of your speech—tell me this : Of what clan and what place are you, and whence is Urla come ; and by what shore was it that the men of Lochlin whom we slew took you and her out of the sea, as you swam against the sun, with waving swords upon the strand when the viking-boat carried you away ?"

"How know you these things?" asked **Ula**, that had been Isla, son of the king of Islay.

"One of the sea-rovers spoke before he died."

"Then let the viking speak again. I have nought to say."

With that the Maormor frowned, but said no more. That eve Ula was seized, as he walked in the dusk by the sea, singing low to himself an ancient song.

"Is it death?" he said, remembering another day when he and Eilidh, that they called Urla, had the same asking upon their lips.

"It is death."

Ula frowned, but spake no word for a time. Then he spake.

"Let me say one word with Urla."

"No word canst thou have. She, too, must die."

Ula laughed low at that.

"I am ready," he said. And they slew him with a spear.

When they told Urla, she rose from the deerskins and went down to the shore. She said no word then. But she stooped, and she put her lips upon his cold lips, and she whispered in his unhearing ear.

That night Coll mac Torcall went secretly

to where Urla was. When he entered, a
groan came to his lips and there was froth
there : and that was because the spear that
had slain Ula was thrust betwixt his shoulders by one who stood in the shadow. He lay
there till the dawn. When they found Coll
the Maormor he was like a seal speared upon
a rock, for he had his hands out, and his head
was between them, and his face was downward.

" Eat dust, slain wolf," was all that Eilidh,
whom they called Urla, said, ere she moved
away from that place in the darkness of the
night.

When the sun rose, Urla was in a glen
among the hills. A man who shepherded
there took her to his mate. They gave her
milk, and because of her beauty and the frozen silence of her eyes, bade her stay with
them and be at peace.

They knew in time that she wished death.
But first, there was the birthing of the
child.

" It was Isla's will," she said to the woman.
Ula was but the shadow of a bird's wing : an
idle name. And she, too, was Eilidh once
more.

" It was death he gave you when he gave
you the child," said the woman once.

" It was life," answered Eilidh, with her eyes filled with the shadow of dream. And yet another day the woman said to her that it would be well to bear the child and let it die : for beauty was like sunlight on a day of clouds, and if she were to go forth young and alone and so wondrous fair, she would have love, and love is best.

" Truly, love is best," Eilidh answered. "And because Isla loved me, I would that another Isla came into the world and sang his songs—the songs that were so sweet, and the songs that he never sang, because I gave him death when I gave him life. But now he shall live again, and he and I shall be in one body, in him that I carry now."

At that the woman understood, and said no more. And so the days grew out of the nights, and the dust of the feet of one month was in the eyes of that which followed after ; and this until Eilidh's time was come.

Dusk after dusk, Ula that was Isla the Singer, waited by the Stone of Sorrow. Then a great weariness came upon him. He made a song there, where he lay in the narrow place ; the last song that he made, for after that he heard no trampling of the hours.

The swift years slip and slide adown the steep;
   The slow years pass; neither will come again.
Yon huddled years have weary eyes that weep,
   These laugh, these moan, these silent frown, these
      plain,
   These have their lips acurl with proud disdain.

O years with tears, and tears through weary years,
   How weary I who in your arms have lain:
Now, I am tired: the sound of slipping spears
   Moves soft, and tears fall in a bloody rain,
   And the chill footless years go over me who am
      slain.

I hear, as in a wood, dim with old light, the rain,
   Slow falling; old, old, weary, human tears:
And in the deepening dark my comfort is my Pain,
   Sole comfort left of all my hopes and fears,
   Pain that alone survives, gaunt hound of the
      shadowy years.

But, at the last, after many days, he stirred. There was a song in his ears.

He listened. It was like soft rain in a wood in June. It was like the wind laughing among the leaves.

Then his heart leaped. Sure, it was the voice of Eilidh!

"*Eilidh! Eilidh! Eilidh!*" he cried. But a great weariness came upon him again. He fell asleep, knowing not the little hand that was in his, and the small, flower-sweet body that was warm against his side.

Then the child that was his looked into the singer's heart, and saw there a mist of rainbows, and midway in that mist was the face of Eilidh, his mother.

Thereafter, the little one looked into his brain that was so still, and he saw the music that was there: and it was the voice of Eilidh his mother.

And, again, the birdeen, that had the blue of Isla's eyes and the dream of Eilidh's, looked into Ula's sleeping soul : and he saw that it was not Isla nor yet Eilidh, but that it was like unto himself, who was made of Eilidh and Isla.

For a long time the child dreamed. Then he put his ear to Isla's brow, and listened. Ah, the sweet songs that he heard. Ah, bittersweet moonseed of song ! Into his life they passed, echo after echo, strain after strain, wild air after wild sweet air.

" Isla shall never die," whispered the child, " for Eilidh loved him. And I am Isla and Eilidh."

Then the little one put his hands above Isla's heart. There was a flame there, that the Grave quenched not.

" O flame of love ! " sighed the child, and he clasped it to his breast : and it was a moonshine glory about the two hearts that he had, the heart of Isla and the heart of Eilidh, that were thenceforth one.

At dawn he was no longer there. Already the sunrise was warm upon him where he lay, new-born, upon the breast of Eilidh.

"It is the end," murmured Isla when he waked. "She has never come. For sure, now, the darkness and the silence."

Then he remembered the words of Maol the Druid, he that was a seer, and had told him of Orchil, the dim goddess who is under the brown earth, in a vast cavern, where she weaves at two looms. With one hand she weaves life upward through the grass; with the other she weaves death downward through the mould; and the sound of the weaving is Eternity, and the name of it in the green world is Time. And, through all, Orchil weaves the weft of Eternal Beauty, that passeth not, though its soul is Change.

And these were the words of Orchil, on the lips of Maol the Druid, that was old, and knew the mystery of the Grave.

When thou journeyest toward the Shadowy Gate take neither Fear with thee nor Hope, for both are abashed hounds of silence in that place; but take only the purple night-

*shade for sleep, and a vial of tears and wine,
tears that shall be known unto thee and old
wine of love. So shalt thou have thy silent
festival, ere the end.*

So therewith Isla, having, in his weariness,
the nightshade of sleep, and in his mind the
slow dripping rain of familiar tears, and deep
in his heart the old wine of love, bowed his
head.

It was well to have lived, since life was
Eilidh. It was well to cease to live, since
Eilidh came no more.

Then suddenly he raised his head. There
was music in the green world above. A sunray opened the earth about him : staring upward he beheld Angus Òg.

"Ah, fair face of the god of youth," he
sighed. Then he saw the white birds that fly
about the head of Angus Òg, and he heard the
music that his breath made upon the harp of
the wind.

"Arise," said Angus ; and, when he smiled,
the white birds flashed their wings and made
a mist of rainbows.

"Arise," said Angus Òg again, and, when
he spoke, the spires of the grass quivered to a
wild, sweet haunting air.

So Isla arose, and the sun shone upon him,

133

F

and his shadow passed into the earth. Orchil wove into it her web of death.

"Why dost thou wait here by the Stone of Sorrow, Isla that was called Ula at the end?"

"I wait for Eilidh, who cometh not."

At that the wind-listening god stooped and laid his head upon the grass.

"I hear the coming of a woman's feet," he said, and he rose.

"Eilidh! Eilidh!" cried Isla, and the sorrow of his cry was a moan in the web of Orchil.

Angus Òg took a branch, and put the cool greenness against his cheek.

"I hear the beating of a heart," he said.

"Eilidh! Eilidh! Eilidh!" Isla cried, and the tears that were in his voice were turned by Angus into dim dews of remembrance in the babe-brain that was the brain of Isla and Eilidh.

"I hear a word," said Angus Òg, "and that word is a flame of joy."

Isla listened. He heard a singing of birds. Then, suddenly, a glory came into the shine of the sun.

"*I have come, Isla my king!*"

It was the voice of Eilidh. He bowed his head, and swayed; for it was his own life that came to him.

"*Eilidh !*" he whispered.

And so, at the last, Isla came into his kingdom.

But are they gone, these twain, who loved with deathless love ? Or is this a dream that I have dreamed ?

Afar in an island-sanctuary that I shall not see again, where the wind chants the blind oblivious rune of Time, I have heard the grasses whisper: *Time never was, Time is not.*

THE WASHER OF THE FORD:

AND OTHER LEGENDARY MORALITIES

It is Loveliness I seek, not lovely things.

TO
C. A. J

PROLOGUE

" I find under the boughs of love and hate,
Eternal Beauty wandering on her way."
(" The Rose upon the Rood of Time.")

Prologue

(To Kathia)

To you, in your far-away home in Provence, I send these tales out of the remote North you love so well, and so well understand. The same blood is in our veins, a deep current somewhere beneath the tide that sustains us. We have meeting-places that none knows of; we understand what few can understand; and we share in common a strange and inexplicable heritage. It is because you, who are called Kathia of the Sunway, are also Kathia nan Ciar, Kathia of the Shadow, it is because you are what you are that I inscribe this book to you. In it you will find much that is familiar to you; for there is a reality, beneath the mere accident of novelty, which may be recognised in a moment as native to the secret life, that lives behind the brain and the wise nerves with their dim ancestral knowledge.

The greater portion of this book deals with the remote life of a remote past. As for

"The Last Supper" and "The Fisher of
Men," they are of no time or date, for they
are founded upon elemental facts which are
modified but not transformed by the changing
years.

It may be the last of its kind I shall write
—at any rate, for a time. I would like it to
be associated with you, to whom not only the
mystery but the pagan sentiment and the old
barbaric emotion are so near. With the second sight of the imagination we can often
see more clearly in the dim subsided waters
than through the foam and spray of the present; and most clearly when we recognise that,
amid the ebb and flow of time and circum-
stance, the present is but a surface-eddy of
that past to which we belong. In the strange
arrogance of our passing hour we are as ships
swinging happily content to anchors which
are linked to us by ropes of sand.

If I am eager to have my say on other
aspects of our Celtic life in the remoter West
Highlands and in the Isles: now with the
idyllic, now with the tragic, now with the
grotesque, the humorous, the pathetic, with
all the medley cast from the looms of Life—
all that

> "... from the looms of Life are spun,
> Warp of shadow and woof of sun——"

and if, too, I long to express anew something
of that wonderful historic romance in which
we of our race and country are so rich, I am
not likely to forget those earlier dreams
which are no whit less realities—realities of
the present seen through an inverted glass—
which have been, and are, so full of inspiration
and of a strange and terrible beauty.

But one to whom life appeals by a myriad
avenues, all alluring and full of wonder and
mystery, cannot always abide where the heart
longs most to be. It is well to remember
that there are Shadowy Waters even in the
cities, and that the Fount of Youth is discov-
erable in the dreariest towns as well as in
Hy Bràsil: a truth apt to be forgotten by
those of us who dwell with ever-wondering
delight in that land of lost romance which had
its own way, as this epoch of a still stranger,
if a less obvious, romance has its own passing
hour.

The titular piece—with its strange name
that will not be unfamiliar to you who know
our ancient Celtic literature, or may bear in
mind the striking image wrought out of the
old local legend, by the author of the Irish
epic, *Congal*—gives the keynote, not only of
this book, but of what has been for hundreds
of years, and to some extent still is, the char-

acteristic of the purely Celtic mind in the
Highlands and the Isles. This characteristic
is a strange complexity of paganism and
Christianity, or rather an apparent complexity
arising from the grafting of Christianity upon
paganism. Columba, St. Patrick, St. Ronan,
Kentigern, all these militant Christian saints
were merely transformed pagans. Even in
the famous dialogue between St. Patrick and
Oisin, which is the folk-telling of the passing
of the old before the new, the thrill of a
pagan sympathy on the part of the uncom-
promising saint is unmistakable. To this day
there are Christian rites and superstitions
which are merely a gloss upon a surviving
antique paganism. I have known an old
woman, in nowise different from her neigh-
bours, who on the day of Beltane sacrificed a
hen: though for her propitiatory rite she had
no warrant save that of vague traditionary
lore, the lore of the *teinntean*, of the hearthside
—where, in truth, are best to be heard the
last echoes of the dim mythologic faith of our
ancestors. What is the familiar "clachan,"
now meaning a hamlet with a kirk, but an
echo of the "Stones," the circles of the
Druids—or of a more ancient worship still,
that perhaps of the mysterious Anait, whose
sole record is a *clach* on a lonely moor, of

which from time immemorial the people have
spoken as the "Teampull na'n Anait"?   A
relative of mine saw, in South Uist, less than
twenty-five years ago, what may have been
the last sun-sacrifice in Scotland, when an old
Gael secretly and furtively slew a lamb on
the summit of a conical grassy knoll at sunrise.
Those who have the Gaelic have their ears
filled with rumours of a day that is gone.
When an evicted crofter laments, *O   mo
chreach, mo chreach!*[1] or some poor soul on
a bed of pain cries, *O mo chradhshlat!*[2] he
who knows the past recognises in the one the
mournful refrain of the time when the sea-
pirates or the hill-robbers pillaged and devas-
tated quiet homesteads ; and, in the other, not
the moan of suffering only, but the cry of torment from the victim racked on the "cradh-
shlat," a bitter ignominious torture used by
the ancient Gaels.   When, in good fellowship
one man says to another, *Tha, a laochain* (yes,
my dear fellow), he recalls Fionn and the
chivalry of eld ; for *laochain* is merely a
contraction for laoch-Fhinn, meaning a companion in war, a hero, literally Fionn's right-
hand man in battle.   To this day, women, ac-

[1] "O, alas, alas!"   Literally, "O, my undoing,"
or "O, my utter ruin."
[2] "Alas, my torment!"

companying a marching regiment, are sometimes heard to say in the Gaelic, "We are going
with the dear souls to the wars"—literally
an echo of the Ossianic *Siubhlaidh sinn le'n
anam do'n araich*, "We shall accompany their
souls to the battle-field." A thousand instances
could be adduced. The language is a her-
ring-net through which the unchanging sea
filtrates even though the net be clogged with
the fish of the hour. Nor is it the pagan atmosphere only that survives : often we breathe
the air of that early day when the mind of
man was attuned to a beautiful piety which
was wrought into nature itself. Of the several
words for the dawn, there is a beautiful
one, *Uinneagachadh*. We have it in the
phrase, *'nuair a bha an latha ag uinneagachadh*, "when the day began to dawn." Now
this word is simply an extension of *Uinneag*,
a window, and the application of the image
dates far back to the days of St Columba
when some devout and poetic soul spoke of
the *uinneagan Nèimh*, the windows of heaven.

Sometimes, among the innumerable legendary moralities which exist fragmentarily in the
West Highlands and in the Isles, there is
a coherent narrative basis—as, for example, in
the Irish and Highland folk-lore about St
Bride, or Brigit, "Muime Chriosd" Some-

times there is simply a phrase survived out of antiquity. I doubt if any now living, either in the Hebrides or in Ireland, has heard even a fragmentary legend of the Washer of the Ford. The name survives, with its atmosphere of a remote past, its dim ancestral memory of a shadowy figure of awe haunting a shadowy stream in a shadowy land. Sir Samuel Ferguson, in *Congal*, has done little more than limm an obscure shadow of that shadow; yet it haunts the imagination. In the passage of paganism, these old myths were too deep-rooted in the Celtic mind to vanish at the bidding of the Cross: fhus came about that strange grafting of the symbolic imagery of the devout Culdee, of the visionary Mariolater, upon the surviving Druidic and pre-historic imagination. In a word, the Washer of the Ford might well have appeared, to a single generation, now as a terrible and sombre pagan goddess of death, now as a symbolic figure in the new faith, foreshadowing spiritual salvation and the mystery of resurrection.

If, in a composition such as " Cathal-of-the Woods," there is the expression of revolt—not ancient only, nor of the hour, but eternal, for the revolt is of the sovereign nature within us whereon all else is an accidental super-

structure—against the Christian ethic of re-
nunciation, with a concurrent echo of our deep
primeval longing for earth-kinship with every
life in Nature : if here there is the breath of
a day that may not come again, there is little
or nothing of the past, save what is merely
accidental, in " The Fisher of Men " or " The
Last Supper." I like to think that these *each-
daireachd spioradail*, these spiritual chronicles,
might as well, in substance, have been told a
thousand years ago or be written a thousand
years hence. That Fisher still haunts the invisible shadowy stream of human tears ; those
mystic Spinners still ply their triple shuttles,
and the fair Weaver of Hope now as of yore
and for ever sends his rainbows adrift across
the hearts and through the minds of men.
What does it matter, again, that the Three
Marvels of Hy are set against the background
of the Iona of St. Columba ? St. Francis
blessed the birds of Assisi, and San Antonio
had a heart as tender for all winged and
gentle creatures ; and there are innumerable
quiet gardens of peace in the world even now,
where the kindred of San Antonio and St.
Francis and St Columba are kith to our fel-
low-beings, knowing them akin one and all to
the seals whom St Molios blessed at the end
of his days, and in his new humbleness hailed

as likewise of the company of the sons of God.

But of this I am sure. If there be spiritual truth in the vision of the Blind Harper who saw the Washer of the Ford, or in that of Molios who hailed the seals as brethren, or in that of Colum, who blessed the birds and the fish of the sea, and even the vagrant flies of the air, and saw the Moon-Child, and in that seeing learned the last mystery of the life of the soul; if in these, as in "The Fisher of Men" and "The Last Supper," I have given faint utterance to the heart-knowledge we all have, I would not have you or any think that the pagan way is therefore to me as the way of darkness. The lost monk who loved the Annir-Choille was doubtless not the less able to see the Uinneagan Nèimh because he was under ban of Colum and all his kin; and there are those of us who would rather be with Cathal of the Woods, and be drunken with green fire, than gain the paradise of the holy Molios who banned him, if in that gain were involved the forfeiture of the sunny green world, the joy of life, and the earth-sweet ancient song of the blood that is in the veins of youth.

These tales, let me add, are not legendary mysteries but legendary moralities. They are

reflections from the mirror that is often obscured but is never dimmed. There is no
mystery in them, or anywhere ; except the
eternal mystery of beauty.

Of the section called Seanachas, the short
barbaric tales, I will say nothing to you, whose
favourite echo from Shelley is that thrilling
line—" The tempestuous loveliness of terror."

You in your far Provence, amid the austere
hills that guard an ancient land of olive and
vine, a land illumined by the blue flowing
light of the Rhone, and girt by desert places
where sun and wind inhabit, and scarce any
other—you there and I here have this in common. Everywhere we see the life of Man in
subservient union with the life of Nature ;
never, in a word, as a sun beset by tributary
stars, but as one planet among the innumerous
concourse of the sky, nurtured, it may be, by
light from other luminaries and other spheres
than we know of. That we are intimately at
one with Nature is a cosmic truth we are all
slowly approaching. It is not only the dog,
it is not only the wild beast and the wood-
dove, that are our close kindred, but the green
tree and the green grass, the blue wave and
the flowing wind, the flower of a day and the
granite peak of an æon. And I for one would
rather have the wind for comrade, and the

white stars and green leaves as my kith and kin, than many a human companion, whose chief claim is the red blood that differs little from the sap in the grass or in the pines, and whose "deathless soul" is, mayhap, no more than a fugitive light blown idly for an hour betwixt dawn and dark. We are woven in one loom, and the Weaver thrids our being with the sweet influences, not only of the Pleiades, but of the living world of which each is no more than a multi-coloured thread: as, in turn, He thrids the wandering wind with the inarticulate cry, the yearning, the passion, the pain, of that bitter clan, the Human.

Truly, we are all one. It is a common tongue we speak, though the wave has its own whisper, and the wind its own sigh, and the lip of man its word, and the heart of woman its silence.

Long, long ago a desert king, old and blind, but dowered with ancestral wisdom beyond all men that have lived, heard that the Son of God was born among men. He rose from his place, and on the eve of the third day he came to where Jesus sat among the gifts brought by the wise men of the East. The little lad sat in Mary's lap, beneath a tree filled with quiet light; and while the folk of

Bethlehem came and went He was only a child as other children are. But when the desert king drew near, the child's eyes deepened with knowledge.

"What is it, my little son?" said Mary the Virgin.

"Sure, Mother dear," said Jesus, who had never yet spoken a word, "it is Deep Knowledge that is coming to me."

"And what will that be, O my Wonder and Glory?"

"That which will come in at the door before you speak to me again."

Even as the child spoke, an old blind man entered and bowed his head.

"Come near, O tired old man," said Mary that had borne a son to Joseph, but whose womb knew him not.

With that the tears fell into the old man's beard. "Sorrow of sorrows," he said, "but that will be the voice of the Queen of Heaven!"

But Jesus said to his mother: "Take up the tears, and throw them into the dark night." And Mary did so: and lo! upon the wilderness, where no light was, and on the dark wave, where seamen toiled without hope, clusters of shining stars rayed downward in a white peace.

Thereupon the old king of the desert said:
"Heal me, O King of the Elements."

And Jesus healed him. His sight was upon
him again, and his grey ancientness was green
youth once more.

"I have come with Deep Knowledge," he
said.

"Ay, sure, I am for knowing that," said the
King of the Elements, that was a little
child.

"Well, if you will be knowing that, you can
tell me who is at my right side?"

"It is my elder brother the Wind."

"And what colour will the shadow be?"

"Now blue as Hope, now green as Compassion."

"And who is on my left?"

"The Shadow of Life."

"And what colour will the Shadow be?"

"That which is woven out of the bowels
of the earth and out of the belly of the
sea."

"Truly, thou art the King of the Elements.
I am bringing you a great gift, I am: I have
come with Deep Knowledge."

And with that the old blind man, whose
eyes were now as stars, and whose youth was
a green garland about him, chanted nine
runes.

The first rune was the Rune of the Four Winds.

The second rune was the Rune of the Deep Seas.

The third rune was the Rune of the Lochs and Rivers and the Rains and the Dews and the many waters.

The fourth rune was the Rune of the Green Trees and of all things that grow.

The fifth rune was the Rune of Man and Bird and Beast, and of everything that lives and moves, in the air, on the earth, and in the sea: all that is seen of man, and all that is unseen of man.

The sixth rune was the Rune of Birth, from the spawn on the wave to the Passion of Woman.

The seventh rune was the Rune of Death, from the quenching of a gnat to the fading of the stars.

The eighth rune was the Rune of the Soul that dieth not, and the Spirit that is.

The ninth rune was the Rune of the Mud and the Dross and the Slime of Evil—that is the Garden of God, wherein He walks with sunlight streaming from the palms of His hands and with stars springing beneath His feet.

Then when he had done, the old man said:

" I have brought you Deep Knowledge." But at that Jesus the Child said:

" All this I heard on my way hither."

The old desert king bowed his head. Then he took a blade of grass, and played upon it. It was a wild, strange air that he played.

" Iosa mac Dhè, tell the woman what song *that* is," cried the desert king.

" It is the secret speech of the Wind that is my Brother," cried the Child, clapping his hands for joy.

" And what will this be ? " and with that the old man took a green leaf, and played a lovely whispering song.

" It is the secret speech of the leaves," cried Jesus the little lad, laughing low.

And thereafter the desert king played upon a handful of dust, and upon a drop of water, and upon a flame of fire ; and the Child laughed for the knowing and the joy. Then he gave the secret speech of the singing bird, and the barking fox, and the howling wolf, and the bleating sheep: of all and every created kind.

" O King of the Elements," he said then, " for sure you knew much ; but now I have made you to know the secret things of the green Earth that is Mother of you and of Mary too."

But while Jesus pondered that one mystery, the old man was gone : and when he got to his people, they put him alive into a hollow of the earth and covered him up, because of his shining eyes, and the green youth that was about him as a garland.

And when Christ was nailed upon the Cross, Deep knowledge went back into the green world, and passed into the grass and the sap in trees, and the flowing wind, and the dust that swirls and is gone.

All this is of the wisdom of the long ago, and you and I are of those who know how ancient it is, how remoter far than when Mary, at the bidding of her little son, threw up into the firmament the tears of an old man.

It is old, old—

> " Thousands of years, thousands of years,
> If all were told."

Is it wholly unwise, wholly the fantasy of a dreamer, to insist, in this late day, when the dust of ages and the mists of the present hide from us the Beauty of the World, that we can regain our birthright only by leaving our cloud-palaces of the brain, and becoming consciously at one with the cosmic life of which, merely as men, we are no more than a perpetual phosphorescence?

LEGENDARY MORALITIES

" . . . . . tell
Of the dim wisdoms old and deep,
That God gives unto man in sleep,
For the elemental beings go
About my table to and fro.
In flow and fire and clay and wind,
They huddle from man's pondering mind
Yet he who treads in austere ways,
May surely meet their ancient gaze.
Man ever journeys on with them
After the red-rose-bordered hem.
Ah, faeries, dancing under the moon,
A Druid land, a Druid tune!"

The Washer of the Ford

When Torcall the Harper heard of the death of his friend, Aodh-of-the-Songs, he made a vow to mourn for him for three seasons—a green-time, an apple-time, and a snow-time.

There was sorrow upon him because of that death. True, Aodh was not of his kindred, but the singer had saved the harper's life when his friend was fallen in the Field of Spears.

Torcall was of the people of the north—of the men of Lochlin. His song was of the fjords and of strange gods, of the sword and the war-galley, of the red blood and the white breast, of Odin and Thor and Freya, of Balder and the Dream-God that sits in the rainbow, of the starry North, of the flames of pale blue and flushing rose that play around the Pole, of sudden death in battle, and of Valhalla.

Aodh was of the south isles, where these shake under the thunder of the western seas. His clan was of the isle that is now called

Barra, and was then Aoidû ; but his mother
was a woman out of a royal rath in Banba,
as men of old called Eiré or Eireann. She was
so fair that a man died of his desire of her.
He was named Ulad, and was a prince. " The
Melancholy of Ulad" was long sung in his
land after his end in the dark swamp, where
he heard a singing, and went laughing glad to
his death. Another man was made a prince
because of her. This was Aodh the Harper,
out of the Hebrid Isles. He won the heart
out of her, and it was his from the day she
heard his music and felt his eyes flame upon
her. Before the child was born, she said,
" He shall be the son of love. He shall be
called Aodh. He shall be called Aodh-of-the-
Songs." And so it was.

Sweet were his songs. He loved, and he
sang, and he died.

And when Torcall that was his friend knew
this sorrow, he rose and made his vow, and
went out for evermore from the place where
he was.

Since the hour of the Field of Spears he
had been blind. Torcall Dall he was upon
men's lips thereafter. His harp had a moonshine wind upon it from that day, it was said :
a beautiful strange harping when he went
down through the glen, or out upon the sandy

162

machar by the shore, and played what the wind sang, and the grass whispered, and the tree murmured, and the sea muttered or cried hollowly in the dark.

Because there was no sight to his eyes, men said he saw and he heard. What was it he heard and saw that they saw not and heard not? It was in the voice that sighed in the strings of his harp, so the saying was.

When he rose and went away from his place, the Maormor asked him if he went north, as the blood sang; or south, as the heart cried; or west, as the dead go; or east, as the light comes.

"I go east," answered Torcall Dall.

"And why so, Blind Harper?"

"For there is darkness always upon me, and I go where the light comes."

On that night of the nights, a fair wind blowing out of the west, Torcall the Harper set forth in a galley. It splashed in the moonshine as it was rowed swiftly by nine men.

"Sing us a song, O Torcall Dall!" they cried.

"Sing us a song, Torcall of Lochlin," said the man who steered. He and all his company were of the Gael: the Harper only was of the Northmen.

"What shall I sing?" he asked. "Shall it be of war that you love, or of women that twine you like silk o' the kine; or shall it be of death that is your need; or of your dread, the Spears of the North?"

A low sullen growl went from beard to beard.

"We are under *ceangal*, Blind Harper," said the steersman, with downcast eyes because of his flaming wrath; "we are under bond to take you safe to the mainland, but we have sworn no vow to sit still under the lash of your tongue. 'Twas a wind-fleet arrow that sliced the sight out of your eyes: have a care lest a sudden sword-wind sweep the breath out of your body."

Torcall laughed a low, quiet laugh.

"Is it death I am fearing now—I who have washed my hands in blood, and had love, and known all that is given to man? But I will sing you a song, I will."

And with that he took his harp, and struck the strings:

A lonely stream there is, afar in a lone dim land:
It hath white dust for shore it has, white bones bestrew the strand:
The only thing that liveth there is a naked leaping sword;
But I, who a seer am, have seen the whirling hand
　　　Of the Washer of the Ford.

The Washer of the Ford

A shadowy shape of cloud and mist, of gloom and
  night, she stands,
      The Washer of the Ford:
She laughs, at times, and strews the dust through the
  hollow of her hands.

She counts the sins of all men there, and slays the
  red-stained horde—
The ghosts of all the sins of men must know the
  whirling sword
      Of the Washer of the Ford.

She stoops and laughs when in the dust she sees a
  writhing limb·
"Go back into the ford," she says, "and hither and
  thither swim;
Then I shall wash you white as snow, and shall take
  you by the hand,
And slay you here in the silence with this my whirling brand,
And trample you into the dust of this white windless
  sand"—

          This is the laughing word
          Of the Washer of the Ford
          Along that silent strand.

There was silence for a time after Torcall
Dall sang that song. The oars took up the
moonshine and flung it hither and thither like
loose shining crystals. The foam at the prow
curled and leaped.

Suddenly one of the rowers broke into a
long, low chant—

Yo, eily-a-ho, ayah-a-ho, eily-ayah-a-ho,
  Singeth the Sword
Eily-a-ho, ayah-a-ho, eily-ayah-a-ho,
  Of the Washer of the Ford!

And at that all ceased from rowing. Standing erect, they lifted up their oars against the stars, and the wild voices of them flew out upon the night—

Yo, eily-a-ho, ayah-a-ho, eily-ayah-a ho,
  Singeth the Sword
Eily-a-ho, ayah-a-ho, eily-ayah-a-ho,
  Of the Washer of the Ford!

Torcall Dall laughed. Then he drew his sword from his side and plunged it into the sea. When he drew the blade out of the water and whirled it on high, all the white shining drops of it swirled about his head like a sleety rain.

And at that the steersman let go the steering-oar and drew his sword, and clove a flowing wave. But with the might of his blow the sword spun him round, and the sword sliced away the ear of the man who had the sternmost oar. Then there was blood in the eyes of all there. The man staggered, and felt for his knife, and it was in the heart of the steersman.

Then because these two men were leaders,

and had had a blood-feud, and because all
there, save Torcall, were of one or the other
side, swords and knives sang a song.

The rowers dropped their oars; and four
men fought against three.

Torcall laughed, and lay back in his place.
While out of the wandering wave the death
of each man clambered into the hollow of the
boat, and breathed its chill upon its man, Torcall the Blind took his harp. He sang this
song, with the swirling spray against his face,
and the smell of blood in his nostrils, and the
feet of him dabbling in the red tide that rose
there.

Oh 'tis a good thing the red blood, by Odin his word!
And a good thing it is to hear it bubbling deep.
And when we hear the laughter of the Sword,
Oh, the corbies croak, and the old wail, and the
    women weep!
And busy will she be there where she stands,
Washing the red out of the sins of all this slaying
    horde;
And trampling the bones of them into white powdery
    sands,
  And laughing low at the thirst of her thirsty
    sword—
        The Washer of the Ford!

When he had sung that song there was only
one man whose pulse still beat, and he was
at the bow.

"A bitter black curse upon you, Torcall Dall !" he groaned out of the ooze of blood that was in his mouth.

"And who will you be ?" said the blind Harper.

"I am Fergus, the son of Art, the son of Fergus of the Two Dûns."

"Well, it is a song for your death I will make, Fergus mac Art mhic Fheargus : and because you are the last."

With that Torcall struck a sob out of his harp, and he sang—

Oh, death of Fergus, that is lying in the boat here
  Betwixt the man of the red hair and him of the
     black beard,
Rise now, and out of your cold white eyes take out
  the fear,
  And let Fergus mac Art mhic Fheargus see his
     weird !
Sure, now, it's a blind man I am, but I'm thinking I
  see
The shadow of you crawling across the dead :
Soon you will twine your arm around his shaking
  knee,
  And be whispering your silence into his listless
    head.
And that is why, O Fergus—

But here the man hurled his sword into the sea and with a choking cry fell forward ; and upon the White Sands he was, beneath the trampling feet of the Washer of the Ford.

II

It was a fair wind beneath the stars that night. At dawn the mountains of Skye were like turrets of a great Dûn against the east.

But Torcall the blind Harper did not see that thing. Sleep, too, was upon him. He smiled in that sleep, for in his mind he saw the dead men, that were of the alien people, his foes, draw near the stream that was in a far place. The shaking of them, poor tremulous frostbit leaves they were, thin and sere, made the only breath there was in that desert.

At the ford—this is what he saw in his vision—they fell down like stricken deer with the hounds upon them.

"What is this stream?" they cried in the thin voice of rain across the moors.

"The River of Blood," said a voice.

"And who are you that are in the silence?"

"I am the Washer of the Ford."

And with that each red soul was seized and thrown into the water of the ford; and when white as a sheep-bone on the hill, was taken in one hand by the Washer of the Ford and flung into the air, where no wind was and where sound was dead, and was then severed this way and that, in four whirling blows of the sword from the four quarters of the world. Then it was that the Washer of the Ford trampled upon what fell to the ground, till under the feet of her was only a white sand, white as powder, light as the dust of the yellow flowers that grow in the grass.

It was at that Torcall Dall smiled in his sleep. He did not hear the washing of the sea ; no, nor any idle splashing of the unoared boat. Then he dreamed, and it was of the woman he had left, seven summer-sailings ago in Lochlin. He thought her hand was in his, and that her heart was against his.

"Ah, dear beautiful heart of woman," he said, "and what is the pain that has put a shadow upon you ? "

It was a sweet voice that he heard coming out of sleep.

" Torcall, it is the weary love I have."

" Ah, heart o' me, dear ! sure 'tis a bitter pain I have had too, and I away from you all these years."

" There's a man's pain, and there's a woman's pain."

" By the blood of Balder, Hildyr, I would have both upon me to take it off the dear heart that is here."

" Torcall ! "

" Yes, white one."

" We are not alone, we two in the dark."

And when she had said that thing, Torcall felt two baby arms go round his neck, and two leaves of a wild-rose press cool and sweet against his lips.

" Ah ! what is this ? " he cried, with his heart beating, and the blood in his body singing a glad song.

A low voice crooned in his ear : a bitter-sweet song it was, passing-sweet, passing-bitter.

" Ah, white one, white one," he moaned ; "ah, the wee fawn o' me ! Baby o' foam, bonnie wee lass, put your sight upon me that I may see the blue eyes that are mine too and Hildyr's."

But the child only nestled closer. Like a fledgling in a great nest she was. If God heard her song, He was a glád God that day. The blood that was in her body called to the blood that was in his body. He could say no word. The tears were in his blind eyes.

Then Hildyr leaned into the dark, and took his harp, and played upon it. It was of the fonnsheen he had learned, far, far away, where the isles are.

She sang : but he could not hear what she sang.

Then the little lips, that were like a cool wave upon the dry sand of his life, whispered into a low song : and the wavering of it was like this in his brain—

> Where the winds gather
>   The souls of the dead,
> O Torcall, my father,
>   My soul is led!
>
> In Hildyr-mead
>   I was thrown, I was sown
> Out of thy seed
>   I am sprung, I am blown!
>
> But where is the way
>   For Hildyr and me,
> By the hill-moss grey
>   Or the grey sea ?
>
> For a river is here,
>   And a whirling Sword—
> And a Woman washing
>   By a Ford !

With that, Torcall Dall gave a wild cry, and sheathed an arm about the wee white one, and put out a hand to the bosom that loved him. But there was no white breast there, and no white babe : and what was against his lips was his own hand red with blood.

" O Hildyr ! " he cried.

But only the splashing of the waves did he hear.

" O white one ! " he cried.

But only the scream of a sea-mew, as it hovered over that boat filled with dead men, made answer.

III

All day the Blind Harper steered the galley of the dead. There was a faint wind moving out of the west. The boat went before it slow, and with a low, sighing wash.

Torcall saw the red gaping wounds of the dead, and the glassy eyes of the nine men.

It is better not to be blind and to see the dead," he muttered, " than to be blind and to see the dead."

The man who had been steersman leaned against him. He took him in his shuddering grip and thrust him into the sea.

But when, an hour later, he put his hand to the coolness of the water, he drew it back with a cry, for it was on the cold, stiff face of the dead man that it had fallen. The long hair had caught in a cleft in the leather where the withes had given.

For another hour Torcall sat with his chin

173

G2

in his right hand, and his unseeing eyes staring upon the dead. He heard no sound at all, save the lap of wave upon wave, and the *suss* of spray against spray, and a bubbling beneath the boat, and the low, steady swish of the body that trailed alongside the steering oar.

At the second hour before sundown he lifted his head. The sound he heard was the sound of waves beating upon rocks.

At the hour before sundown he moved the oar rapidly to and fro, and cut away the body that trailed behind the boat. The noise of the waves upon the rocks was now a loud song.

When the last sunfire burned upon his neck, and made the long hair upon his shoulders ashine, he smelt the green smell of grass. Then it was too that he heard the muffled fall of the sea, in a quiet haven, where shelves of sand were.

He followed that sound, and while he strained to hear any voice the boat grided upon the sand, and drifted to one side. Taking his harp, Torcall drove an oar into the sand, and leaped on to the shore. When he was there, he listened. There was silence. Far, far away he heard the falling of a mountain-torrent, and the thin, faint cry of an eagle, where the sun-flame dyed its eyrie as with streaming blood.

So he lifted his harp, and, harping low, with an old broken song on his lips, moved away from that place, and gave no more thought to the dead.

It was deep gloaming when he came to a wood. He felt the cold green breath of it

"Come," said a voice, low and sweet.

"And who will *you* be?" asked Torcall the Harper, trembling because of the sudden voice in the stillness.

"I am a child, and here is my hand, and I will lead you, Torcall of Lochlin."

The blind man had fear upon him.

"Who are you that in a strange place are for knowing who I am?"

"Come."

"Ay, sure, it is coming I am, white one; but tell me who you are, and whence you came, and whither we go."

Then a voice that he knew sang:

> O where the winds gather
>   The souls of the dead,
> O Torcal, my father,
>   My soul is led!
>
> But a river is here,
>   And a whirling Sword—
> And a Woman washing
>   By a Ford!

Torcall Dall was as the last leaf on a tree at that.

"Were you on the boat?" he whispered hoarsely.

But it seemed to him that another voice answered: "*Yea, even so.*"

"Tell me, for I have blindness: Is it peace?"

"It is peace."

Are you man, or child, or of the Hidden People?"

"I am a shepherd."

"A shepherd? Then, sure, you will guide me through this wood? And what will be beyond this wood?"

"A river."

"And what river will that be?"

"Deep and terrible. It runs through the Valley of the Shadow."

"And is there no ford there?"

"Ay, there is a ford."

"And who will guide me across that ford?"

"She."

"Who?"

"The Washer of the Ford."

But hereat Torcall Dall gave a sore cry and snatched his hand away, and fled sidelong into an alley of the wood.

It was moonshine when he lay down, weary. The sound of flowing water filled his ears.

"Come," said a voice.

So he rose and went. When the cold breath of the water was upon his face, the guide that led him put a fruit into his hand.

"Eat, Torcall Dall!"

He ate. He was no more Torcall Dall. He felt his sight coming upon him again. Out of the blackness shadows came; out of the shadows, the great boughs of trees; from the boughs, dark branches and dark clusters of leaves; above the branches, white stars; below the branches, white flowers; and beyond these, the moonshine on the grass and the moonfire on the flowing of a river dark and deep.

"Take your harp, O Harper, and sing the song of what you see."

Torcall heard the voice, but saw no one. No shadow moved. Then he walked out upon the moonlit grass; and at the ford he saw a woman stooping and washing shroud after shroud of woven moonbeams: washing them there in the flowing water, and singing low a song that he did not hear. He did not see her face. Bnt she was young, and with long

black hair that fell like the shadow of night
over a white rock.

So Torcall took his harp, and he sang :

Glory to the great Gods, it is no Sword I am seeing;
Nor do I see aught but the flowing of a river,
And I see shadows on the flow that are ever fleeing,
And I see a woman washing shrouds for ever and
    ever.

Then he ceased, for he heard the woman
sing :

Glory to God on high, and to Mary, Mother of Jesus,
Here am I washing away the sins of the shriven,
O Torcall of Lochlin, throw off the red sins that ye
    cherish
And I will be giving you the washen shroud that they
    wear in Heaven.

Filled with a great awe, Torcall bowed his
head.   Then once more he took his harp,
and he sang :

O well it is I am seeing, Woman of the Shrouds,
That you have not for me any whirling of the Sword ;
I have lost my gods, O woman, so what will the name
    be
Of thee and thy gods, O woman that art Washer of
    the Ford ?

But the woman did not look up from the
dark water, nor did she cease from washing
the shrouds made of the woven moonbeams.

The Harper heard this song above the sighing of the water :

It is Mary Magdalene my name is, and I loved Christ.
And Christ is the Son of God and of Mary the Mother
of Heaven.
And this river is the river of death, and the shadows
Are the fleeing souls that are lost if they be not
shriven.

Then Torcall drew closer to the stream. A melancholy wind was upon it.

"Where are all the dead of the world ?" he said.

But the woman answered not.

"And what is the end, you that are called Mary ?"

Then the woman rose.

"Would you cross the Ford, O Torcall the Harper ?"

He made no word upon that. But he listened. He heard a woman singing faint and low, far away in the dark. He drew more near.

"Would you cross the Ford, O Torcall ?"

He made no word upon that ; but once more he listened. He heard a little child crying in the night.

"Ah, lonely heart of the white one," he sighed, and his tears fell.

179

Mary Magdalene turned and looked upon him.

It was the face of Sorrow she had. She stooped and took up the tears.

"They are bells of joy," she said. And he heard a faint, sweet ringing in his ears.

A prayer came out of his heart. A blind prayer it was, but God gave it wings. It flew to Mary, who took and kissed it, and gave it song.

"It is the Song of Peace," she said. And Torcall had peace.

"What is best, O Torcall?" she asked,—rustling-sweet as rain among the trees her voice was. "What is best?" The sword, or peace?"

"Peace," he answered; and he was white now, and was old.

"Take your harp," Mary said, "and go in unto the Ford. But, lo, now I clothe you with a white shroud. And if you fear the drowning flood, follow the bells that were your tears; and if the dark affright you, follow the song of the prayer that came out of your heart."

So Torcall the Harper moved into the whelming flood, and he played a new strange air like the laughing of a child.

Deep silence there was. The moonshine lay

upon the obscure wood, and the darkling river flowed sighing through the soundless gloom.

The Washer of the Ford stooped once more. Low and sweet, as of yore and for ever, over the drowning souls she sang her immemorial song.

ST BRIDE OF THE ISLES

To the beautiful memory of
S. F. Alden.

SLOINNEADH BRIGHDE, MUIME CHRIOSD

Brighde nighean Dughaill Duinn,
'Ic Aoidth, 'ic Arta, 'ic Cuinn.
Gach la is gach oidhche
Ni mi cuimhneachadh air sloinneadh Brighde
Cha mharbhar mi,
Cha ghonar mi,
Cha mho, dh' fhagas Criosd an dearmad mi;
Cha loisg teine gniomh Shatain mi;
'S cha bhath uisge no saile mi;
'S mi fo chomraig Naoimh Moire
'S mo chaomh mhuime, Brighde.

The Genealogy of St Brigit or St Bride
Foster-Mother of Christ.

St Brigit, the daughter of Dùghall Donn,
Son of Hugh, son of Art, son of Conn,
Each day and each night
I will meditate on the genealogy of St Brigit.
[Whereby] I will not be killed,
I will not be wounded,
I will not be bewitched;
Neither will Christ forsake me :
Satan's fire will not burn me;
Neither water nor sea shall drown me ;
For I am under the protection of the Virgin Mary,
And my gentle foster-mother St Brigit.

St Bride of the Isles

I

Before ever St Colum came across the Moyle to the island of Iona, that was then by strangers called Innis-nan-Dhruidhneach, the Isle of the Druids, and by the natives Ioua, there lived upon the south-east slope of Dun-I a poor herdsman named Dùvach. Poor he was, for sure, though it was not for this reason that he could not win back to Ireland, green Banba, as he called it : but because he was an exile thence, and might never again

NOTE.—This legendary romance is based upon the ancient and still current (though often hopelessly contradictory) legends concerning Brighid, or Bride, commonly known as "Muime Chriosd"—i.e., the Foster-Mother of Christ. From the universal honour and reverence in which she was and is held—second only in this respect to the Virgin herself—she is also called "Mary of the Gael." Another name, frequent in the West, is "Brighde-nam-Brat "—i.e. St Bride of the Mantle, a name explained in the course of this legendary story. Brigit the Christian saint should not, however, be confused with a much earlier and remoter Brigit, the ancient Celtic Muse of Song.

smell the heather blowing over Sliabh-Gorm
in what of old was the realm of Aoimag.

He was a prince in his own land, though
none on Ioua save the Arch-Druid knew what
his name was. The high priest, however,
knew that Dùvach was the royal Dùghall,
called Dùghall Donn, the son of Hugh the
King, the son of Art, the son of Conn. In
his youth he had been accused of having done
wrong against a noble maiden of the blood.
When her child was born he was made to
swear across her dead body that he would be
true to the daughter for whom she had given
up her life, that he would rear her in a holy
place, but away from Eiré, and that he would
never set foot within that land again. This
was a bitter thing for Dùghall Donn to do :
the more so as, before the King, and the
priests, and the people, he swore by the Wind,
and by the Moon, and by the Sun, that he
was guiltless of the thing of which he was
accused. There were many there who be-
lieved him because of that sacred oath : others,
too, forasmuch as that Morna the Princess
had herself sworn to the same effect. Moreover, there was Aodh of the Golden Hair, a
poet and seer, who avowed that Morna had
given birth to an immortal, whose name would
one day be as a moon among the stars for

glory. But the King would not be appeased, though he spared the life of his youngest son. So it was that, by the advice of Aodh of the Druids, Dùghall Donn went northwards through the realm of Clanadon and so to the sea-loch that was then called Loc Feobal. There he took boat with some wayfarers bound for Alba. But in the Moyle a tempest arose, and the frail galley was driven northward, and at sunrise was cast like a fish, spent and dead, upon the south end of Ioua, that is now Iona. Only two lived: Dùghall Donn and the little child. This was at the place where, on a day of the days in a year that was not yet come, St Colum landed in his coracle, and gave thanks on his bended knees.

When, warmed by the sun, they rose, they found themselves in a waste place. Ill was Dùghall in his mind because of the portents, and now to his fear and amaze the child Bridget knelt on the stones, and, with claspt hands, small and pink as the sea-shells round about her, sang a song of words which were unknown to him. This was the more marvellous, as she was yet so young, and could say no word even of Erse, the only tongue she had heard.

At this portent, he knew that Aodh had spoken seeingly. Truly this child was not of

human parentage. So he, too, kneeled, and,
bowing before her, asked if she were of the
race of Tuatha de Danann, or of the older
gods, and what her will was, that he might
be her servant. Then it was that the kneel-
ing babe looked at him, and sang in a low
sweet voice in Erse:

> I am but a little child,
> Dùghall, son of Hugh, son of Art,
> But my garment shall be laid
> On the lord of the world,
> Yea, surely it shall be that He
> The King of the Elements Himself
> Shall lean against my bosom,
> And I will give him peace,
> And peace will I give to all who ask
> Because of this mighty Prince,
> And because of his Mother that is the Daughter
>   of Peace.

And while Dùghall Donn was still marvelling at this thing, the Arch-Druid of Iona
approached, with his white-robed priests. A
grave welcome was given to the stranger.
While the youngest of the servants of God
was entrusted with the child, the Arch-Druid
took Dùghall aside and questioned him. It
was not till the third day that the old man
gave his decision. Dùghall Donn was to
abide on Iona if he so willed : but the child

was to stay. His life would be spared, nor
would he be a bondager of any kind, and a
little land to till would be given him, and all
that he might need. But of his past he was
to say no word. His name was to become as
nought, and he was to be known simply as
Dùvach. The child, too, was to be named
Bride, for that was the way the same Brigit
was called in the Erse of the Isles.

To the question of Dùghall, that was
thenceforth Dùvach, as to why he laid so
great stress on the child, that was a girl, and
the reputed offspring of shame at that, Cathal
the Arch-Druid replied thus: "My kinsman
Aodh of the Golden Hair who sent you here,
was wiser than Hugh the King and all the
Druids of Aoimag' Truly this child is an
Immortal. There is an ancient prophecy concerning her: surely of her who is now here,
and no other. There shall be, it says, a spot-
less maid born of a virgin of the ancient
immemorial race in Innisfail. And when for
the seventh time the sacred year has come, she
will hold Eternity in her lap as a white flower.
Her maiden breasts shall swell with milk for
the Prince of the World. She shall give suck
to the King of the Elements. So I say unto
you, Dùvach, go in peace. Take unto thyself
a wife, and live upon the place I will give

thee on the east side of Iona. Treat Bride as
though she were thy spirit, but leave her
much alone, and let her learn of the sun and
the wind. In the fulness of time the prophecy
shall be fulfilled."

So was it, from that day of the days.
Dùvach took a wife unto himself, who weaned
the little Bride, who grew in beauty and
grace, so that all men marvelled. Year by
year for seven years the wife of Dùvach bore
him a son, and these grew apace in strength,
so that by the beginning of the third year of
the seventh cycle of Bride's life there were
three stalwart youths to brother her, and three
comely and strong lads, and one young boy
fair to see. Nor did anyone, not even Bride
herself, saving Cathal the Arch-Druid, know
that Dùvach the herdsman was Dùghall Donn,
of a princely race in Innisfail.

In the end, too, Dùvach came to think that
he had dreamed, or at the least that Cathal
had not interpreted the prophecy aright. For
though Bride was of exceeding beauty, and of
a strange piety that made the young Druids
bow before her as though she were a bàndia,
yet the world went on as before, and the days
brought no change. Often, while she was
still a child, he had questioned her about the
words she had said as a babe, but she had

no memory of them. Once in her ninth year, he came upon her on the hillside of Dun-I singing these self-same words. Her eyes dreamed far away. He bowed his head, and, praying to the Giver of Light, hurried to Cathal. The old man bade him speak no more to the child concerning the mysteries.

Bride lived the hours of her days upon the slopes of Dun-I, herding the sheep, or in following the kye upon the green hillocks and grassy dunes of what then as now was called the Machar. The beauty of the world was her daily food. The spirit within her was like sunlight behind a white flower. The birdeens in the green bushes sang for joy when they saw her blue eyes. The tender prayers that were in her heart for all the beasts and birds, for helpless children, and tired women, and for all who were old, were often seen flying above her head in the form of white doves of sunshine.

But when the middle of the year came that was, though Dùvach had forgotten it, the year of the prophecy, his eldest son, Conn, who was now a man, murmured against the virginity of Bride, because of her beauty and because a chieftain of the mainland was eager to wed her. "I shall wed Bride or raid Ioua," was the message he had sent.

So, one day, before the great fire of the summer-festival, Conn and his brothers reproached Bride.

" Idle are these pure eyes, O Bride, not to be as lamps at Thy marriage-bed."

" Truly, it is not by the eyes that we live," replied the maiden gently, while to their fear and amazement she passed her hand before her face and let them see that the sockets were empty.

Trembling with awe at this portent, Dùvach intervened.

" By the Sun I swear it, O Bride, that thou shalt marry whomsoever thou wilt and none other, and when thou willest, or not at all if such be thy will."

And when he had spoken, Bride smiled, and passed her hand before her face again, and all there were abashed because of the blue light as of morning that was in her shining eyes.

II

The still weather had come, and all the isles lay in beauty, Far south, beyond vision, ranged the coasts of Eiré : westward, leagues of quiet ocean dreamed into unsailed wastes whose waves at last laved the shores of Tir-

ná'n-Og, the Land of Eternal Youth : northward, the spell-bound waters sparkled in the
sunlight, broken here and there by purple
shadows, that were the isles of Staffa and
Ulva, Lunga and the isles of the columns,
misty Coll, and Tiree that is the land beneath
the wave, with, pale-blue in the heat-haze, the
mountains of Rûm called Haleval, Haskeval,
and Oreval, and the sheer Scuir-na-Gillian and
the peaks of the Cuchullins in remote Skye.

All the sweet loveliness of a late spring
remained, to give a freshness to the glory of
summer. The birds had song to them still.

It was while the dew was yet wet on the
grass that Bride came out of her father's
house, and went up the steep slope of Dun-I.
The crying of the ewes and lambs at the
pastures came plaintively against the dawn.
The lowing of the kye arose from the sandy
hollows by the shore, or from the meadows on
the lower slopes. Through the whole island
went a rapid trickling sound, most sweet to
hear : the myriad voices of twittering birds,
from the dotterel in the seaweed to the larks
climbing the blue spirals of heaven.

This was the morning of her birth, and she
was clad in white. About her waist was a
girdle of the sacred rowan, the feathery green
leaves of it flickering dusky shadows upon her

robe as she moved. The light upon her yellow
hair was as when morning wakes, laughing
low with joy amid the tall corn. As she went
she sang, soft as the crooning of a dove. If
any had been there to hear he would have
been abashed, for the words were not in Erse,
and the eyes of the beautiful girl were as those
of one in a vision.

When, at last, a brief while before sunrise,
she reached the summit of the Scuir, that is
so small a hill and yet seems so big in Iona
where it is the sole peak, she found three
young Druids there, ready to tend the sacred
fire the moment the sun-rays should kindle it.
Each was clad in a white robe, with fillets of
oak leaves ; and each had a golden armlet.
They made a quiet obeisance as she approached. One stepped forward with a flush
in his face because of her beauty, that was as
a sea-wave for grace, and a flower for purity,
and sunlight for joy, and moonlight for peace,
and the wind for fragrance.

" Thou mayst draw near if thou wilt, Bride,
daughter of Dùvach," he said, with something
of reverence as well as of grave courtesy in
his voice : " for the holy Cathal hath said that
the Breath of the Source of All is upon thee.
It is not lawful for women to be here at this
moment, but thou hast the law shining upon

thy face and in thine eyes. Hast thou come
to pray ?"

But at that moment a low cry came from
one of his companions. He turned, and re-
joined his fellows. Then all three sank upon
their knees, and with outstretched arms hailed
the rising of God.

As the sun rose, a solemn chant swelled
from their lips, ascending as incense through
the silent air. The glory of the new day came
soundlessly. Peace was in the blue heaven,
on the blue-green sea, on the green land.
There was no wind, even where the currents
of the deep moved in shadowy purple. The
sea itself was silent, making no more than a
sighing slumber-breath round the white sands
of the isle, or a hushed whisper where the
tide lifted the long weed that clung to the
rocks.

In what strange, mysterious way, Bride did
not see ; but as the three Druids held their
hands before the sacred fire there was a faint
crackling, then three thin spirals of blue smoke
rose, and soon dusky red and wan yellow
tongues of flame moved to and fro. The
sacrifice of God was made. Out of the im-
measurable heaven He had come, in His golden
chariot. Now, in the wonder and mystery
of His love, he was re-born upon the world,

re-born a little fugitive flame upon a low hill
in a remote isle. Great must be His love
that He could die thus daily in a thousand
places : so great His love that He could give
up His own body to daily death, and suffer
the holy flame that was in the embers He
illumined to be lighted and revered and then
scattered to the four quarters of the world.

Bride could bear no longer the mystery of
this great love. It moved her to an ecstasy.
What tenderness of divine love that could thus
redeem the world daily : what long-suffering
for all the evil and cruelty done hourly
upon the weeping earth : what patience with
the bitterness of the blind fates ! The beauty
of the worship of Be'al was upon her as a
golden glory. Her heart leaped to a song
that could not be sung. The inexhaustible
love and pity in her soul chanted a hymn
that was heard of no Druid or mortal anywhere, but was known of the white spirits of
Life.

Bowing her head, so that the glad tears fell
warm as thunder-rain upon her hands, she rose
and moved away.

Not far from the summit of Dun-I is a hidden pool, to this day called the Fountain of
Youth. Hitherward she went, as was her
wont when upon the hill at the break of day,

at noon, or at sundown. Close by the huge boulder, which hides it from above, she heard a pitiful bleating, and soon the healing of her eyes was upon a lamb which had become fixed in a crevice in the rock. On a crag above it stood a falcon, with savage cries, lusting for warm blood. With swift step Bride drew near. There was no hurt to the lambkin as she lifted it in her arms. Soft and warm was it there, as a young babe against the bosom that mothers it. Then with quiet eyes she looked at the falcon, who hooded his cruel gaze.

" There is no wrong in thee, Seobhag," she said gently ; "but the law of blood shall not prevail for ever. Let there be peace this morn."

And when she had spoken this word, the wild hawk of the hills flew down upon her shoulder, nor did the heart of the lambkin beat the quicker, while with drowsy eyes it nestled as against its dam. When she stood by the pool she laid the little woolly creature among the fern. Already the bleating of it was sweet against the forlorn heart of a ewe. The falcon rose, circled above her head, and with swift flight sped through the blue air. For a time Bride watched its travelling shadow : when it was itself no

H

more than a speck in the golden haze, she
turned, and stooped above the Fountain of
Youth.

Beyond it stood then, though for ages past
there has been no sign of either, two quicken-
trees. Now they were gold-green in the
morning light, and the brown-green berries
that had not yet reddened were still small.
Fair to see was the flickering of the long
finger shadows upon the granite rocks and
boulders.

Often had Bride dreamed through their
foliage ; but now she stared in amaze. She
had put her lips to the water, and had started
back because she had seen, beyond her own
image, that of a woman so beautiful that her
soul was troubled within her, and had cried
its inaudible cry, worshipping. When, trembling, she had glanced again, there was none
beside herself. Yet what had happened ?
For, as she stared at the quicken-trees, she
saw that their boughs had interlaced, and
that they now became a green arch. What was
stranger still was that the rowan-clusters hung
in blood-red masses, although the late heats
were yet a long way off.

Bride rose, her body quivering because of
the cool sweet draught of the Fountain of
Youth, so that almost she imagined the water

was for her that day what it could be once
in each year to every person who came to it,
a breath of new life and the strength and
joy of youth. With slow steps she advanced
toward the arch of the quickens. Her heart
beat as she saw that the branches at the summit had formed themselves into the shape of
a wreath or crown, and that the scarlet berries
dropped therefrom a steady rain of red drops
as of blood. A sigh of joy breathed from her
lips when, deep among the red and green, she
saw the white merle of which the ancient poets
sang, and heard the exceeding wonder of its
rapture, which was now the pain of joy and
now the joy of pain.

The song of the mystic bird grew wilder
and more sweet as she drew near. For a
brief while she hesitated. Then, as a white
dove drifted slow before her under and
through the quicken-boughs, a dove white as
snow but radient with sunfire, she moved forward to follow with a dream-smile upon her
face and her eyes full of the sheen of wonder
and mystery, as shadowy waters flooded with
moonshine.

And this was the passing of Bride, who
was not seen again of Dùvach or her foster-
brothers for the space of a year and a day.
Only Cathal, the aged Arch-Druid, who died

seven days thence, had a vision of her, and
wept for joy.

III

When the strain of the white merle ceased,
though it had seemed to her scarce longer
than the vanishing song of the swallow on
the wing, Bride saw that the evening was
come. Through the violet glooms of dusk
she moved soundlessly, save for the crispling
of her feet among the hot sands. Far as she
could see to right or left there were hollows
and ridges of sand ; where, here and there,
trees or shrubs grew out of the parched soil,
they were strange to her. She had heard the
Druids speak of the sunlands in a remote,
nigh unreachable East, where there were trees
called palms, trees in a perpetual sunflood yet
that perished not, also tall dark cypresses,
black-green as the holy yew. These were the
trees she now saw. Did she dream, she wondered ? Far down in her mind was some
memory, some floating vision only, mayhap,
of a small green isle far among the northern
seas. Voices, words, faces, familiar yet unfamiliar when she strove to bring them near,
haunted her.

The heat brooded upon the land. The sigh
of the parched earth was " Water, water."

As she moved onward through the gloaming she descried white walls beyond her : white walls and square white buildings, looming ghostly through the dark, yet home-sweet as the bells of the cows on the sea-pastures, because of the yellow lights every here and there agleam.

A tall figure moved toward her, clad in white, even as those figures which haunted her unremembering memory. When he drew near she gave a low cry of joy. The face of her father was sweet to her.

" Where will be the pitcher, Brigit ? " he said, though the words were not the words that were near her when she was alone. Nevertheless she knew them, and the same manner of words was upon her lips.

" My pitcher, father ? "

" Ah, dreamer, when will you be taking heed ! It is leaving your pitcher you will be, and by the Well of the Camels, no doubt : though little matter will that be, since there is now no water, and the drought is heavy upon the land. But . . . Brigit . . . "

" Yes, my father ? "

" Sure now, it is not safe for you to be on the desert at night. Wild beasts come out of the darkness, and there are robbers and wild men who lurk in the shadow.

Brigit . . . Brigit . . . is it dreaming you are
still ? "

"I was dreaming of a cool green isle in
northern seas, where . . ."

"Where you have never been, foolish lass,
and are never like to be. Sure, if any wayfarer
were to come upon us you would scarce
be able to tell him that yonder village is Bethlehem, and that I am Dùghall Donn the inn-
keeper, Dùghall, the son of Hugh, son of Art,
son of Conn. Well, well, I am growing old,
and they say that the old see wonders. But I
do not wish to see this wonder, that my daughter Brigit forgets her own town, and the good
inn that is there, and the strong sweet
ale that is cool against the thirst of the weary,
Sure, if the day of my days is near it is near.
"Green be the place of my rest," I cry, even
as Oisìn the son of Fionn of the hero-line of
Trenmor cried in his old age ; though if Oisìn
and the Fiànn were here not a green place
would they find now, for the land is burned
dry as the heather after a hill-fire. But now,
Brigit, let us go back into Bethlehem, for I
have that for the saying which must be said at
once."

In silence the twain walked through the
gloaming that was already the mirk, till they
came to the white gate where the asses and

camels breathed wearily in the sultry darkness, with dry tongues moving round parched
mouths. Thence they fared through narrow
streets, where a few white-robed Hebrews and
sons of the desert moved silently, or sat in
niches. Finally, they came to a great yard,
where more than a score of camels lay
huddled and growling in their sleep. Beyond
this was the inn, which was known to all the
patrons and friends of Dùghall Donn as the
" Rest and Be Thankful," though formerly as
the Rest of Clan-Ailpean, for was he not himself through his mother MacAlpine of the
Isles, as well as blood-kin to the great Cormac
the Ard-Righ, to whom his father, Hugh, was
feudatory prince ?

As Dùghall and Bride walked along the
stone flags of a passage leading to the inner
rooms, he stopped and drew her attention to
the water-tanks.

" Look you, my lass," he said sorrowfully,
"of these tanks and barrels nearly all are
empty. Soon there will be no water whatever, which is an evil thing though I whisper
it in peace, to the Stones be it said. Now,
already the folk who come here murmur. No
man can drink ale all day long, and those
wayfarers who want to wash the dust of their
journey from their feet and hands complain

bitterly. And . . . what is that you will be saying? The kye? Ay, sure, there is the kye; but the poor beasts are o'ercome with the heat, and there's not a Cailliach on the hills who could win a drop more of milk from them than we squeeze out of their udders now, and that only with rune after rune till all the throats of the milking lassies are as dry as the salt grass by the sea.

"Well, what I am saying is this: 'tis months now since any rain will be falling, and every crock of water has been for the treasuring as though it had been the honey of Moy-Mell itself. The moon had been full twice since we had the good water brought from the mountain-springs; and now they are for drying up too. The seers say that the drought will last. If that is a true word, and there be no rain till the winter comes, there will be no inn in Bethlehem called 'The Rest and Be Thankful'; for already there is not enough good water to give peace even to your little thirst, my birdeen. As for the ale, it is poor drink now for man or maid, and as for the camels and asses, poor beasts, they don't understand the drinking of it."

"That is true, father; but what is to be done?"

"That's what I will be telling you, my lin-

tie. Now, I have been told by an oganach
out of Jerusalem, that lives in another place
close by the great town, that there is a quench-
less well of pure water, cold as the sea with a
north wind in it, on a hill there called the
Mount of Olives. Now, it is to that hill I will
be going. I am for taking all the camels
and all the horses, and all the asses, and will
lade each with a burthen of water-skins, and
come back home again with water enough to
last us till the drought breaks."

That was all that was said that night. But
at the dawn the inn was busy, and all the folk
in Bethlehem were up to see the going abroad
of Dùghall Donn and Ronald McIan, his
shepherd, and some Macleans and Macallums
that were then in that place. It was a fair
sight to see as they went forth through the
white gate that is called the Gate of Nazareth.
A piper walked first, playing the Gathering of
the Swords : then came Dùghall Donn on a
camel, and McIan on a horse, and the herds-
men on asses, and then there were the collies
barking for joy.

Before he had gone, Dùghall took Bride out
of the hearing of the others. There was only
a little stagnant water, he said ; and as for the
ale, there was no more than a flagon left of
what was good. This flagon and the one jar

HQ

of pure water he left with her. On no account was she to give a drop to any wayfarer, no matter how urgent he might be; for he, Dùghall, could not say when he would get back, and he did not want to find a dead daughter to greet him on his return, let alone there being no maid of the inn to attend to customers. Over and above that, he made her take an oath that she would give no one, no, not even a stranger, accomodation at the inn, during his absence.

Afternoon and night came, and dawn and night again, and yet again. It was on the afternoon of the third day, when even the crickets were dying of thirst, that Bride heard a clanging at the door of the inn.

When she went to the door she saw a weary grey-haired man, dusty and tired. By his side was an ass with drooping head, and on the ass was a woman, young, and of a beauty that was as the cool shadow of green leaves and the cold ripple of running waters. But beautiful as she was it was not this that made Bride start: no, nor the heavy womb that showed the woman was with child. For she remembered her of a dream—it was a dream, sure—when she had looked into a pool on a mountain-side, and seen, beyond her own image, just this fair and beautiful face, the most beautiful that ever man saw since Naois, of the Sons of Usnach, beheld Deirdrê in the forest—ay, and lovelier far even than she, the peerless among women.

"Gu'm beannaicheadh Dia an tigh," said the grey-haired man in a weary voice, "the blessing of God on this house."

"Soraidh leat," replied Bride gently, "and upon you likewise."

"Can you give us food and drink, and, after that, good rest at this inn? Sure it is grateful we will be. This is my wife Mary, upon whom is a mystery : and I am Joseph, a carpenter in Arimathea."

"Welcome, and to you too, Mary : and peace. But there is neither food nor drink here, and my father has bidden me give shelter to none who comes here against his return."

The carpenter sighed, but the fair woman on the ass turned her shadowy eyes upon Bride, so that the maiden trembled with joy and fear.

"And is it forgetting me you will be, Brighde-Alona," she murmured, in the good sweet Gaelic of the Isles ; and the voice of her was like the rustle of leaves when a soft rain is falling in a wood.

"Sure, I remember," Bride whispered filled

with deep awe, Then without a word she turned, and beckoned them to follow : which having left the ass by the doorway, they did.

" Here is all the ale that I have," she said, as she gave the flagon to Joseph : "and here, Mary, is all the water that there is. Little there is, but it is you that are welcome to it."

Then, when they had quenched their thirst she brought out oatcakes and scones and brown bread, and would fain have added milk, but there was none.

"Go to the byre, Brigit," said Mary, "and the first of the kye shall give milk."

So Bride went, but returned saying that the creature would not give milk without a *sian* or song, and that her throat was too dry to sing.

" Say this *sian*," said Mary.

> Give up thy milk to her who calls
> Across the low green hills of Heaven
> And stream-cool meads of Paradise

And sure enough, when Bride did this, the milk came : and she soothed her thirst, and went back to her guests rejoicing. It was sorrow to her not to let them stay where they were, but she could not, because of her oath.

The man Joseph was weary, and said he

was too tired to seek far that night, and asked if there was no empty byre or stable where he and Mary could sleep till morning. At that, Bride was glad : for she knew there was a clean cool stable close to the byre where her kye were : and thereto she led them, and returned with peace at her heart.

When she was in the Inn again, she was afraid once more : for lo, though Mary and Joseph had drunken deep of the jar and the flagon, each was now full as it had been. Of the food, too, none seemed to have been taken, though she had herself seen them break the scones and the oatcakes.

It was dusk when her reverie was broken by the sound of the pipes. Soon thereafter Dùghall Donn and his following rode up to the inn, and all were glad because of the cool water, and the grapes, and the green fruits of the earth, that they brought with them.

While her father was eating and drinking, merry because of the ale that was still in the flagon, Bride told him of the wayfarers. Even as she spoke, he made a sign of silence, because of a strange, unwonted sound that he heard.

"What will that be meaning?" he asked, in a low, hushed voice.

"Sure it is the rain at last, father. That is a glad thing. The earth will be green again. The beasts will not perish. Hark, I hear the noise of it coming down from the hills as well." But Dùghall sat brooding.

"Ay," he said at last, "is it not foretold that the Prince of the World is to be born in this land, during a heavy falling of rain, after a long drought? And who is for knowing that Bethlehem is not the place, and that this is not the night of the day of the days? Brigit, Brigit, the woman Mary must be the mother of the Prince, who is to save all mankind out of evil and pain and death!"

And with that he rose and beckoned to her to follow. They took a lantern, and made their way through the drowsing camels and asses and horses, and past the byres where the kye lowed gently, and so to the stable.

"Sure that is a bright light they are having." Dùghall muttered uneasily; for, truly, it was as though the shed were a shell filled with the fires of sunrise.

Lightly they pushed back the door. When they saw what they saw they fell upon their knees. Mary sat with her heavenly beauty upon her like sunshine on a dusk land: in her lap, a Babe, laughing sweet and low.

Never had they seen a Child so fair. He was as though wrought of light.

" Who is it ? " murmured Dùghall Donn, of Joseph, who stood near, with rapt eyes.

" It is the Prince of Peace."

And with that Mary smiled, and the Child slept.

" Brigit, my sister dear "—and, as she whispered this, Mary held the little one to Bride.

The fair girl took the Babe in her arms, and covered it with her mantle. Therefore it is that she is known to this day as Brigde-nam-Brat, St Bride of the Mantle.

And all through that night, while the mother slept, Bride nursed the Child with tender hands and croodling crooning songs. And this was one of the songs that she sang :

> Ah, Baby Christ, so dear to me,
>   Sang Brigit Bride :
> How sweet thou art,
> Heart of my heart !

> Heavy her body was with thee,
> Mary, beloved of One in Three,
>   Sang Brigit Bride—
> Mary, who bore thee, little lad :
> But light her heart was, light and glad
> With God's love clad.

Sit on my knee,
  Sang Brigit Bride:
  Sit here
O Baby dear,
Close to my heart, my heart:
For I thy foster-mother am,
My helpless lamb!
O have no fear,
  Sang good St Bride.

None, none,
No fear have I:
So let me cling
Close to thy side
Whilst thou dost sing,
O Brigit Bride!

My Lord, my Prince I sing:
My baby dear, my King!
  Sang Brigit Bride.

It was on this night that, far away in Iona, the Arch-Druid Cathal died. But before the breath went from him he had his vision of joy, and last words were:

Brighde 'dol air a glùn
Righ nan dùl a shuidh 'na h-uchd!
(Brigit Bride upon her knee,
The King of the Elements asleep on her breast?)

At the coming of dawn Mary awoke, and took the Child. She kissed Bride upon the brows, and said this thing to her: "Brigit,

my sister dear, thou shalt be known unto all
time as Muime Chriosd."

IV

No sooner had Mary spoken than Bride fell
into a deep sleep. So profound was this
slumber that when Dùghall Donn came to see
to the wayfarers, and to tell them that the
milk and the porridge were ready for the
breaking of their fast, he could get no word
of her at all. She lay in the clean, yellow
straw beneath the manger, where Mary had
laid the Child. Dùghall stared in amaze.
There was no sign of the mother, nor of the
Babe that was the Prince of Peace, nor of the
douce, quiet man that was Joseph the carpenter. As for Bride, she not only slept so sound
that no word of his fell against her ears, but
she gave him awe. For as he looked at her
he saw that she was surrounded by a glowing
light. Something in his heart shaped itself
into a prayer, and he knelt beside her, sobbing
low. When he rose, it was in peace. Mayhap an angel had comforted his soul in its
dark shadowy haunt of his body.

It was late when Bride awoke, though she
did not open her eyes, but lay dreaming. For
long she thought she was in Tir-Tairngire,

the Land of Promise, or wandering on the honey-sweet plain of Magh-Mell ; for the wind of dreamland brought exquisite odours to her, and in her ears were confused songs of great joy.

All round her there was music of rejoicing. Voices, lovelier than any she had ever heard, resounded ; glad voices full of winged rapture. There was a pleasant tumult of harps and trumpets, and as from across blue hills and over calm water came the sound of the bagpipes. She listened with tears. Loud and glad were the pipes at times, full of triumph, as when the heroes of old marched with Cuchullin or went down to battle with Fionn : again, they were low and sweet, like humming of bees when the heather is heavy with the honey-ooze. The songs and wild music of the angels lulled her into peace : for a time no thought of the woman Mary came to her, nor of the Child that was her foster-child.

Suddenly it was in her mind as though the pipes played the chant that is called the "Aoibhneas a Shlighe," "the joy of his way," a march played before a bridegroom going to his bride.

Out of this glad music came a solitary voice, like a child singing on the hillside.

"The way of wonder shall be thine, O Brighde-Naomha!"

This was what the child-voice sang. Then it was as though all the harpers of the west were playing "air clàrsach" : and the song of a multitude of voices was this :

"Blessed art thou, O Brigit, who nursed the King of the Elements in thy bosom : blessed thou, the Virgin Sister of the Virgin Mother, for unto all time thou shalt be called Muime Chriosd, the Foster-Mother of Jesus that is the Christ."

With that, Bride remembered all, and opened her eyes. Nought strange was there to see, save that she lay in the stable. Then as she noted that the gloaming had come, she wondered at the soft light that prevailed in the shed, though no lamp or candle burned there.

In her ears, too, still lingered a wild and beautiful music.

It was strange. Was it all a dream, she pondered. But even as she thought thus, she saw half of her mantle lying upon the straw in the manger. Much she marvelled at this, but when she took the garment in her hand she wondered more. For though it was no more than a half of the poor mantle wherewith she had wrapped the Babe, it was all wrought with mystic gold lines and with precious stones more glorious than ever Arch Druid or Island Prince had seen. The marvel gave her awe at last, when, as she placed the garment upon her shoulder, it covered her completely.

She knew now that she had not dreamed, and that a miracle was done. So with gladness she went out of the stable, and into the inn. Dùghall Donn was amazed when he saw her, and then rejoiced exceedingly.

"Why are you so merry, my father," she asked.

"Sure it is glad that I am. For now the folk will be laughing the wrong way. This very morning I was so pleased with the pleasure, that while the pot was boiling on the peats I went out and told every one I met that the Prince of Peace was come, and had just been born in the stable behind the 'Rest and Be Thankful.' Well, that saying was just like a weasel among the rabbits, only it was an old toothless weasel : for all Bethlehem mocked me, some with jeers, some with hard words, and some with threats. Sure, I cursed them right and left. No, not for all my cursing— and by the blood of my fathers, I spared no man among them, wishing them sword and fire, the black plague and the grey death— would they believe. So back it was that I

came, and going through the inn I am come to
the stable. 'Sorrow is on me like a grey mist,'
said Oisin, mourning for Oscur, and sure it
was a grey mist that was on me when not a
sign of man, woman, or child was to be seen,
and you so sound asleep that a March gale in
the Moyle wouldn't have roused you. Well,
I went back, and told this thing, and all the
people in Bethlehem mocked at me. And the
Elders of the People came at last, and put a
fine upon me : and condemned me to pay three
barrels of good ale, and a sack of meal, and
three thin chains of gold, each three yards
long : and this for causing a false rumour, and
still more for making a laughing-stock of the
good folk of Bethlehem. There was a man
called Murdoch-Dhu, who is the chief smith in
Nazareth, and it's him I'm thinking will have
laughed the Elders into doing this hard thing."

It was then that Bride was aware of a marvel
upon her, for she blew an incantation off the
palm of her hand, and by that frith she knew
where the dues were to be found.

"By what I see in the air that is blown off
the palm of my hand, father, I bid you go into
the cellar of the inn. There you will find
three barrels full of good ale, and beside them
a sack of meal, and the sack is tied with three
chains of gold, each three yards long."

But while Dùghall Donn went away rejoicing, and found that which Bride had foretold,
she passed out into the street. None saw her
in the gloaming, or as she went toward the
Gate in the East. When she passed by the
Lazar-house she took her mantel off her back
and laid it in the place of offerings. All the
jewels and fine gold passed into invisible birds
with healing wings : and these birds flew about
the heads of the sick all night, so that at dawn
every one arose, with no ill upon him, and
went on his way rejoicing. As each went out
of Bethlehem that morning of the mornings
he found a clean white robe and new sandals
at the first mile ; and, at the second, food and
cool water ; and, at the third, a gold piece and
a staff.

The guard that was at the Eastern Gate did
not hail Bride. All the gaze of him was upon
a company of strange men, shepherd-kings,
who said they had come out of the East led
by a star. They carried rare gifts with them
when they first came to Bethlehem : but no
man knew whence they came, what they
wanted, or whither they went.

For a time Bride walked along the road that
leads to Nazareth. There was fear in her
gentle heart when she heard the howling of
hyenas down in the dark hollows, and she was

glad when the moon came out and shone quietly upon her.

In the moonlight she saw that there were steps in the dew before her. She could see the black print of feet in the silver sheen on the wet grass, for it was on a grassy hill that she now walked, though a day ago every leaf and sheath there had lain brown and withered. The footprints she followed were those of a woman and of a child.

All night through she tracked those wandering feet in the dew. They were always fresh before her, and led her away from the villages, and also where no wild beasts prowled through the gloom. There was no weariness upon her, though often she wondered when she should see the fair wondrous face she sought. Behind her also were footsteps in the dew, though she knew nothing of them. They were those of the Following Love. And this was the Lorgadh-Brighde of which men speak to this day : the Quest of the holy St Bride.

All night she walked ; now upon the high slopes of a hill. Never once did she have a glimpse of any figure in the moonlight, though the steps in the dew before her were newly made, and none lay in the glisten a short way ahead.

Suddenly she stopped. There were no more footprints. Eagerly she looked before her. On a hill beyond the valley beneath her she saw the gleaming of yellow stars. These were the lights of a city. " Behold, it is Jerusalem," she murmured, awe-struck, for she had never seen the great town.

Sweet was the breath of the wind that stirred among the olives on the mount where she stood. It had the smell of heather, and she could hear the rustle of it among the bracken on a hill close by.

" Truly, this must be the Mount of Olives," she whispered, " The Mount of which I have heard my father speak, and that must be the hill called Calvary."

But even as she gazed marvelling, she sighed with new wonder; for now she saw that the yellow stars were as the twinkling of the fires of the sun along the crest of a hill that is set in the east. There was a living joy in the dawntide. In her ears was a sweet sound of the bleating of ewes and lambs. From the hollows in the shadows came the swift singing rush of the flowing tide. Faint cries of the herring gulls filled the air; from the weedy boulders by the sea the skuas called wailingly.

Bewildered, she stood intent. If only she

could see the footprints again, she thought. Whither should she turn, whither go? At her feet was a yellow flower. She stooped and plucked it.

"Tell me, O little sun-flower, which way shall I be going?" and as she spoke a small golden bee flew up from the heart of it, and up the hill to the left of her. So it is that from that day the dandelion is called am-Bèarnàn-Brighde.

Still she hesitated. Then a sea-bird flew by her with a loud whistling cry.

"Tell me, O eisireùn," she called, "which way shall I be going?"

And at this the eisireùn swerved in its flight, and followed the golden bee, crying, "This way, O Bride, Bride, Bride, Bride, Bri-i-i-ide!"

So it is that from that day the oyster-catcher has been called the Gille-Brighde, the Servant of St Brigit.

Then it was that Bride said this sian:

Dia romham;
Mhoire am dheaghuidh;
'S am Mac a thug Righ nan Dull
Mis' air do shlios, a Dhia,
Is Dia ma'm luirg.
Mac' 'oire, a's Righ nan Dul,
A shoillseachadh gach ni dheth so,
Le a ghras, mu'm choinneamh.

God before me;
The Virgin Mary after me;
And the Son sent by the King of the Elements.
I am to windward of thee, O God!
And God on my footsteps.
May the Son of Mary, King of the Elements,
Reveal the meaning of each of these things
Before me, through His grace.

And as she ended she saw before her two quicken-trees, of which the boughs were inter-wrought so that they made an arch. Deep in the green foliage was a white merle that sang a wondrous sweet song. Above it the small branches were twisted into the shape of a wreath or crown, lovely with the sunlit rowan-clusters, from whose·scarlet berries red drops as of blood fell.

Before her flew a white dove, white as milk become white fire. She followed, and passed beneath the quicken arch.

Fading sweet was the song of the merle, that was then no more; sweet the green shadow of the rowans, that now grew straight as young pines. Sweet the far song in the sky, where the white dove flew against the sun.

Bride looked, and her eyes were glad. Homesweet the blooming of the heather on the slopes of Dun-I. Iona lay green and gold, isled in her blue waters. From the sheiling of Dùvach, her father, rose a thin column of pale blue smoke. The collies, seeing her, barked loudly with welcoming joy.

The bleating of the sheep, the lowing of the kye, the breath of the salt wind from the open sea beyond, the song of the flowing tide in the Sound beneath : dear the homing.

With a starry light in her eyes she moved down through the heather and among the green bracken : white, wonderful, fair to see.

THE FISHER OF MEN

But now I have grown nothing, being all,
And the whole world weighs down upon my heart
                                    (Fergus and the Druid.)

The Fisher of Men

When old Sheen nic Lèoid came back to
the croft, after she had been to the burn at the
edge of the green airidh, where she had
washed the *claar* that was for the potatoes at
the peeling, she sat down before the peats.

She was white with years. The mountain
wind was chill, too, for all that the sun had
shone throughout the midsummer day. It was
well to sit before the peat-fire.

The croft was on the slope of a mountain,
and had the south upon it. North, south, east,
and west, other great slopes reached upward
like hollow green waves frozen into silence
by the very wind that curved them so, and
freaked their crests into peaks and jagged pinnacles. Stillness was in that place for ever
and ever. What though the Gorromalt Water
foamed down Ben Nair, where the croft was,
and made a hoarse voice for aye surrendering
sound to silence ? What though at times the
stones fell from the ridges of Ben Chaisteal
and Maolmòr, and clattered down the barren
declivities till they were slung in the tangled
meshes of whin and juniper ? What though

on stormy dawns the eagle screamed as he
fought against the wind that graved a thin line
upon the aged front of Ben Mulad, where his
eyrie was : or that the kestrel cried above the
rabbit-burrows in the strath : or that the hill-
fox barked, or that the curlew wailed, or that
the scattered sheep made an endless mournful
crying ? What were these but the ministers
of silence ?

There was no blue smoke in the strath except from the one turf cot. In the hidden valley beyond Ben Nair there was a hamlet, and
nigh upon three-score folk lived there ; but
that was over three miles away. Sheen Macleod was alone in that solitary place, save for
her son Alasdair Mòr Òg. "Young Alasdair " he was still, though the grey feet of fifty
years had marked his hair. Alasdair Òg he
was while Alasdair Ruadh mac Chalum mhic
Lèoid, that was his father, lived. But when
Alasdair Ruadh changed, and Sheen was left
a mourning woman, he that was their son was
Alasdair Òg still.

She had sore weariness that day. For all
that, it was not the weight of the burden that
made her go in and out of the afternoon sun,
and sit by the red glow of the peats, brooding
deep.

When, nigh upon an hour later, Alasdair

came up the slope, and led the kye to the byre, she did not hear him: nor had she sight of him, when his shadow flickered in before him and lay along the floor.

"Poor old woman," he said to himself, bending his head because of the big height that was his, and he there so heavy and strong, and tender, too, for all the tangled black beard and the wild hill-eyes that looked out under bristling grey-black eyebrows.

"Poor old woman, and she with the tired heart that she has. Ay, ay, for sure the weeks lap up her shadow, as the sayin' is. She will be thinkin' of him that is gone. Ay, or maybe the old thoughts of her are goin' back on their own steps, down this glen an' over that hill an' away beyont that strath, an' this corrie an' that moor. Well, well, it is a good love, that of the mother. Sure a bitter pain it will be to me when there's no old grey hair there to stroke. It's quiet here, terrible quiet, God knows, to Himself be the blessin' for this an' for that; but when she has the white sleep at last, then it'll be a sore day for me, an' one that I will not be able to bear to hear the sheep callin', callin,' callin' through the rain on the hills here, and Gorromalt Water an' no other voice to be with me on that day of the days."

She heard a faint sigh, and stirred a moment, but did not look round.

"Muim'-à-ghraidh, is it tired you are, an' this so fine a time, too?"

With a quick gesture, the old woman glanced at him.

"Ah, child, is that you indeed? Well, I am glad of that, for I have the trouble again."

"What trouble, Muim' ghaolaiche?"

But the old woman did not answer. Wearily she turned her face to the peat-glow again.

Alasdair seated himself on the big wooden chair to her right. For a time he stayed silent thus, staring into the red heart of the peats. What was the gloom upon the old heart that he loved? What trouble was it?

At last he rose and put meal and water into the iron pot, and stirred the porridge while it seethed and sputtered. Then he poured boiling water upon the tea in the brown jenny, and put the new bread and the sweet-milk scones on the rude deal board that was the table.

"Come, dear tired old heart," he said, "and let us give thanks to the Being."

"Blessings and thanks," she said, and turned round.

Alasdair poured out the porridge, and watched the steam rise. Then he sat down, with a knife in one hand and the brown-white loaf in the other.

"O God," he said, in the low voice he had in the kirk when the Bread and Wine were given—"O God, be giving us now thy blessing, and have the thanks. And give us peace."

Peace there was in the sorrowful old eyes of the mother. The two ate in silence. The big clock that was by the bed *tick-tacked*, *tick-tacked*. A faint sputtering came out of a peat that had bog-gas in it. Shadows moved in the silence, and met and whispered and moved into deep, warm darkness. There was peace.

There was still a red flush above the hill in the west when the mother and son sat in the ingle again.

"What is it, mother-my-heart?" Alasdair asked at last, putting his great red hand upon the woman's knee.

She looked at him for a moment. When she spoke she turned away her gaze again.

"Foxes have holes," and the fowls of the air have their places of rest, but the Son of Man hath not where to lay his head."

"And what then, dear? Sure, it is the deep meaning you have in that grey old head that I'm loving so."

"A, lennav-aghray, there is meaning to my words. It is old I am, and the hour of my hours is near. I heard a voice outside the window last night. It is a voice I will not be hearing, no, not for seventy years. It was cradle-sweet, it was."

She paused, and there was silence for a time.

"Well, dear," she began again, wearily, and in a low weak voice, "it is more tired and more tired I am every day now this last month. Two Sabbaths ago I woke, and there were bells in the air: and you are for knowing well, Alasdair, that no kirk-bells ever rang in Strath-Nair. At edge o' dark on Friday, and by the same token the thirteenth day it was, I fell asleep and dreamed the mools were on my breast, and that the roots of the white daisies were in the hollows where the eyes were that loved you, Alasdair, my son."

The man looked at her with troubled gaze. No words would come. Of what avail to speak when there is nothing to be said? God sends the gloom upon the cloud, and there is rain: God sends the gloom upon the hill, and there is mist: God sends the gloom upon the sun, and there is winter. It is God, too, sends the gloom upon the soul, and there is change. The swallow knows when to lift up her wing overagainst the shadow that creeps out of the

232

north : the wild swan knows when the smell
of snow is behind the sun : the salmon, lone in
the brown pool among the hills, hears the deep
sea, and his tongue pants for salt, and his fins
quiver, and he knows that his time is come,
and that the sea calls. The doe knows when
the fawn hath not yet quaked in her belly : is
not the violet more deep in the shadowy dewy
eyes ? The woman knows when the babe hath
not yet stirred a little hand : is not the wild-
rose on her cheek more often seen, and are
not the shy tears moist on quiet hands in the
dusk ? How, then, shall the soul not know
when the change is nigh at last ? Is it a less
thing than a reed, which sees the yellow birch-
gold adrift on the lake, and the gown of the
heather grow russet when the purple has passed
into the sky, and the white bog-down
wave grey and tattered where the loneroid
grows dark and pungent—which sees, and
knows that the breath of the Death-Weaver at
the Pole is fast faring along the frozen norland
peaks. It is more than a reed, it is more
than a wild doe on the hills, it is more than a
swallow lifting her wing against the coming
of the shadow, it is more than a swan drunken
with the savour of the blue wine of the waves
when the green Arctic lawns are white and
still. It is more than these, which has the

Son of God for brother, and is clothed with light. God doth not extinguish at the dark tomb what he hath litten in the dark womb.

Who shall say that the soul knows not when the bird is aweary of the nest, and the nest is aweary of the wind? Who shall say that all portents are vain imaginings? A whirling straw upon the road is but a whirling straw: yet the wind is upon the cheek almost ere it is gone.

It was not for Alasdair Og, then, to put a word upon the saying of the woman that was his mother, and was age-white, and could see with the seeing of old wise eyes.

So all that was upon his lips was a sigh, and the poor prayer that is only a breath out of the heart.

"You will be telling me, grey sweetheart," he said lovingly, at last—"you will be telling me what was behind the word that you said: that about the foxes that have holes for the hiding, poor beasts, and the birdeens wi' their nests, though the Son o' Man hath not where to lay his head?"

"Ay, Alastair, my son that I bore long syne an' that I'm leaving soon, I will be be for telling you that thing, an' now too, for I am knowing what is in the dark this night o' the nights."

Old Sheen put her head back wearily on the chair, and let her hands lie, long and white, palm-downward upon her knees. The peat-glow warmed the dull grey that lurked under her closed eyes and about her mouth, and in the furrowed cheeks. Alasdair moved nearer and took her right hand in his, where it lay like a tired sheep between two scarped rocks. Gently he smoothed her hand, and wondered why so frail and slight a creature as this small old wizened woman could have mothered a great swarthy man like himself—he a man now, with his twoscore and ten years, and yet but a boy there at the dear side of her.

"It was this way, Alasdair-mochree," she went on in her low thin voice—like a wind worn leaf, the man that was her son thought. "It was this way. I went down to the burn to wash the *claar*, and when I was there I saw a wounded fawn in the bracken The big sad eyes of it were like those of Maisie, poor lass, when she had the birthing that was her going-call. I went through the bracken, and down by the Gorromalt, and into the Glen of The Willows.

"And when I was there, and standing by the running water, I saw a man by the stream-side. He was tall, but spare and weary: and the clothes upon him were poor and worn.

235

He had sorrow. When he lifted his head at me, I saw the tears. Dark, wonderful, sweet eyes they were. His face was pale. It was not the face of a man of the hills. There was no red in it, and the eyes looked in upon themselves. He was a fair man, with the white hands that a woman has, a woman like the Bantighearna of Glenchaisteal over yonder. His voice, too, was a voice like that: in the softness, and the sweet, quiet sorrow, I am meaning.

"The word that I gave him was in the English: for I thought he was like a man out of *Sasunn*, or of the southlands somewhere. But he answered me in the Gaelic: sweet, good Gaelic like that of the Bioball over there, to Himself be the praise.

"'And is it the way down the Strath you are seeking,' I asked: 'and will you not be coming up to the house yonder, poor cot though it is, and have a sup of milk, and a rest if it's weary you are?'

"'You are having my thanks for that,' he said, 'and it is as though I had both the good rest and the cool sweet drink. But I am following the flowing water here.'

"'Is it for the fishing?' I asked.

"'I am a Fisher,' he said, and the voice of him was low and sad.

" He had no hat on his head, and the light that streamed through a rowan-tree was in his long hair. He had the pity of the poor in his sorrowful grey eyes.

" ' And will you not sleep with us ? ' I asked again : ' that is, if you have no place to go to, and are a stranger in this country, as I am thinking you are ; for I have never had sight of you in the home-straths before. '

" ' I am a stranger," he said, ' and I have no home, and my father's house is a great way off.'

" ' Do not tell me, poor man,' I said gently, for fear of the pain, ' do not tell me if you would fain not ; but it is glad I will be if you will give me the name you have.'

" ' My name is Mac-an-t'-Saoir,' he answered with the quiet deep gaze that was his. And with that he bowed his head, and went on his way, brooding deep.

" ' Well, it was with a heavy heart I turned, and went back through the bracken. A heavy heart, for sure, and yet, oh peace too, cool dews of peace. And the fawn was there: healed, Alasdair, healed, and whinny-bleating for its doe, that stood on a rock wi' lifted hoof an' stared down the glen to where the Fisher was.

" When I was at the burnside, a woman

237

12

came down the brae. She was fair to see, but the tears were upon her.

"'Oh,' she cried, 'have you seen a man going this way?'"

"'Ay, for sure,' I answered, 'But what man would he be?'

"'He is called Mac-an-t'-Saoir.'

"'Well, there are many men that are called Son of the Carpenter. What will his own name be?'

"Iosa,' she said.

"And when I looked at her, she was weaving the wavy branches of a thorn near by, and sobbing low, and it was like a wreath or crown that she made.

"'And who will you be, poor woman?' I asked.

"'O my Son, my Son,' she said, and put her apron over her head and went down into the Glen of the Willows, she weeping sore, too, at that, poor woman.

"So now, Alasdair, my son, tell me what thought you have about this thing that I have told you. For I know well whom I met on the brae there, and who the Fisher was. And when I was at the peats here once more I sat down, and my mind sank into myself. And it is knowing the knowledge I am."

"Well, well, dear, it is sore tired you are.

238

Have rest now. But sure there are many men called Macintyre."

"Ay, an' what Gael that you know will be for giving you his surname like that."

Alasdair had no word for that. He rose to put some more peats on the fire. When he had done this, he gave a cry.

The whiteness that was on the mother's hair was now in the face. There was no blood there, or in the drawn lips. The light in the old, dim eyes was like water after frost.

He took her hand in his. Clay-cold it was. He let it go, and it fell straight by the chair, stiff as the cromak he carried when he was with the sheep.

"Oh my God and my God," he whispered, white with the awe, and the bitter cruel pain.

Then it was that he heard a knocking at the door.

"Who is there?" he cried hoarsely.

"Open, and let me in." It was a low, sweet voice, but was that grey hour the time for a welcome?

"Go, but go in peace, whoever you are. There is death here."

"Open, and let me in."

At that, Alasdair, shaking like a reed in the wind, unclasped the latch. A tall fair man, ill-clad and weary, pale, too, and with dreaming eyes, came in.

"*Beannachd Dhe an Tigh*," he said, "God's blessing on this house, and on all here."

"The same upon yourself," Alasdair said, with the weary pain in his voice. "And who will you be? and forgive the asking."

"I am called Mac-an-t'-Saoir, and Iosa is the name I bear—Jesus, the Son of the Carpenter."

"It is a good name. And is it good you are seeking this night?"

"I am a Fisher."

"Well, that's here an' that's there. But will you go to the Strath over the hill, and tell the good man that is there, the minister, Lachlan MacLachlan, that old Sheen nic Lèoid, wife of Alasdair Ruadh, is dead."

"I know that, Alasdair Òg."

"And how will you be knowing that, and my name too, you that are called Macintyre?"

"I met the white soul of Sheen as it went down by the Glen of the Willows a brief while ago. She was singing a glad song, she was. She had green youth in her eyes. And a man was holding her by the hand. It was Alasdair Ruadh."

At that Alasdair fell on his knees. When

he looked up there was no one there. Through the darkness outside the door, he saw a star shining white, and leaping like a pulse.

It was three days after that day of shadow that Sheen Macleod was put under the green turf.

On each night, Alasdair Og walked in the Glen of the Willows, and there he saw a man fishing, though ever afar off. Stooping he was, always, and like a shadow at times. But he was the man that was called Iosa Mac-an-t'-Saoir—Jesus, the Son of the Carpenter.

And on the night of the earthing he saw the Fisher close by.

" Lord God," he said, with the hush on his voice, and deep awe in his wondering eyes : " Lord God ! "

And the Man looked at him.

" Night and day Alasdair MacAlasdair," he said, " night and day I fish in the waters of the world. And these waters are the waters of grief, and the waters of sorrow, and the waters of despair. And it is the souls of the living I fish for. And lo, I say this thing unto you, for you shall not see me again : *Go in peace.* Go in peace, good soul of a poor man, for thou hast seen the Fisher of Men."

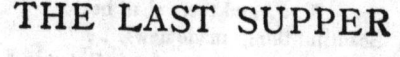

THE LAST SUPPER

" . . . and there shall be
Beautiful things made new . . . "
(Hyperion.)

The Last Supper

The last time that the Fisher of Men was
seen in Strath-Nair was not of Alasdair Macleod but of the little child, Art Macarthur, him
that was born of the woman, Mary Gilchrist,
that had known the sorrow of women.

He was a little child, indeed, when, because
of his loneliness and having lost his way, he
lay sobbing among the bracken by the stream-
side in the Shadowy Glen.

When he was a man, and had reached the
gloaming of his years, he was loved of men
and women, for his songs are many and sweet,
and his heart was true, and he was a good man
and had no evil against any one.

It is he who saw the Fisher of Men when
he was but a little lad : and some say that it
was on the eve of the day that Alasdair Og
died, though of this I know nothing. And
what he saw, and what he heard, was a moonbeam that fell into the dark sea of his mind,
and sank therein, and filled it with light for
all the days of his life. A moonlit mind was
that of Art Macarthur. He had music always
in his mind. I asked him once why he heard

what so few heard, but he smiled and said only: "When the heart is full of love, cool dews of peace rise from it and fall upon the mind: and that is when the song of Joy is heard."

It must have been because of this shining of his soul that some who loved him thought of him as one illumined. His wind was a shell that held the haunting echo of the deep seas: and to know him was to catch a breath of the infinite ocean of wonder and mystery and beauty of which he was the quiet oracle. He has peace now, where he lies under the heather upon a hillside far away: but the Fisher of Men will send him hitherward again, to put a light upon the wave and a gleam upon the brown earth.

I will try to tell this *sgeul* much as Art Macarthur told it to me, though, as he said himself, not all of it was what he dreamed as a child, for there had come to it in the drift of years new awakenings of memory, and new interpretations, as colour and fragrance come to a flower.

.   .   .   .   .

Often and often it is to me all as a dream that comes unawares. Often and often have I striven to see into the green glens of the mind whence it comes, and whither, in a flash,

in a rainbow gleam, it vanishes. When I seek
to draw close to it, to know whether it is a
winged glory out of the soul, or was indeed a
thing that happened to me in my tender years,
lo—it is a dawn drowned in day, a star lost
in the sun, the falling of dew.

But I will not be forgetting: no, never: no,
not till the silence of the grass is over my
eyes: I will not be forgetting that gloaming.

Bitter tears are those that children have.
All that we say with vain words is said by
them in this welling spray of pain. I had the
sorrow that day. Strange hostilities lurked in
the familiar bracken. The soughing of the
wind among the trees, the wash of the brown
water by my side, that had been companion-
able, were voices of awe. The quiet light
upon the grass flamed.

The fierce people that lurked in shadow had
eyes for my helplessness. When the dark
came I thought I should be dead, devoured
of I knew not what wild creature. Would
mother never come, never come with saving
arms, with eyes like soft candles of home?

Then my sobs grew still, for I heard a step.
With dread upon me, poor wee lad that I was,
I looked to see who came out of the wilderness. It was a man, tall and thin and worn,
with long hair hanging adown his face. Pale

he was as a moonlit cot on the dark moor, and his voice was low and sweet. When I saw his eyes I had no fear upon me at all. I saw the mother-look in the grey shadow of them.

"And is that you, Art lennavan-mo?" he said, as he stooped and lifted me.

I had no fear. The wet was out of my eyes.

"What is it you will be listening to now, my little lad?" he whispered, as he saw me lean, intent, hearkening to I know not what.

"Sure," I said, "I am not for knowing: but I thought I heard a music away down there in the wood."

I heard it, for sure. It was a wondrous sweet air as of one playing the feadan in a dream. Callum Dall, the piper, could give no rarer music than that was; and Callum was a seventh son, and was born in the moonshine.

"Will you come with me this night of the nights, little Art?" the man asked me, with his lips touching my brow and giving me rest.

"That I will indeed and indeed," I said. And then I fell asleep.

When I awoke we were in the huntsman's booth, that is at the far end of the Shadowy Glen.

There was a long rough-hewn table in it,

and I stared when I saw bowls and a great jug of milk and a plate heaped with oat-cakes, and beside it a brown loaf of rye-bread.

"Little Art," said he who carried me, "are you for knowing now who I am?"

"You are a prince, I'm thinking," was the shy word that came to my mouth.

"Sure, lennav-aghràp, it is so. It is called the Prince of Peace I am."

"And who is to be eating all this?" I asked.

"This is the last supper," the prince said, so low that I could scarce hear; and it seemed to me that he whispered, "For I die daily, and ever ere I die the Twelve break bread with me."

It was then I saw that there were six bowls of porridge on the one side and six on the other.

"What is your name, O Prince?"

"Iosa."

"And will you have no other name than that?"

"I am called Iosa mac Dhe."

"And is it living in this house you are"

"Ay. But Art, my little lad, I will kiss your eyes, and you shall see who sup with me."

And with that the prince that was called Iosa kissed me on the eyes, and I saw.

"You will never be quite blind again," he

whispered, and that is why all the long years of my years I have been glad in my soul.

What I saw was a thing strange and wonderful. Twelve men sat at that table, and all had eyes of love upon Iosa. But they were not like any men I had ever seen. Tall and fair and terrible they were, like morning in a desert place; all save one, who was dark, and had a shadow upon him and in his wild eyes.

It seemed to me that each was clad in radiant mist. The eyes of them were as stars through that mist.

And each, before he broke bread, or put spoon to the porridge that was in the bowl before him, laid down upon the table three shuttles.

Long I looked upon the company, but Iosa held me in his arms, and I had no fear.

" Who are these men ? " he asked me.

" The Sons of God," I said, I not knowing what I said, for it was but a child I was.

He smiled at that. " Behold," he spoke to the twelve men who sat at the table, " behold the little one is wiser than the wisest of ye." At that all smiled with the gladness and the joy, save one; him that was in the shadow. He looked at me, and I remembered two black lonely tarns upon the hillside, black with the terror because of the kelpie and the drowner.

"Who are these men?" I whispered, with the tremor on me that was come of the awe I had.

"They are the Twelve Weavers, Art, my little child."

" And what is their weaving?"

"They weave for my Father, whose web I am."

At that I looked upon the prince, but I could see no web.

" Are you not Iosa the Prince?"

" I am the Web of Life, Art Iennavan-mo."

"And what are the three shuttles that are beside each Weaver?"

I know now that when I turned my child's-eyes upon these shuttles I saw that they were alive and wonderful, and never the same to the seeing.

"They are called *Beauty* and *Wonder* and *Mystery*."

And with that Iosa mac Dhe sat down and talked with the Twelve. All were passing fair, save him who looked sidelong out of dark eyes. I thought each as I looked at him, more beautiful than any of his fellows : but most I loved to look at the twain who sat on either side of Iosa

" He will be a dreamer among men," said the prince ; " so tell him who ye are."

251

Then he who was on the right turned his eyes upon me. I leaned to him, laughing low with the glad pleasure I had because of his eyes and shining hair, and the flame as of the blue sky that was his robe.

"I am the Weaver of Joy," he said. And with that he took his three shuttles that were called Beauty and Wonder and Mystery, and he wove an immortal shape, and it went forth of the room and out into the green world, singing a rapturous sweet song.

Then he that was upon the left of Iosa the Life looked at me, and my heart leaped, He, too, had shining hair, but I could not tell the colour of his eyes for the glory that was in them. "I am the Weaver of Love," he said, "and I sit next the heart of Iosa." And with that he took his three shuttles that were called Beauty and Wonder and Mystery and he wove an immortal shape, and it went forth of the room and into the green world singing a rapturous sweet song.

Even then, child as I was, I wished to look on no other. None could be so passing fair, I thought, as the Weaver of Joy and the Weaver of Love.

But a wondrous sweet voice sang in my ears, and a cool, soft hand laid itself upon my head. and the beautiful lordly one who had spoken said, "I am the Weaver of Death," and the lovely whispering one who had lulled me with rest said, "I am the Weaver of Sleep." And each wove with the shuttles of Beauty and Wonder and Mystery, and I knew not which was the more fair, and Death seemed to me as Love, and in the eyes of Dream I saw Joy.

My gaze was still upon the fair wonderful shapes that went forth from these twain—from the Weaver of Sleep, an immortal shape of star-eyed Silence, and from the Weaver of Death a lovely Dusk with a heart of hidden flame—when I heard the voice of two other of the Twelve. They were like the laughter of the wind in the corn, and like the golden fire upon that corn. 'And the one said, " I am the Weaver of Passion," and when he spoke I thought that he was both Love and Joy, and Death and Life, and I put out my hands. " It is Strength I give," he said, and he took and kissed me. Then, while Iosa took me again upon his knee, I saw ths Weaver of Passion turn to the white glory beside him, him that Iosa whispered to me was the secret of the world, and that was called "The Weaver of Youth." I know not whence nor how it came, but there was a singing of skiey birds when these twain took the shuttles of Beauty and

Wonder and Mystery, and wove each an immortal shape, and bade it go forth out of the room into the green world, to sing there for ever and ever in the ears of man a rapturous sweet song.

"O Iosa," I cried, "are these all thy brethren? for each is fair as thee, and all have lit their eyes at the white fire I see now in thy heart."

But, before he spake, the room was filled with music. I trembled with the joy, and in my ears it has lingered ever, nor shall ever go. Then I saw that it was the breathing of the seventh and eighth, of the ninth and the tenth of those star-eyed ministers of Iosa whom he called the Twelve: and the names of them were the Weaver of Laughter, the Weaver of Tears, the Weaver of Prayer, and the Weaver of Peace. Each rose and kissed me there. "We shall be with you to the end, little Art," they said: and I took hold of the hand of one, and cried, "O my beautiful one, be likewise with the woman my mother," and there came back to me the whisper of the Weaver of Tears: "I will, unto the end."

Then, wonderingly, I watched him likewise take the shuttles that were ever the same and yet never the same, and weave an immortal shape. And when this Soul of Tears went forth of the room, I thought it was my mother's voice singing that rapturous sweet song, and I cried out to it.

The fair immortal turned and waved to me. "I shall never be far from thee, little Art," it sighed, like summer rain falling on leaves: "but I go now to my home in the heart of women."

There were now but two out of the Twelve Oh the gladness and the joy when I looked at him who had his eyes fixed on the face of Iosa that was the Life! He lifted the three shuttles of Beauty and Wonder and Mystery, and he wove a Mist of Rainbows in that room; and in the glory I saw that even the dark twelfth one lifted up his eyes and smiled.

"O what will the name of you be?" I cried, straining my arms to the beautiful lordly one. But he did not hear, for he wrought Rainbow after Rainbow out of the mist of glory that he made, and sent each out into the green world, to be for ever before the eyes of men.

"He is the Weaver of Hope," whispered Iosa mac Dhe; "and he is the soul of each that is here."

Then I turned to the twelfth, and said "Who art thou, O lordly one with the shadow in the eyes."

But he answered not, and there was silence

in the room. And all there, from the Weaver
of Joy to the Weaver of Peace, looked down,
and said nought. Only the Weaver of Hope
wrought a rainbow, and it drifted into the
heart of the lonely Weaver that was twelfth.

"And who will this man be, O Iosa mac
Dhe ? " I whispered.

" Answer the little child," said Iosa, and his
voice was sad.

Then the Weaver answered :

" I am the Weaver of Glory—— ," he began, but Iosa looked at him, and he said no
more.

" Art, little lad," said the Prince of Peace,
" he is the one who betrayeth me for ever.
He is Judas, the Weaver of Fear."

And at that the sorrowful shadowed-eyed man
that was the twelfth took up the three shuttles
that were before him.

"And what are these, O Judas ? " I cried
eagerly, for I saw that they were black.

When he answered not, one of the Twelve
leaned forward and looked at him. It was
the Weaver of Death who did this thing.

"The three shuttles of Judas the Fear-
Weaver, O little Art," said the Weaver of
Death, "are called Mystery, and Despair, and
the Grave."

And with that Judas rose and left the room.

But the shape that he had woven went forth with him as his shadow : and each fared out into the dim world, and the Shadow entered into the minds and into the hearts of men, and betrayed Iosa that was the Prince of Peace.

Thereupon, Iosa rose and took me by the hand, and led me out of that room. When, once, I looked back I saw none of the Twelve save only the Weaver of hope, and he sat singing a wild sweet song that he had learned of the Weaver of Joy, sat singing amid a mist of rainbows and weaving a radiant glory that was dazzling as the sun.

And at that I woke, and was against my mother's heart, and she with the tears upon me. and her lips moving in a prayer.

THE DARK NAMELESS
ONE

The Dark Nameless One

One day this summer I sailed with Pâdruig Macrae and Ivor McLean, boatmen of Iona, along the south-western reach of the Ross of Mull.

The whole coast of the Ross is indescribably wild and desolate. From Feenafort (Fhionnphort), opposite Balliemore of Icolmkill, to the hamlet of Earraid Lighthouse, it were hardly exaggeration to say that the whole tract is uninhabited by man and unenlivened by any green thing. It is the haunt of the cormorant and the seal.

No one who has not visited this region can realize its barrenness. Its one beauty is the faint bloom which lies upon it in the sunlight —a bloom which becomes as the glow of an inner flame when the sun westers without cloud or mist. This is from the ruddy hue of the granite, of which all that wilderness is wrought.

It is a land tortured by the sea, scourged by the sea-wind. A myriad lochs, fiords, inlets,

passages, serrate its broken frontiers, Innumerable islets and reefs, fanged like ravenous
wolves, sentinel every shallow, lurk in
every strait. He must be a skilled boat-
man who would take the Sound of Earraid and penetrate the reaches of the
Ross.

There are many days in the months of
peace, as the islanders call the period from
Easter till the autumnal equinox, when Earraid and the rest of Ross seem under a spell.
It is the spell of beauty. Then the yellow light
of the sun is upon the tumbled masses and
precipitous shelves and ledges, ruddy petals or
leaves of that vast Flower of Granite. Across
it the cloud shadows trail their purple phantoms, their scythe-sweep curves, and abrupt
evanishing floodings of warm dusk. From
wet boulder to boulder, from crag to shelly
crag, from fissure to fissure, the sea cease-
lessly weaves a girdle of foam. When the
wide luminous stretch of waters beyond—
green near the land, and farther out all of a
living blue, interspersed with wide alleys of
amethyst—is white with the sea-horses, there
is such a laughter of surge and splash all the
way from Slugan-dubh to the Rudha-nam-
Maol-Mòra, or to the tide-swept promontory
of the Sgeireig-a'-Bhochdaidh, that, looking

inland, one sees through a rainbow-shimmering veil of ever-flying spray.

But the sun spell is even more fugitive upon the face of this wild land than the spell of beauty upon a woman. So runs one of our proverbs : as the falling of the wave, as the fading of the leaf, so is the beauty of a woman, unless—ah, that *unless*, and the indiscoverable fount of joy that can only be come upon by hazard once in life, and thereafter only in dreams, and the Land of the Rainbow that is never reached, and the green sea-doors of Tir-na-thonn, that open now no more to any wandering wave

It was from Pâdruig, on that day, I heard the strange tale of his kinsman Murdoch, the tale of "The Judgment o' God" that I have told elsewhere. It was Pàdruig, too, who told me of the Sea-witch of Earraid.

"Yes," he said, "I have heard of the *each-uisge* (the sea-beast, sea-kelpie, or water-horse), but I have never seen it with the eyes. My father and my brother knew of it. But this thing I know, and this what we call *an-cailleach-uisge* (the siren or water-witch) ; the *cailliach*, mind you, not the *maighdeannmhàra* (the mermaid), who means no harm. May she hear me saying it ! The cailliach is old and clad in weeds, but her voice is young, and

263

she always sits so that the light is in the eyes
of the beholder. She seems to him young
also, and fair. She has two familiars in the
form of seals, one black as the grave, and the
other white as the shroud that is in the grave ;
and these sometimes upset a boat, if
the sailor laughs at the song of the water-
witch.

"A man netted one of those seals, more
than a hundred years ago, with his herring-
trawl, and dragged it into the boat ; but the
other seal tore at the net so savagely, with its
head and paws over the bows, that it was clear
no net would long avail. The man heard
them crying and screaming, and then talking
law and muttering, like women in a frenzy.
In his fear he cast the nets adrift, all but a
small portion that was caught in the thwarts.
Afterwards, in this portion, he found a tress of
woman's hair. And that is just so : to the
Stones be it said.

" The grandson of this man, Tòmais McNair,
is still living, a shepherd on Eilean-
Uamhain, beyond Lunga in the Cainburg
Isles. A few years ago, off Callachan Point,
he saw the two seals, and heard, though he
did not see, the caillaich. And that which I
tell you—Christ's Cross before me—is a true
thing."

All the time that Pàdruig was speaking, I saw that Ivor McLean looked away : either as though he heard nothing, or did not wish to hear. There was dream in his eyes ; I saw that, so said nothing for a time.

"What is it, Ivor ? " I asked at last, in a low voice. He started, and looked at me strangely.

"What will you be asking that for ? What are you doing in my mind, that is secret ? "

"I see that you are brooding over something. Will you not tell me ? "

"Tell her," said Pàdruig quietly.

But Ivor kept silent. There was a look in his eyes which I understood. Thereafter we sailed on, with no word in the boat at all.

That night, a dark, rainy night it was, with an uplift wind beating high over against the hidden moon, I went to the cottage where Ivor McLean lived with his old deaf mother, deaf nigh upon twenty years, ever since the night of the nights when she heard the women whisper that Callum, her husband, was among the drowned, after a death-wind had blown.

When I entered, he was sitting before the flaming coal-fire ; for on Iona now, by decree of MacCailin Mòr, there is no more peat burned.

"You will tell me now, Ivor ? " was all I said.

" Yes ; I will be telling you now. And the reason why I did not tell you before was because it is not a wise or a good thing to tell ancient stories about the sea while still on the running wave. Macrae should not have done that thing. It may be we shall suffer for it when next we go out with the nets. We were to go to-night ; but no, not I, no, no, for sure, not for all the herring in the Sound."

" Is it an ancient *sgeul*, Ivor ? "

" Ay. I am not for knowing the age of these things. It may be as old as the days of the Féinn for all I know. It has come down to us. Alasdair MacAlasdair of Tiree, him that used to boast of having all the stories of Colum and Brighde, it was he told it to the mother of my mother, and she to me."

" What is it called ? "

" Well, this and that ; but there is no harm in saying it is called the Dark Nameless One."

" The Dark Nameless One ! "

" It is this way. But will you ever have been hearing of the MacOdrums of Uist ? "

" Ay : the Sliochd-nan-ròn."

" That is so. God knows. The Sliochd-nan-ròn . . . the progeny of the Seal. . . . Well, well, no man knows what moves in the shadow of life. And now I will be telling you

266

that old ancient tale, as it was given to me by
the mother of my mother.

On a day of the days, Colum was walking
alone by the sea-shore. The monks were at
the hoe or the spade, and some milking the
kye, and some at the fishing. They say it was
on the first day of the *Faoilleach Geamhraidh*,
the day that is called *Am fheill Brighde*.

The holy man had wandered on to where
the rocks are, opposite to Soa. He was praying and praying, and it is said that whenever
he prayed aloud, the barren egg in the nest
would quicke. and the blighted bud enfold,
and the butterfly cleave its shroud.

Of a sudden he came upon a great black seal,
lying silent on the rocks, with wicked eyes.

"My blessing upon you, O Ròn," he said
with the good kind courteousness that was his.

"*Droch spadadh ort,*" answered the seal,
"A bad end to you, Colum of the Gown."

"Sure, now," said Colum angrily. "I am
knowing by that curse that you are no friend
of Christ, but of the evil pagan faith out of
the north. For here I am known ever as
Colum the White, or as Colum the Saint; and
it is only the Picts and the wanton Normen
who deride me because of the holy white robe
I wear."

"Well, well," replied the seal, speaking the good Gaelic as though it were the tongue of the deep sea, as God knows it may be for all you, I, or the blind wind can say ; " Well, well, let that thing be : it's a wave-way here or a wave-way there. But now if it is a Druid you are, whether of Fire or of Christ, be telling me where my woman is, and where my little daughter."

At this, Colum looked at him for a long while. Then he knew.

" It is a man you were once, O Ròn ? "

" Maybe ay and maybe no."

" And with that thick Gaelic that you have it will be out of the north isles you come ? "

" That is a true thing."

" Now I am for knowing at last who and what you are. You are one of the race of Odrum the Pagan."

" Well, I am not denying it, Colum. And what is more, I am Angus MacOdrum, Aonghas mac Torcall mhic Odrum, and the name I am known by is Black Angus."

" A fitting name too," said Colum the Holy, " because of the black sin in your heart, and the black end God has in store for you."

At that Black Angus laughed.

" Why is there laughter upon you, Man-Seal ? "

"Well, it is because of the good company I'll be having. But, now, give me the word : Are you for having seen or heard aught of a woman called Kirsteen McVurich ? "

"Kirsteen—Kirsteen—that is the good name of a nun it is, and no sea-wanton ! "

"Oh, a name here or a name there is soft sand. And so you cannot be for telling me where my woman is ? "

" No."

" Then a stake for your belly, and the nails through your hands, thirst on your tongue, and the corbies at your eyne ! "

And, with that, Black Angus louped into the green water, and the hoarse wild laugh of him sprang into the air and fell dead against the cliff like a wind-spent mew.

Colum went slowly back to the brethren, brooding deep. "God is good," he said in a low voice, again and again ; and each time that he spoke there came a fair sweet daisy into the grass, or a yellow bird rose up, with song to it for the first time wonderful and sweet to hear.

As he drew near to the House of God he met Murtagh, an old monk of the ancient old race of the isles.

" Who is Kirsteen McVurich, Murtagh ? " he asked.

"She was a good servant of Christ, she was, in the south isles, O Colum, till Black Angus won her to the sea."

"And when was that?"

"Nigh upon a thousand years ago."

At that Colum stared in amaze. But Murtagh was a man of truth, nor did he speak in allegories. "Ay, Colum, my father, nigh upon a thousand years ago."

"But can mortal sin live as long as that?"

"Ay, it endureth. Long, long ago, before Oisìn sang, before Fionn before Cuchullin was a glorious great prince, and in the days when the Tuatha-De Danànn were sole lords in all green Banba, Black Angus made the woman Kirsteen McVurich leave the place of prayer and go down to the sea-shore, and there he leaped upon her and made her his prey, and she followed him into the sea."

"And is death above her now?"

"No. She is the woman that weaves the sea-spells at the wild place out yonder that is known as Earraid: she that is called *an-Cailleach-uisge*, the sea-witch."

"Then why was Black Angus for the seeking her here and the seeking her there?"

"It is the Doom. It is Adam's first wife she is, that sea-witch over there, where the foam is ever in the sharp fangs of the rocks."

" And who will he be ? "

" His body is the body of Angus the son of Torcall of the race of Odrum, for all that a seal he is to the seeming ; but the soul of him is Judas."

" Black Judas, Murtagh ? "

" Ay, Black Judas, Colum."

But with that, Ivor McLean rose abruptly from before the fire, saying that he would speak no more that night. And truly enough there was a wild, lone, desolate cry in the wind, and a slapping of the waves one upon the other with an eerie laughing sound, and the screaming of a sea-mew that was like a human thing.

So I touched the shawl of his mother, who looked up with startled eyes and said, " God be with us " ; and then I opened the door, and the salt smell of the wrack was in my nostrils, and the great drowning blackness of the night.

THE THREE MARVELS
OF HY

———

The Three Marvels
of Hy

I

THE FESTIVAL OF THE BIRDS

Before dawn, on the morning of the hundredth Sabbath after Colum the White had made glory to God in Hy, that was theretofore called Ioua, and thereafter I-shona and is now Iona, the Saint beheld his own Sleep in a vision.

Much fasting and long pondering over the missals, with their golden and azure and sea-green initials and earth-brown branching letters, had made Colum weary. He had brooded much of late upon the mystery of the living world that was not man's world.

On the eve of that hundredth Sabbath, which was to be a holy festival in Iona, he had talked long with an ancient greybeard out of a remote isle in the north, the wild Isle of the Mountains, where Scathach the Queen hanged the men of Lochlin by their yellow hair.

This man's name was Ardan, and he was of the ancient people. He had come to Hy because of two things. Maolmòr, the King of the northern Picts, had sent him to learn of Colum what was this god-teaching he had brought out of Eiré : and for himself he had come, with his age upon him, to see what manner of man this Colum was, who had made Ioua, that was "Innis-nan-Dhruidh-neach"—the Isle of the Druids—into a place of new worship.

For three hours Ardan and Colum had walked by the sea-shore. Each learned of the other. Ardan bowed his head before the wisdom. Colum knew in his heart that the Druid saw mysteries.

In the first hour they talked of God. Colum spake, and Ardan smiled in his shadowy eyes. It is for the knowing," he said, when Colum ceased.

"Ay, sure," said the Saint : " And now, O Ardan the wise, is my God thy God ?"

But at that Arden smiled not. He turned his eyes to the west. With his right hand he pointed to the Sun that was like a great golden flower. "Truly, he is thy God and my God." Colum was silent. Then he said,

" Thee and thine, O Ardan, from Maolmór the Pictish king to the least of thy slaves, shall have a long weariness in Hell. That fiery globe yonder is but the Lamp of the World : and sad is the case of the man who knows not the torch from the torch-bearer."

And in the second hour they talked of Man. Ardan spake, and Colum smiled in his deep, grey eyes.

" It is for laughter that," he said, when Ardan ceased.

" And why will that be, O Colum of Eiré ? " said Ardan. Then the smile went out of Colum's grey eyes, and he turned and looked about him.

He beheld, near, a crow, a horse, and a hound.

" These are thy brethren," he said scornfully.

But Ardan answered quietly, " Even so."

The third hour they talked about the beasts of the earth and the fowls of the air.

At the last Ardan said : "The ancient wisdom hath it that these are the souls of men and women that have been, or are to be."

Whereat Colum answered : " The new wisdom, that is old as eternity, declareth that God created all things in love. Therefore are we at one, O Ardan, though we sail to

277

the Isle of Truth from the West and the East.
Let there be peace between us."

" Peace," said Ardan.

That eve, Ardan of the Picts sat with the
monks of Iona. Colum blessed him and said
a saying. Oran of the songs sang a hymn of
beauty. Ardan rose, and put the wine of
guests to his lips, and chanted this rune :

> O Colum and Monks of Christ,
> It is peace we are having this night :
> Sure, peace is a good thing,
> And I am glad with the gladness.
>
> We worship one God,
> Though ye call him Dè—
> And I say not, *O Dia !*
> But cry *Bea'uil !*
>
> For it is one faith for man,
> And one for the living world,
> And no man is wiser than another—
> And none knoweth much.
>
> None knoweth a better thing than this :
> The Sword, Love, Song, Honour, Sleep.
> None knoweth a surer thing than this :
> Birth, Sorrow, Pain, Weariness, Death.
>
> Sure, peace is a good thing ;
> Let us be glad of Peace :
> We are not men of the Sword,
> But of the Rune and the Wisdom.

278

The Three Marvels of Hy

I have learned a truth of Colum,
He too hath learned of me:
All ye on the morrow shall see
A wonder of the wonders.

The thought is on you, that the Cross
Is known only of you:
Lo, I tell you the birds know it
That are marked with the Sorrow.

Listen to the Birds of Sorrow,
They shall tell you a great Joy:
It is peace you will be having,
With the Birds.

No more would Ardan say after that, though all besought him.

Many pondered long that night. Oran made a song of mystery. Colum brooded through the dark ; but before dawn he slept upon the fern that strewed his cell. At dawn, with waking eyes, and weary, he saw his Sleep in a vision.

It stood grey and wan beside him.

"What art thou, O spirit ?" he said.

"I am thy Sleep, Colum."

"And is it peace ?"

"It is peace."

"What wouldest thou ?"

"I have wisdom. Thy heart and thy brain were closed. I could not give you what I brought. I brought wisdom."

"Give it."

" Behold ! "

And Colum, sitting upon the strewed fern
that was his bed, rubbed his eyes that were
heavy with weariness and fasting and long
prayer. He could not see his Sleep now. It
was gone as smoke that is licked up by the
wind.

But on the ledge of the hole that was in
the eastern wall of his cell he saw a bird. He
leaned his elbow upon the leabhar-aifrionn that
was by his side.[1] Then he spoke.

" Is there song upon thee, O Bru-dhearg ? "

Then the Red-breast sang, and the singing
was so sweet that tears came into the eyes of
Colum, and he thought the sunlight that was
streaming from the east was melted into
that lilting sweet song. It was a hymn that
the Bru-dhearg sang, and it was this :

> Holy, Holy, Holy,
> Christ upon the Cross ;
> My little nest was near,
> Hidden in the moss.
>
> Holy, Holy, Holy,
> Christ was pale and wan :
> His eyes beheld me singing
> *Bron, Bron, mo Bron !* [2]

[1] The "leabhar-aifrionn" (pron. lyo-ur eff-runn) is
a missal : literally a mass-book, or chapel-book.
Bru-dhearg is literally red-breast.

[2] "O my Grief, my Grief.'

The Three Marvels of Hy

Holy, Holy, Holy,
  "Come near, O wee brown bird!"
Christ spake: and lo, I lighted
  Upon the Living Word.

Holy, Holy, Holy,
  I heard the mocking scorn!
But *Holy, Holy, Holy*,
  I sang against a thorn!

Holy, Holy, Holy,
  Ah, his brow was bloody:
Holy, Holy, Holy,
  All my breast was ruddy.

Holy, Holy, Holy,
  Christ's-Bird shalt thou be:
Thus said Mary Virgin
  There on Calvary.

Holy, Holy, Holy,
  A wee brown bird am I:
But my breast is ruddy
  For I saw Christ die.

Holy, Holy, Holy,
  By this ruddy feather,
Colum, call thy monks, and
  All the birds together.

And at that Colum rose. Awe was upon him, and joy.

He went out and told all to the monks. Then he said Mass out on the green sward.

281

The yellow sunshine was warm upon his grey hair. The love of God was warm in his heart.

" Come, all ye birds ! " he cried.

And lo, all the birds of the air flew nigh. The golden eagle soared from the Cuchullins in far-off Skye, and the osprey from the wild lochs of Mull ; the gannet from above the clouds, and the fulmar and petrel from the green wave : the cormorant and the skua from the weedy rock, and the plover and the kestrel from the machar : the corbie and the raven from the moor, and the snipe and the bittern and the heron : the cuckoo and cushat from the woodland : the crane from the swamp, the lark from the sky, and the mavis and the merle from the green bushes : the yellowyite, the shilfa, and the lintie, the gyalvonn and the wren and the redbreast, one and all, every creature of the wings, they came at the bidding.

" Peace ! " cried Colum.

" Peace ! " cried all the Birds, and even the Eagle, the Kestrel, the Corbie, and the Raven cried *Peace, Peace!*

" I will say the Mass," said Colum the White.

And with that he said the Mass. And he blessed the birds.

When the last chant was sung, only the Bru-dhearg remained.

"Come, O Ruddy-Breast," said Colum, "and sing to us of the Christ."

Through a golden hour thereafter the Red-breast sang.   Sweet was the joy of it.

At the end Colum said, " Peace ! In the name of the Father, the Son, and the Holy Ghost."

Thereat Ardan the Pict bowed his head, and in a loud voice repeated—

" *Sith* (shee) ! *An ainm an Athar*, *'s an Mhic, 's an Spioraid Naoimh !* "

And to this day the song of the Birds of Colum, as they are called in Hy, is *Sith— Sith—Sith—an—ainm—Chriosd*——

" Peace—Peace—Peace—in the name of Christ ! "

II

THE SABBATH OF THE FISHES AND FLIES.

For three days Colum had fasted, save for a mouthful of meal at dawn, a piece of rye-bread at noon, and a mouthful of dulse and spring-water at sundown. On the night of the third day, Oran and Keir came to him in his cell. Colum was on his knees, lost in prayer. There was no sound there, save the faint whispered muttering of his lips, and on the plastered wall the weary buzzing of a fly.

"Master !" said Oran in a low voice, soft with pity and awe, "Master !"

But Colum took no notice. His lips still moved, and the tangled hairs below his nether lip shivered with his failing breath.

"Father !" said Keir, tender as a woman, "Father !"

Colum did not turn his eyes from the wall. The fly droned his drowsy hum upon the rough plaster. It crawled wearily for a space, then stopped. The slow hot drone filled the cell.

"Master," said Oran, "it is the will of the brethren that you break your fast. You are old, and God has your glory. Give us peace."

"Father," urged Keir, seeing that Colum kneeled unnoticingly, his lips still moving above his grey beard, with the white hair of him falling about his head like a snowdrift slipping from a boulder. "Father, be pitiful! We hunger and thirst for your presence. We can fast no longer, yet have we no heart to break our fast if you are not with us. Come, holy one, and be of our company, and eat of the good broiled fish that awaiteth us. We perish for the benediction of thine eyes."

Then it was that Colum rose, and walked slowly toward the wall.

"Little black beast," he said to the fly that droned its drowsy hum and moved not at all; "little black beast, sure it is well I am knowing what you are. You are thinking you are going to get my blessing, you that have come out of hell for the soul of me!"

At that the fly flew heavily from the wall, and slowly circled round and round the head of Colum the White.

"What think you of that, brother Oran,

brother Keir ?" he asked in a low voice, hoarse because of his long fast and the weariness that was upon him.

"It is a fiend," said Oran.

"It is an angel," said Keir.

Thereupon the fly settled upon the wall again, and again droned his drowsy hot hum.

"Little black beast," said Colum, with the frown coming down into his eyes, "is it for peace you are here, or for sin ? Answer, I conjure you in the name of the Father, the Son, and the Holy Ghost ! "

"*An ainm an Athar, 's an Mhic, 's an Spioraid Naoimh,*" repeated Oran below his breath.

"*An ainm an Athar, 's an Mhic, 's an Spioraid Naoimh,*" repeated Keir below his breath.

Then the fly that was upon the wall flew up to the roof and circled to and fro. And it sang a beautiful song, and its song was this :

I

Praise be to God, and a blessing too at that, and a blessing!
For Colum the White, Colum the Dove, hath worshipped;
Yea, he hath worshipped and made of a desert a garden,
And out of the dung of men's souls hath made a sweet savour of burning.

II

A savour of burning, most sweet, a fire for the altar,
This he hath made in the desert; the hell-saved all
    gladden,
Sure he hath put his benison, too, on milch-cow and
    bullock,
On the fowls of the air, and the man-eyed seals, and
    the otter.

III

But where in his Dûn in the great blue mainland of
    Heaven
God the All-Father broodeth, where the harpers are
    harping his glory;
There where He sitteth, where a river of ale poureth
    ever,
His great sword broken, His spear in the dust, He
    broodeth,

IV

And this is the thought that moves in his brain, as a
    cloud filled with thunder
Moves through the vast hollow sky filled with the
    dust of the stars:
What boots it the glory of Colum, since he maketh a
    Sabbath to bless me,
And hath no thought of my sons in the deeps of the air
    and the sea?

And with that the fly passed from their
vision. In the cell was a most wondrous sweet
song, like the sound of far-off pipes over
water.

Oran said in a low voice of awe, "O our God!"

Keir whispered, white with fear, "O God, my God!"

But Colum rose, and took a scourge from where it hung on the wall. "It shall be for peace, Oran," he said, with a grim smile flitting like a bird above the nest of his black beard; "it is for peace, Keir!"

And with that he laid the scourge heavily upon the bent backs of Keir and Oran, nor stayed his hand, nor let his three days' fast weaken the deep piety that was in the might of his arm, and because of the glory to God.

Then, when he was weary, peace came into his heart, and he sighed "*Amen!*"

"Amen!" said Oran the monk.

"Amen!" said Keir the monk.

"And this thing hath been done," said Colum, "because of the evil wish of you and the brethren, that I should break my fast, and eat of fish, till God willeth it. And lo, I have learned a mystery. Ye shall all witness to it on the morrow, which is the Sabbath."

That night the monks wondered much. Only Oran and Keir cursed the fishes in the deeps of the sea and the flies in the deeps of the air.

On the morrow, when the sun was yellow

on the brown sea-weed, and there was peace on the isle and upon the waters, Colum and the brotherhood went slowly toward the sea.

At the meadows that are close to the sea, the Saint stood still. All bowed their heads.

"O winged things of the air," cried Colum, "draw near!"

With that the air was full of the hum of innumerous flies, midges, bees, wasps, moths, and all winged insects. These settled upon the monks, who moved not, but praised God in silence. "Glory and praise to God," cried Colum, "behold the Sabbath of the children of God that inhabit the deeps of the air! Blessing and peace be upon them."

"Peace! Peace!" cried the monks, with one voice.

"In the name of the Father, the Son, and the Holy Ghost!" cried Colum the White, glad because of the glory to God.

"*An ainm an Athar, 's an Mhic, 's an Spioraid Naoimh.*" cried the monks, bowing reverently, and Oran and Keir deepest of all, because they saw the fly that was of Colum's cell leading the whole host, as though it were their captain, and singing to them a marvellous sweet song.

Oran and Keir testified to this thing, and

all were full of awe and wonder, and Colum praised God.

Then the Saints and the brotherhood moved onward and went upon the rocks. When all stood ankle-deep in the sea-weed that was swaying in the tide, Colum cried :

"O finny creatures of the deep, draw near !"

And with that the whole sea shimmered as with silver and gold.

All the fishes of the sea, and the great eels, and the lobsters and the crabs, came in a swift and terrible procession. Great was the glory.

Then Colum cried, "O fishes of the Deep, who is your king ?"

Whereupon the herring, the mackerel, and the dog-fish swam forward, and each claimed to be king. But the echo that ran from wave to wave said, *The Herring is King.*

Then Colum said to the mackerel : "Sing the song that is upon you !"

And the mackerel sang the song of the wild rovers of the sea, and the lust of pleasure.

Then Colum said, "But for God's mercy, I would curse you, O false fish."

Then he spake likewise to the dog-fish : and the dog-fish sang of slaughter and the chase, and the joy of blood.

And Colum said : " Hell shall be your portion."

And there was peace   And the Herring said :

" In the name of the Father, the Son, and the Holy Ghost ! "

Whereat all that mighty multitude, ere they sank into the deep, waved their fins and their claws, each after his kind, and repeated as with one voice :

"*An ainm an Athar, 's an Mhic, 's an Spioraid Naoimh !*"

And the glory that was upon the Sound of Iona was as though God trailed a starry net upon the waters, with a shining star in every little hollow, and a flowing moon of gold on every wave.

Then Colum the White put out both his arms, and blessed the children of God that are in the deeps of the sea and that are in the deeps of the air.

That is how Sabbath came upon all living things upon Hy that is called Iona, and within the air above Hy, and within the sea that is around Hy.

And the glory is Colum's.

III

THE MOON-CHILD

A year and a day before God bade Colum arise to the Feast of Eternity, Pòl the Freckled, the youngest of the brethren, came to him, on a night of the nights.

"The moon is among the stars, O Colum. By his own will, and yours, old Murtagh that is this day with God, is to be laid in the deep dry sand at the east end of the isle."

So the holy Saint rose from his bed of weariness, and went and blessed the place where Murtagh lay in, and bade neither the creeping worm nor any other creature to touch the sacred dead. "Let God only," he said, "Let God alone strip that which he made to grow."

But on his way back sleep passed from him. The sweet salt smell of the sea was in his nostrils : he heard the running of a wave in all his blood.

At the cells he turned, and bade the brethren go in. " Peace be with you," he sighed wearily.

Then he moved downwards toward the sea

A great tenderness of late was upon Colum the Bishop. Ever since he had blessed the fishes and the flies, the least of the children of God, his soul had glowed in a white flame. There was deep compassion in his blue-grey eyes. One night he had waked, because God was there.

"O Christ," he cried, bowing low his old grey head. "Sure, ah sure, the gladness and the joy, because of the hour of the hours."

But God said : " Not so Colum, who keepest me upon the Cross. It is Murtagh, Murtagh the Druid that was, whose soul I am taking to the glory,"

With that Colum rose in awe and great grief. There was no light in his cell. In the deep darkness, his spirit quailed. But lo, the beauty of his heart wrought a soft gleam about him, and in that moonshine of good deeds he rose and made his way to where Murtagh lay.

The old monk slept indeed. It was a sweet breath he drew—he, young and fair now, and laughing with peace under the apples in Paradise.

"O Murtagh," Colum cried, "and thee I thought the least of the brethren, because that thou wast a Druid, and loved not to see thy pagan kindred put to the sword if they would not repent. But, true, in my years I am becoming as a boy who learns, knowing nothing. God wash the sin of pride out of my life!"

At that a soft white shining as of one winged and beautiful, stood beside the dead.

"Art thou Murtagh?" whispered Colum, in deep awe.

"No, I am not Murtagh," came as the breath of vanishing song.

"What art Thou?"

"I am Peace," said the glory."

Thereupon Colum sank to his knees, sobbing with joy, for the sorrow that had been and was no more.

"Tell me, O White Peace, he murmured, "can Murtagh hearken, there under the apples where God is?"

"God's love is a wind that blows hitherward and hence. Speak, and thou shalt hear."

Colum spake. "O Murtagh my brother, tell me in what way it is that I still keep God crucified upon the Cross."

There was a sound in the cell as of the morning-laughter of children, of the singing of birds, of the sunlight streaming through the blue fields of Heaven.

Then Murtagh's voice came out of Paradise, sweet with the sweetness ; honey-sweet it was, and clothed with deep awe because of the glory.

"Colum, servant of Christ, arise !"

Colum rose, and was as a leaf there, a leaf that is in the wind.

"Colum, thine hour is not yet come. I see it, bathing in the white light which is the Pool of Eternal life, that is in the abyss where deep-rooted are the Gates of Heaven."

"And my sin, O Murtagh, my sin ?"

"God is weary because thou has not repented."

"O my God and my God ! Sure, Murtagh, if that is so, it is so, but it is not for knowledge to me.   Sure, O God, it is a blessing I have put on man and woman, on beast and bird and fish, on creeping things and flying things, on the green grass and the brown earth and the flowing wave, on the wind that cometh and goeth, and on the mystery of the flame ! Sure, O God, I have sorrowed for all my sins : there is not one I have not fasted and prayed for. Sorrow upon me !—Is it accursed I am, or what is the evil that holdeth me by the hand ? "

Then Murtagh, calling through sweet dreams and the rainbow-rain of happy tears that make that place so wondrous and so fair, spake once more :

"O Colum, blind art thou. Hast thou yet repented because after that thou didst capture the great black seal, that is a man under spells, thou, with thy monks, didst crucify him upon the great rock at the place where, long ago, thy coracle came ashore ? "

"O Murtagh, favoured of God, will you not be explaining to Him that is King of the Elements, that this was because the seal who was called Black Angus wrought evil upon a mortal woman, and that of the sea-seed was sprung one who had no soul ? "

But no answer came to that, aud when Colum looked about him, behold there was no no soft shining, but only the body of Murtagh the old monk. With a heavy heart, and his soul like a sinking boat in a sea of pain, he turned and went out into the night.

A fine, wonderful night it was. The moon lay low above the sea, and all the flowing gold and flashing silver of the rippling running water seemed to be a flood going that way and falling into the shining hollow splendour.

Through the sea-weed the old Saint moved

weary and sad. When he came to a sandy
place he stopped. There, on a rock, he saw
a little child. Naked she was, though clad
with soft white moonlight. In her hair were
brown weeds of the sea, gleaming golden because of the glow. In her hands was a great
shell, and at that shell was her mouth. And
she was singing this song; passing sweet to
hear it was, with the sea-music that was in
it:

> A little lonely child am I
>   That have not any soul:
> God made me but a homeless wave,
>   Without a goal.
>
> A seal my father was, a seal
>   That once was man:
> My mother loved him tho' he was
>   'Neath mortal ban.
>
> He took a wave and drownèd her,
>   She took a wave and lifted him:
> And I was born where shadows are
>   I the sea-depths dim.
>
> All through the sunny blue-sweet hours
>   I swim and glide in waters green;
> Never by day the mournful shores
>   By me are seen.
>
> But when the gloom is on the wave
>   A shell unto the shore I bring:
> And then upon the rocks I sit
>   And plaintive sing.

O what is this wild song I sing,
  With meanings strange and dim?
No soul am I, a wave am I,
  And sing the Moon-Child's hymn.

Softly Colum drew nigh.

"Peace," he said. "Peace, little one. Ah tender little heart, peace!"

The child looked at him with wide sea-dusky eyes.

"Is it Colum the Holy you will be?"

"No, my fawn, my white dear babe: it is not Colum the Holy I am, but Colum the poor fool that knew not God!"

"Is it you, O Colum, that put the sorrow on my mother, who is the Sea-woman that lives in the whirlpool over there?"

"Ay, God forgive me!"

"Is it you, O Colum, that crucified the seal that was my father: him that was a man once, and that was called Black Angus?"

"Ay, God forgive me!"

"Is it you, O Colum, that bade the children of Hy run away from me, because I was a moon-child, and might win them by the sea-spell into the green wave?"

"Ay, God forgive me!"

"Sure, dear Colum, it was to the glory of God, it was?"

"Ay, He knoweth it, and can hear it, too, from Murtagh, who died this night."

"Look!"

And at that Colum looked, and in a moon-gold wave he saw Black Angus, the seal-man, drifting dark, and the eyes in his round head were the eyes of love. And beside the man-seal swam a woman fair to see, and she looked at him with joy, and with joy at the Moon-Child that was her own, and at Colum with joy.

Thereupon Colum fell upon his knees and cried—

"Give me thy sorrow, wild woman of the sea!"

"Peace to you, Colum," she answered, and sank into the shadow-thridden wave.

"Give me thy death and crucifixion, O Angus-dhu!" cried the Saint, shaking with the sorrow.

"Peace to you, Colum," answered the man-seal, and sank into the dusky quietudes of the deep.

"Ah, bitter heart 'o me! Teach me the way to God, O little child," cried Colum the old, turning to where the Moon-Child was!

But lo, the glory and the wonder!

It was a little naked child that looked at him with healing eyes, but there were no seaweeds in her hair, and no shell in the little wee hands of her. For now, it was a male Child that was there, shining with a light from within : and in his fair sunny hair was a shadowy crown of thorns, and in his hand was a pearl of great price.

" O Christ, my God," said Colum, with failing voice.

" It is thine now, O Colum," said the Moon-Child, holding out to him the shining pearl of great price.

" What is it, O Lord my God ? " whispered the old servant of God that was now glad with the gladness : " what is this, thy boon ? "

"Perfect Peace."

And that is all.

(To God be the Glory. Amen)

THE WOMAN WITH
THE NET

The Woman With
the Net

When Artan had kissed the brow of every
white-robed brother on Iona, and had been
thrice kissed by the aged Colum, his heart was
filled with gladness.

It was late summer. In the afternoon
light peace lay on the green waters of the
Sound, on the green grass of the dunes, on
the white and brown domed cells of the Culdees over whom the holy Colum ruled, and
on the little rock-strewn hill which rose above
where stood Colum's wattled church of sun-
baked mud.

The abbot walked slowly by the side of the
young man. Colum was tall, with hair long
and heavy but white as the canna, and with a
beard that hung low on his breast, grey as the
moss on old firs. His blue eyes were tender.
The youth—for though he was a grown man
he seemed a youth beside Colum—had beauty.
He was tall and comely, with yellow curling
hair, and dark-blue eyes, and a skin so white
that it troubled some of the monks who

dreamed old dreams and washed them away in tears and scourgings.

"You have the bitter fever of youth upon you, Artan," said Colum, as they crossed the dunes beyond Dun-I ; "but you have no fear, and you will be a flame among these Pictish idolaters, and you will be a lamp to show them the way."

"And when I come again, there will be clappings of hands, and hymns and many rejoicings ? "

"I do not think you will come again," said Colum. "The wild folk of these northlands will burn you, or crucify you, or put you upon the crahslat, or give you thirst and hunger till you die. It will be a great joy for you to die like that, Artan, my son ? ,'

"Ay, a great joy," answered the young monk, but with his eyes dreaming away from his words.

There was silence between them as they neared the cove where a large coracle lay, with three men in it.

"Will God be coming to Iona when I am away ? " asked Artan.

Colum stared at him.

"Is it likely that God would come here in a coracle ? " he asked, with scornful eyes.

The young man looked abashed. For sure,

God would not come in a coracle, just as he himself might come. He knew by that how Colum had reproved him. He would come in a cloud of fire, and would be seen from far and near. Artan wondered if the place he was going to was too far north for him to see that greatness ; but he feared to ask.

"Give me a new name," he asked; "give me a new name, my Father."

"What name will you have ? "

"Servant of Mary."

"So be it, Artan Gille-Mhoire."

With that Colum kissed him and bade farewell, and Artan sat down in the coracle, and covered his head with his mantle, and wept and prayed.

The last word he heard was *Peace !*

"That is a good word, and a good thing," he said to himself ; "and because I am the Servant of Mary, and the Brother of Jesu the Son, I will take peace to the *Cruitnè*, who know nothing of that blessing of the blessings."

When he unfolded his mantle, the coracle was already far from Iona. The south wind blew, and the tides swept northward, and the boat moved swiftly across the water. The sea was ashine with froth and small waves leaping like lambs.

In the boat were Thorkeld, a helot of Iona, and two dark wild-eyed men of the north. They were Picts, but could speak the tongue of the Gael. Myrdu, the Pictish king of Skye, had sent them to Iona, to bring back from Colum a Culdee who could show wonders.

"And tell the Chief Druid of the crossed Tree," Myrdu had said, "that if his Culdee does not show me good wonders, and make me believe in his two gods and the woman, I will put an ash-shaft through his body from his hips and out at his mouth, and send him back on the north-tide to the Isle of the White-Robes."

The sun was lying among the outer isles when the coracle passed near the Isle of the Columns. A great noise was in the air : the noise of the waves in the caverns, and the noise of the tide like sea-wolves growling, and like bulls bellowing in a narrow pass of the hills.

A sudden current caught the boat, and it began to drift toward great reefs white with ceaseless torn streams.

Thorkeld leaned from the helm, and shouted to the two Picts. They did not stir, but sat staring, idle with fear.

Artan knew now that it was as Colum had said. God would give him glory soon.

So he took the little clàrsach he had for hymns, for he was the best harper on Iona, anh struck the strings, and sang. But the Latin words tangled in his throat, and he knew too that the men in the boat would not under stand what he sang ; also that the older gods still came far south, and in the caves of the Isle of Columns were demons. There was only one tongue common to all ; and since God had wisdom beyond that of Colum himself, He would know the song in Gaelic as well as though it were sung in Latin.

So Artan let the wind take his broken hymn, and he made a song of his own, and sang—

O Heavenly Mary, Queen of the Elements,
And you, Brigit the fair, with the little harp,
And all the saints, and all the old gods,
Speak to the Father, that He may save us from
    drowning.

Then, seeing that the boat drifted closer, he sang again—

Save us from the rocks and the sea, Queen of
    Heaven !
And remember that I am a culdee of Iona,
And that Colum has sent me to the *Cruitnè*
To sing them the song of peace lest they be damned
    for ever !

Thorkeld laughed at that

"Can the woman put swimming upon you?" he said roughly. "I would rather have the good fin of a great fish now than any woman in the skies."

"You will burn in hell for that," said Artan, the holy zeal warm at his heart

But Thorkeld answered nothing. His hand was on the helm, his eyes on the foaming rocks Besides, what had he to do with the culdee's hell or heaven? When he died, he, who was a man of Lochlann, would go to his own place.

One of the dark men stood, holding the mask. His eyes shone Thick words swung from his lips, like seaweed thrown out of a hollow by an ebbing wave.

The coracle swerved, and the four men were wet with the heavy spray

Thorkeld put his oar in the water and the swaying craft righted.

"Glory to God!" said Artan

"There is no glory to your god in this," said Thorkeld scornfully. "Did you not hear what Necta sang? He sang to the woman in there that drags men into the caves, and throws their bones on the next tide. He put an incantation upon her, and she shrank, and the boat slid away from the rocks."

"That is a true thing," thought Artan. He wondered if it was because he had not sung his hymn in the holy Latin.

When the last flame died out of the west, and the stars came like sheep gathering at the call of the shepherd, Artan remembered that he had not said the prayers nor sung the Vesper hymn

He lay back and listened. There were no bells calling across the water. He looked into the depths. It was Manann's kingdom, and he had never heard that God was there; but he looked. Then he stared into the dark-blue, star-strewn sky.

Suddenly he touched Thorkeld.

"Tell me," he said, "how far north has the Cross of Christ come?"

"By the sea-way it has not come here yet. Murdoch the Freckled came with it this way, but he was pulled into the sea, and he died."

"Who pulled him into the sea?"

Thorkeld stared into the running wave. He had no words.

Artan lay still a long while.

"It will go ill with me," he thought, "if Mary cannot see me so far away from Iona, and if God will not listen to me. Colum should have known that, and given me a holy leaf with the fair branching letters on it, and the Latin words that are the words of God."

Then he spoke to the man who had sung.

"Who is the Woman with the Net," he said, "of whom you sang?"

Necta turned his head away.

"I said it when I sang," he said sullenly

"Tell me."

"She? She is the Woman who stands on the banks of the river"

"What river?"

"I do not know the name of the river."

"Is it north?"

"I do not know. It is the great river. The banks have mist and shadow She has a great net. And when she nets men they are dead. She takes them out of the net, and some she throws into a caldron in the rocks, filled with green flame, and some she puts beneath her feet and tramples into dust. That is how the sand is made."

Artan shivered with the thought that leaped in his mind. All those white sands of Iona . . . were they fair beautiful women trampled into white sand by the feet of the Woman with the Net?

"What of those in the caldron?" he asked.

"They are thrown out on the wind. They

pass into trees and grass and reeds, and deer
and wolves, and men and women."

"Where?"

The man stared idly.

"There are three there," he said, "who
watch the Woman with the Net. One sits on
a great stone and is blind; one whirls a flaming sword; one stands and leans on a great
spear."

"Who are these three?" asked Artan.

The man stared idly.

"There is fire on the ground below that
sword. There is blood on the ground below
that spear. The man with the sword puts it
into the blackness of the shadow that is about
the great stone, but he does not know what is
there. The man with the spear puts it into the
blackness about the great stone, but he does
not know what is there. The blind man on
the stone has his feet in the blackness of the
shadow, but he does not know what is there."

"It will be Mary," said Artan, brooding
deep; "it will be Mary, and God, and the
Son, and the Spirit."

But Necta the Pict stared at him.

"What have these ancient ones to do with
your Iona gods, White-robe?"

Artan frowned.

"The curse of the God of Peace upon you

for that," he said angrily : "do you not know that you have hell for your dwelling-place if you speak evil of God the Father, and the Son, and the Mother of God ?"

"How long have they been in Iona, White-Robe ?"

The man spoke scornfully. Artan knew they had not been there many years. He had no words.

"My fathers worshipped the Sun on the Holy Isle before ever your great Druid that is called Colum crossed the Moyle. Were your three gods in the coracle with Colum ? They were not on the Holy Isle when he came."

"They were coming there," answered Artan confusedly. "It is a long way from . . . from . . . from the place they were sailing from."

Necta listened sullenly.

"Let them stay on Iona," he said : "gods though they be, it would fare ill with them if they came upon the Woman with the Net."

Then he turned on his side, and lay by the man Darach, who was staring at the moon and muttering words that neither Artan nor Thorkeld knew.

For a time the Culdee and the helot spoke in low voices. Thorkeld spoke of his gods. Then he laughed when he spoke of the

312

women-haters, as he called the holy men of
Iona. Artan said nothing. Why should he
hate women, he thought? They were very
fair, he remembered, and made the heart beat.

Thorkeld smiled. He spoke of women.
Artan heard a song in the sea. The stars
shone like fires in a haven. He put his hand
in the water, and put that water against his dry
lips. The salt stung him.

Thorkeld slept. A white calm had fallen.
The boat lay like a shell on a silent pool.
There was nothing between that dim wilderness and the vast sweeping blackness filled
with quivering stars, but the coracle, that a
wave could crush.

Artan could not sleep; it was easier to forget
God, and the Son, and the Spirit, than those
white women of whom Thorkeld had spoken.
He felt hands touch him, white and warm.
A fever was in his blood.

Then he slept, and dreamed that he was on
a misty bank by a great river. The river was
salt, and moans and cries filled the lamentable
rushing noise.

A great fear came upon him. He drew
back, and something came out of the darkness
and swept past him. The cold air of it
made him stagger and shiver. He put his
hands to a bush, and they went through it,

and he fell. There was a great spear on the ground. He put his hand on it, and it was dust.

Then he rose and cried—

O Mary, Mother of God, Queen of the Elements,
Have mercy upon Artan the Culdee!
For it is a good deed I do coming here to the heathen,
And Colum will tell you that, Cólum of Iona!

But something swept again out of the darkness, and Artan was caught in a net, and was swung across the river. And in that net there were fish beyond count, and all were men and women, and all were dead, and were calling upon many gods.

Then he saw a white face in the dusk. Great stars shone in the hair about the brows ; bats flew in the hollow caverns of the eyes and a hand, grey white as clay, plucked at the mass that was in the net. Some were thrown out, and were trampled into dust, and a wind blew the dust into the river, and the grains were borne to the lips of all isles and shores, and were idle sand thenceforth. And some were plucked by the hand, and were thrown into the great caldron of green fire. Artan was of these. And as he swam hither and thither in that immortal water that was as green fire, he saw the Blind Man on the

Stone, and the Man who whirled a flaming Sword, and the Man with the Spear.

The Man with the Sword cleaved him in two parts, and Artan swam as two swim, but knew not the one part from the other, or which he was. Then the Man with the spear drove the spear through the two parts as they swam, and they were made one. And Artan's heart shook with wonder, for in that same moment, as it seemed, he was in a dim wood, and stood by a tree, and by another tree was a woman, like a flame of pale green, and more beautiful than his dreams. He heard the wind in the grass, and saw a star among dark branches, and in the moonshine a bird sang. The woman threw a white flower at his feet, and he gave a cry, and her breast warmed his breast, and her breath was as flame, and all his youth was upon him again, and Colum was far away, and the Others were not there in that place,

Then Artan woke, and saw the cold shine of the stars, and heard the dawn-wind on the sea. To the east, the mountain-peaks of Skye rose dark, but pale light travelled along their summits. It was day.

For three years Artan dwelt among the Picts. He was called the Dart-Thrower because of his skill in war. He had to wife

Oona, the daughter of Myrdu the king, and three women loved him and were held by him. But Oona only he loved. He knew no Latin words now; but once the sea-rovers brought a coracle with three Culdees in it, and he heard one singing the old words as he died slowly on the tall tree where he was crucified. For one was blinded and led naked into the woods; and one was thrust through with an ash-shaft, from the hips to the mouth, and thrown upon the tide; and one was tied to a sappling, and was crucified upon a tall tree.

"I have no Latin now," said Artan to the monk, "but tell me this: Are God and the Son and the Spirit still upon Iona?"

The monk cursed him and died.

That curse went out, and lay upon Oona, and she withered, and lay down, and life went from her.

Artan took a great galley that held a score men. He set sail for Iona.

But God was now come further north than Iona; for between the Holy Isle and the Isle of the Columns the boat filled and sank.

Colum beheld this in a vision, and in a hymn praised God. Artan alone did not drown, but swam on a spar, and was washed on to the sands at Iona.

The Culdees took him.

"In the name of God," said Colum, with fierce anger in his eyes: "in the name of God, put Artan, the servant of Mary, into the cell below the ground; and let him rest and pray there through the night; and at dawn we shall take him out upon the shore, and shall drive a stake through his breast, and the demon that is within him shall go out of him, and he himself shall go to God the Father. For he has had the holy water on him, and is of those who dwell with the saints."

For Colum knew all that Artan had done.

So Artan the Culdee lay in darkness that night. And before dawn he made this song—

It is but a little thing to sit here in the silence and the
    dark;
For I remember the blazing noon when I saw Oona
    the White.
I remember the day when we sailed the Strait in our
    skin-built bark,
And I remember Oona's lips on mine in the heart of
    the night.

So it is a little thing to sit here, hearing nought, seeing
    nought;
When the dawn breaks they will hurry me hence to
    the new-dug grave:
It will be quiet there, if it be true what the good
    Colum has taught,
And I shall hear Oona's voice as a sleeping seal hears
    the moving wave.

CATHAL OF THE WOODS

Cathal of the Woods

(The Annir Choille.[1])

When Cathal mac Art, that was called
Cathal Gille-Mhoire, Cathal the Servant of
Mary, walked by the sea, one night of the
nights in a green May, there was trouble in his
heart.

It was not long since he had left Iona.
The good St Colum, in sending the youth to
the Isle of Â-rinn, as it was then called, gave
him a writing for St Molios, the holy man
who lived in the sea-cave of the small Isle of
the Peak, that is in the eastward hollow at
the south end of Arran   A sorrow it was to
him to leave the fair isle in the west. He
had known glad years there—since, in one
of the remote isles of the north, he had seen
his father slain by a man of Lochlin, and his
mother carried away in a galley oared by
fierce yellow-haired men. No kith or kin had
he but the old priest, that was the brother of

[1] The English equivalent of Annir-Choille would
be the Wood-nymph. The word *Annir* is an ancient
compound Gaelic word for a maiden.

his father, Cathal Gille-Chriosd, Cathal the
Servant of Christ.

On Iona he had learned the way of Christ.
He had a white robe; and could, with a
shaven stick and a thin tuft of seal-fur, or
with the feather-quill of a wild swan or a
solander, write the holy words upon strained
lambskin or parchment, and fill the big letters,
that were here and there, with earth-brown
and sky-blue and shining green, with scarlet
of blood and gold of sun-warm sands.
He could sing the long holy hymns, too, that
Colum loved to hear; and it was his voice
that had the sweetest clear-call of any on the
island. He was in the nineteenth year of his
years when a Frankish prince, who had come
to Iona for the blessing of the Saint, wanted
him to go back with him to the Southlands.
He promised many things because of that
voice. Cathal dreamed often, in the hot
drowsy afternoons of the month that followed,
of the long white sword that would slay so
well; and of the white money that might be
his to buy fair apparel with, and a great black
stallion accoutred with trappings wrought with
gold, and a bed of down; and of white hands,
and white breasts, and the white song of
youth.

He had not gone with the Frankish prince.

But, afterward, he dreamed often. It was on a day of dream that he lay on his back in the hot grass upon a dune, near where the cells of the monks were The sun-glow bathed the isle in a golden haze. The strait was a shimmering dazzle, and the blue wavelets that made curves in the soft white sand seemed to spill gold flakes and change them straightway into little jets of foam or bubbles of rainbow-spray. Cathal had made a song for his delight. His pain was less when he had made it. Now, lying there, and dreaming at times of the words of the Frankish prince, and remembering at times the stranger words of the old pagan helot, Neis, who had come with him out of the north, he felt fire burn in his veins ; and he sang :

O where in the north, or where in the south, or where
  in the east or west
Is she who hath the flower-white hands and the
  swandown breast ?
O, if she be west, or east she be, or in the north or
  south,
A sword will leap, a horse will prance, ere I win to
  Honey-Mouth.

She has great eyes, like the doe on the hill, and warm
  and sweet she is,
O, come to me, Honey-Mouth, bend to me, Honey.
  Mouth, give me thy kiss !

White Hands her name is, where she reigns amid the
    princes fair :
White hands she moves like swimming swans athrough
    her dusk-wave hair :
White hands she puts about my heart, white hands
    fan up my breath :
White hands take out the heart of me, and grant me
    life or death !

White hands make better songs than hymns, white
    hands are young and sweet :
O, a sword for me, O Honey-Mouth, and a war-horse
    fleet !

O wild sweet eyes ! O glad wild eyes ! O mouth, how
    sweet it is !
O, come to me, Honey-Mouth ! bend to me, Honey-
    Mouth ! give me thy kiss !

When he had ceased he saw a shadow fall
upon the white sand beyond the dune. He
looked up, and beheld Colum the Saint.

"Who taught you that song ? " said the
white holy one, in a voice hard and stern.

" No one, O Colum."

" Then the Evil One is indeed here,
Cathal, I promised that you would be having
a holy name soon, but that name I will not
be giving you now. You must come to me
in sackcloth and with dust upon your head,
with pain upon you, and with deep grief in
your heart. Then only shall I bless you be-

fore the brothers and call you Cathal Gille-
Mhoire, Cathal the Servant of Mary."

A bitter, sad waiting it was for him who
had fire in his young blood and was told to
weave frost there, and to put silence upon the
welling song in his heart. But at the end
of the week Cathal was a holy monk again,
and sang the hymns that Colum had taught
him.

It was on the eve of the day when Colum
blessed him before the brethren, and called
him Gille-Mhoire, that he walked alone,
brooding upon the evil of women and the
curse they brought, and praying to Mary to
save him from the sins of which he scarce
knew the meaning. On his way back to his
cell he passed old Neis, the helot, who said
to him mockingly :

" It is a good thing that sorrow, Cathal
mac Art—and yet, sure, it is true that but for
the hot love the slain man your father had for
Foam that was your mother, you would not
be here to praise your God or serve the woman
whom the Arch-Druid yonder says is the
Mother of God."

Cathal bade the man eat silence, or it would
go ill with him. But the words rankled. That
night in his cell he woke, with on his lips his
own sinful words :

White hands make better songs than hymns, white
    hands are young and sweet;
O, a sword for me, O Honey-Mouth, and a war-horse
    fleet!

On the morrow he went to Colum and told
him that the Evil One would not give him
peace. That night the Saint bade him make
ready to go east to the Isle of Arran—the
sole isle, then, where the Pictish folk would
let the white robes of the Culdees go scathe-
less. To the holy Molios he was to go, him
that dwelled in the sea-cave of the Isle of the
Peak, that men already called the Holy Isle
because of the preaching and the miracles of
Molios.

"He is a wise man," said Colum to himself, "and he was a pagan Cruithne once, and
a prince at that, and he knows the sweetness
of sin, and will keep Cathal away from the
snares that are set. With fasting, and much
peril by day and weariness by night, the blood
of the youth will forget the songs the Evil
One has put into his mind and it will sing
holy hymns. Great will be the glory Cathal
Gille-Mhoire will be a holy man while he has
yet his youth upon him; and he will be a
martyr to the flesh by day and by night and
by night and by day, till the heathen put him
to death because of the faith that is his."

Thus it was that Cathal was blessed by Colum, and sent east among the wild Picts.

It was with joy that he served Molios. For four months he gave him all he had to give. The old saint passed word to Colum that Cathal was a saint and was assured of the crown of martyrdom, and lovingly he urged that the youth should be sent to the Isle of Mist in the north, the great isle that was ruled by Scathach the Queen. There, at the last Summer-sailing, the pagans had flayed a monk alive. A fair happy end : and Cathal was now worthy—and withal might triumph, and might even convert the heathen queen. "She is wondrous fair to see," he added, "and Cathal is a comely youth."

But Colum had answered that the young monk was to bide where he was, and to seek to win souls in the pagan Isle of Arran, where the Cross was still feared.

But with the coming of May and golden weather, the blood of Cathal grew warm. At times, even, he dreamed of the Frankish prince and the evil sweet words he had said.

Then a day of the days came. Molios and Cathal went to a hill-dûn where the Pict chieftain lived, and converted him and all the people in the dûn and all in the rath that was beyond the dûn. That eve the daughter of the warrior came upon Cathal walking in a solitary place, among the green pines beyond the rath. She was most sweet to look upon: tall and fair, with eyes like the sea in a cloudless noon, and hair like westward wheat turned back upon itself.

"What is the name men call you by, young Druid?" she said. "I am Ardanna, the daughter of Ecta."

"Your beauty is sweet to look upon, Ardanna. I am Cathal the son of Art the son of Aodh of the race of Alpein, from the isles of the sea. But I am not a Druid. I am a priest of Christ a servant of Mary the Mother of God, and a son of God."

Ardanna looked at him. A flush came into his face. In his eyes the same light flamed that was there when the Frankish prince told him of the delights of the world.

"Is it true, O Cathal, that the Druids—that the priests of Christ and the two other gods, the white-robed men whom we call Culdees, and of whom you are one, is it true that they will have nought to do with women?"

Cathal looked upon the woman no more, but on the ground at his feet.

"It is true, Ardanna."

The girl laughed. It was a low, sweet, mocking laugh, but it went along Cathal's blood like cloud-fire along the sky. It was to him as though somewhat he had not seen was revealed.

"And is it a true thing that you holy men look at women askance, and as snares of peril and evil?"

"It is true, Ardanna; but not so upon those who are sisters of Christ, and whose eyes are upon heavenly things."

"But what of those who are not sisters of your god, and are only women, fair to look upon, fair to woo, fair to love?"

Cathal again flushed. His eyes were still upon the ground. He made no answer.

Ardanna laughed low.

"Cathal!"

"Yes, fair daughter of Ecta?"

"Is it never longing for love you are?"

"There is but one love for us who have taken the vows of chastity."

"What is chastity?"

Cathal raised his eyes and glanced at Ardanna. Her dark-blue eyes looked at him pure and sweet, though a smile was upon her mouth. He sighed.

"It is the sanctity of the body, Ardanna."

"I do not understand," she said simply. "But tell me this, poor Cathal——"

"Why do you call me poor Cathal?"

" Because you have put your manhood from you—and you so young, and strong, and comely—and are not a warrior, and care neither for the sword, nor the chase, nor the harp, nor for women."

Cathal was troubled. He looked again and again at Ardanna. The sunset light was in her yellow hair, which was about her as a glory. He had seen the moon as wondrous pale as her beautiful face. Like lilies her white hands were. He had dreamed of that flamelight in the eyes.

" I care," he said.

She drew nearer, and leaned a little forward, and looked at him.

" You are good to look upon, Cathal—the comeliest youth I have ever seen."

The monk flushed. This was the devil-tongue of which Colum had warned him. But how sweet the words were : like a harp that low voice. Sure, sweeter is a waking dream than a dream in sleep.

" I care," he repeated dully.

" Look, Cathal."

Slowly he raised his eyes. As his gaze moved upward it rested on the white breast which was like sea-foam swelling out of brown sea-weed, for she had a tanned fawn-skin belted and gold-claspt over the white

robe she wore, and that had disparted for the
warm air to play upon her bosom.

It troubled him. He let his eyes fall again.
The red was on his face.

" Cathal ! "

" Yes, Ardanna."

"And you will never put your kiss upon a
woman's lips? Never put your heart upon
a woman's heart ? Is it of cold sea water you
are made—for even the running water in the
streams is warmed by the sun ? Tell me,
Cathal, would you leave Molios the Culdee,
—if——"

The monk of Christ suddenly flashed his
eyes upon the woman.

" If what, Ardanna ? " he asked abruptly ;
" if what, Ardanna that is so witching fair ? "

" If *I* loved you, Cathal ? If I, the daughter
of Ecta the chief, loved you, and took you to
be my man, and you took me to be your
woman, would you be content so ? "

He stared at her as one in a dream. Then
suddenly all the foolish madness that had
been put upon him by Colum fell away.
What did these old men, Colum and Molios,
know ? It is only the young who know what
life is. They were old, and their blood was
gelid.

He put up his arms, as though in prayer.

Then he smiled. Ardanna saw a light in his eyes that sprang into her heart and sang a song there that whirled in her ears and dazzled her eyes and made her feel as though she had fallen over a great height and were still falling.

Cathal was no longer pale. A red flame burned in either cheek. The sunset-light behind him filled his hair with fire. His eyes were beacons.

" Cathal, Cathal ! "

" Come, Ardanna ! "

That was all. What need to say more. She was in his arms, and her heart throbbing against his that leapt in his body like a wolf fallen in a snare.

He stooped and kissed her. She lifted her eyes, and his brain swung. She kissed him, and he kissed her till she gave a low cry and gently thrust him back. He laughed.

" Why do you laugh, Cathal ? "

" I ? It is I who laugh now. The old men put a spell upon me. I am no more Cathal Gille-Mhoire, but Cathal mac Art. Nay, I am Cathal Gille-Ardanna."

With that he plucked the branch of a rowan that grew near. He stripped it of its leaves, and threw them from him north, south, east, and west.

332

" Why do you that, Cathal-aluinn ? " Ardanna asked, looking at him with eyes of love, and she like a summer morning there, because of the sunshine in her hair, and the wild roses on her face, and the hill-tarn blue of her eyes.

"These are all the hymns that Colum taught me. I give them back. I am knowing them no more. They are idle, foolish songs."

Then the monk took the branch and broke it, and threw the pieces upon the ground and trampled upon them.

"Why do you that, Cathal-aluinn ? " asked Ardanna, wondering at him with her home-call eyes.

"That is the branch of all the wisdom Colum taught me. Old Neis, the helot, was wise. It is a madness, all that. See, it is gone ; it is beneath my feet. I am a man now."

"But O Cathal, Cathal ! this very day of the days, Ecta, my father, has become a man of the Christ-faith, him and his ; and he would do what Molios asked now. And Molios would ask your death."

" Death is a dream."

With that Cathal leaned forward and kissed Ardanna upon the lips twice. "A kiss for

333

life that," he said; "and that a kiss for death."

Ardanna laughed a low laugh. "The monk can kiss," she whispered; "can the monk love?"

He put his arm about her, and they went into the dim dark greenness.

The moon rose slowly, a globe of pale golden fire which spilled unceasingly a yellow flame upon the suspended billows of the forest. Star after star emerged. Deep silence was in the woods, save for the strange, passionate churring of a night-jar, where he leaned low from a pine branch and called to his mate, whose heart throbbed a flight-away amid the dewy shadows.

The wind was still. The white rays of the stars wandered over the moveless, over the shadowless and breathless green lawns of the tree-tops.

"What is that sound?" said Ardanna, a dim shape in the darkness, where she lay in the arms of Cathal.

"I know not," said the youth; for the fevered blood in his veins sang a song against his ears.

"Listen!"

Cathal listened. He heard nothing. His eyes dreamed again into the silence.

334

"What is that sound?" she whispered against his heart once again. "It is not from the sea, nor is it of the woods."

"It is the moan of Heaven," answered Cathal wearily; "*an acain Pàras.*"

II

They found them there in the twilight of the dawn. For long Ecta looked at them and pondered. Then he glanced at Molios. There were tears in the heart of the holy man, but in his eyes a deep anger.

"Bind him," said Ecta.

Cathal woke with the thongs. His gaze fell upon Molios. He made no sign, and spake never a word; but he smiled.

"What now, O Molios?" asked Ecta.

"Take the woman away. Do with her as you will—spare or slay. It matters not. She is but a woman, and she hath wrought evil upon this man. To slay were well."

"She is my daughter."

"Spare, then, if you will; but take her away. Give her to a man. She shall never see this renegade again."

With that, two men led Ardanna away. She gave a glance at Cathal, who smiled. No tears were in her eyes ; but a proud fire was there, and she brooked no man's hand upon her, and walked free.

When she was gone, Molios spake,

" Cathal, that was called Cathal Gille-Mhoire, why have you done this thing ? "

" Because I was weary of vain imaginings, and I am young ; and Ardanna is fair, and we loved."

" Such love is death."

" So be it, Molios. Such death is sweet as love."

" No ordinary death shalt thou have, blas-phemer. Yet even now I would be merciful if I could. Dost thou call upon God ? "

" I call upon the gods of my fathers."

" Fool, they shall not save you."

" Nevertheless, I call. I have nought to do with thy three gods, O Christian."

" Hast thou no fear of hell ? "

" I am a warrior, and the son of my father, and of a race of heroes. Why should I fear ? "

Molios brooded a while.

" Take him," he said at last, " and bury him alive where his gods perchance will hear his cries and come and save him ! Find me a hollow tree."

" There is a great oak near here," said Ecta, wondering, " a great hollow oak whose belly

336

would hold five men, each standing upon the other."

With that he led them to an ancient tree.

"Dost thou repent, Cathal?" Molios asked.

"Ay," the young man answered grimly; "I repent. I repent that I wasted the good days serving you and your three false gods."

"Blaspheme no more. Thou knowest that these three are one God."

Cathal laughed mockingly.

"Hearken to him, Ecta," he cried; "this old Druid would have you believe that two men and a woman make one person! Believe that if you will! As for me, I laugh."

But with that, at a sign from Molios, they lifted and slung him amid the branches of the oak, and let him slide feet foremost into the deep hollow heart of the tree.

When the law was done, Molios bade all near kneel in a circle round the oak. Then he prayed for the soul of the doomed man. As he ended this prayer, a laugh flew up among the high wind-swayed leaves. It was as though an invisible bird were there, mocking like a jay.

One by one, with bowed heads, Molios and Ecta and those with him withdrew, all save two young men who were bidden to stay

Upon these was bond laid, that they would
not stir from that place for three days. They
were to let none draw nigh : and no food was
to be given to the victim: and if he cried to
them, they were to take no heed,—nay, not
though he called upon God or the Mother of
God or upon the White Christ.

All that day there was no sound from the
hollow tree. At the setting of the sun a black-
bird lit upon a small branch that drooped over
the aperture, and sang a brave lilt. Then the
dark came, and the moon rose, and the stars
glimmered through the dew.

At midnight the moon was overhead. A
flood of pale gold rays lit up the branches of
the oak, and turned the leaves into a lustrous
bronze. The watchers heard a voice singing
in the silence of the night—a voice muffled
and obscure, as from one in a pit, or as that
of a shepherd straying in a narrow corrie.
Words they caught, though not all ; and this
was what they heard : [1]

O yellow lamp of Ioua that is having a cold pale flame
　　there,
Put thy honey-sheen upon me who am close-caverned
　　with Death:

[1] *Ioua* was one of the early Celtic names of the
moon. The allusion (in the fourth line) to the sun,
in the feminine, is in accordance with ancient usage

Cathal of the Woods

Sure it is nought I see now who have seen too much
    and too little:
O moon, thy breast is softer and whiter than hers
    who burneth the day.

Put thy white light on the grave where the dead man
    my father is,
               And waken him, waken him, wake!
And put thy soft shining on the breast of the woman
    my mother,
So that she stir in her sleep and say to the Viking
    beside her,
"Take up thy sword, and let it lap blood, for it thirsts
    with long thirst."

And O Ioua, be as the sea-calm upon the hot heart of
    Ardanna, the girl:
Tell her that Cathal loves her, and that memory is
    sweeter than life.
I list her heart beating here in the dark and the
    silence,
And it is not lonely I am, because of that, and
    remembrance.

O yellow flame of Ioua, be a spilling of blood out of
    the heart of Ecta,
So that he fall dead, inglorious, slain from within, as
    a grey-beard;
And light a fire in the brain of Molios, so that he shall
    go moonstruck,
And men will jeer at him, and he will die at the last,
    idly laughing.

For lo, I worship thee, Ioua; and if you can give my
    message to Neis,—

Neis the helot out of Aoidû, who is in Iona, bondman
    to Colum,—
Tell him I hail you as Bandia, as god-queen and
    mighty,
And that he had the wisdom and I was a fool with
    trickling ears of moss.

But grant me this, O goddess, a bitter moon-drinking
    for Colum!
May he have the moonsong in his brain, and in his
    heart the moonfire:
Flame burn him in heart of flame, and may he wane
    as wax at the furnace,
And his soul drown in tears, and his body be a
    nothingness upon the sands!

The watchers looked at each other, but said
no word. On the pale face of each was fear
and awe. What if this new god-teaching
were false, and if Cathal was right, and the
old gods were the lords of life and death!
The moonlight fell upon them, and they saw
doubt in the eyes of each other. Neither
looked at the white fire. Out of the radiance,
cold eyes might stare upon them: when at that,
sure they would leap to the woods, laughing
wild, and be as the beasts of the forest.

While it was still dark, an hour before the
dawn, one of the twain awoke from a brief
slumber. His gaze wandered from vague tree
to tree. Thrice he thought he saw dim shapes
glide from bole to bole or from thicket

to thicket. Suddenly he discerned a tall figure, silent as a shadow, standing at the verge of the glade.

His low cry aroused his companion.

" What is it, Mûrta ? " the young man asked in a whisper.

" A woman."

When they looked again she was gone.

" It was one of the Hidden People," said Mûrta, with restless eyes roaming from dusk to dusk.

" How are you for knowing that, Mûrta ? "

"She was all in green, just like a green shadow she was, and I saw the green fire in her eyes."

" Have you not thought of one that it might be ? "

" Who ? "

" Ardanna."

With that the young man rose and ran swiftly to the place where he had seen the figure. But he could see no one. Looking at the ground he was troubled : for in the moonshine-dew he descried the imprint of small feet.

Thereafter they saw or heard nought, save the sights and sounds of the woodland.

At sunrise the two youths rose. Mûrta lifted up his arms, then sank upon his knees with bowed head.

"Why do you do that forbidden thing?" said Diarmid, that was his companion. " Have you forgotten Cathal the monk that is up there alone with death ? If Molios the holy one saw you worshipping the Light he would do unto you as he had done unto Cathal."

But before Mûrta answered they heard the voice of Cathal once more—hoarse and dry it was, but scarce weaker than when it thrilled them at the rising of the moon.

This was what he chanted in his muffled voice out of his grave there in the hollow oak :

O hot yellow fire that streams out of the sky, sword-
  white and golden,
Be a flame upon the monks who are praying in their
  cells in Ioua !
Be a fire in the veins of Colum, and the hell that he
  preacheth be his,
And be a torch to the men of Lochlin that they
  discover the isle and destroy it !

For I see this thing, that the old gods are the gods
  that die not :
All else is a seeming, a dream, a madness, a tide ever
  ebbing.
Glory to thee, O Grian, lord of life, first of the gods
  Allfather,
Swords and spears are thy beams, thy breath a fire
  that consumeth.

And upon this isle of Â-rinn send sorrow and death
  and disaster,

Upon one and all save Ardanna, who gave me her
bosom,
Upon one and all send death, the curse of a death
slow and swordless,
From Molios of the Cave to Mûrta and Diarmid my
doomsmen!

At that Mûrta moved close to the oak.

"Hail, O Cathal!" he cried. There was
silence.

"Art thou a living man still, or is it the
death of thee that is singing there in the hollow oak?

"My limbs perish, but I die not yet," answered the muffled voice that had greeted the
sun.

"I am Mûrta mac Mûrta mac Neisa, and
my heart is sore for thee, Cathal!"

There was no word to this. A thrush upon
a branch overhead lifted its wings, sang a wild
sweet note, and swooped arrowly through the
greengloom of the leaves.

"Cathal, that wert a monk, which is the
true thing? Is it Christ, or the gods of our
fathers?"

Silence. Three oaks away a woodpecker
thrust its beak into the soft bark, tap-tapping,
tap-tapping.

"Cathal, is it death you are having, there in
the dark and the silence?"

Mûrta strained his ears, but he could hear no sound. Over the woodlands a voice floated, drowsy-warm and breast-white—the voice of a cuckoo calling a love-note from cool green shadow to shadow across a league of windless blaze.

Then Mûrta that was a singer, went to where the bulrushes grew by a little tarn that was in the moss an arrow-flight away. He plucked a last-year reed, straight and brown, and with his knife cut seven holes in it. With a thinner reed he scooped the hollow clean.

Thereupon he returned to the oak. Diarmid, who had begun to eat of the food that had been left with them, sat still, with his eyes upon him.

Mûrta put his hollow reed to his lips, and he played. It was a forlorn, sweet air that he had heard from a shepherding woman upon the hills. Then he played a burying-song of the islanders, wherein the wash of the sea and the rippling of the waves upon the shore was heard. Then he played the song of love, and the beating of hearts was heard, and sighs, and a voice like a distant bird-song rose and fell.

When he ceased, a voice came out of the hollow oak—

" Play me a death-song, Mûrta mac Mûrta mac Neisa."

344

Mûrta smiled, and he played again the song of love.

After that there was silence for a brief while. Then Mûrta played upon his reed for the time it takes a heron to mount her seventh spiral. Then he ceased, and threw away the reed, and stood erect, staring into the greenness. In his eyes was a strange shine. He sang:

Out of the wild hills I am hearing a voice, O Cathal!
And I am thinking it is the voice of a bleeding sword.
Whose is that sword? I know it well: it is the sword
    of the Slayer—
Him that is called Death, and the song that it sings
    I know:—
O where is Cathal mac Art, that is the cup for the thirst
    of my lips?

Out of the cold greyness of the sea I am hearing, O
    Cathal,
I am hearing a wave-muffled voice, as of one who
    drowns in the depths:
Whose is that voice? I know it well: it is the voice
    of the Shadow—
Her that is called the Grave, and the song that she
    sings I know:—
O where is Cathal mac Art, he has warmth for the chill
    that I have!

Out of the hot greenness of the wood I am hearing,
    O Cathal,
I am hearing a rustling step, as of one stumbling
    blind.

Whose is that rustling step? I know it well: the
    rustling walk of the Blind One—
She that is called Silence, and the song that she sings
    I know:—
O where is Cathal mac Art, that has tears to water my
    stillness?

After that there was silence. Mûrta moved
away. When he sat by Diarmid and ate, there
was no word spoken. Diarmid did not look
at him, for he had sung a song of death, and
the shadow was upon him. He kept his gaze
upon the moss: if he raised his eyes might he
not see the Slayer, or the Shadow, or the Blind
One?

Noon came. None drew nigh: not a face
was seen shadowily afar off. Sometimes the
hoofs of the deer rustled among the bracken.
The snarling of young foxes in an oak-root
hollow was like a red pulse in the heat. At
times, in the sheer abyss of blue sky to the
north, a hawk suspended: in the white-blaze
southerly a blotch like swirled foam appeared
for a moment at long intervals, as a gannet
swung from invisible pinnacles of air to the
invisible sea.

The afternoon drowsed through the sun-
flood. The green leaves grew golden, saturated
with light. At sundown a flight of wild
doves rose out of the pines, wheeled against

the shine of the west and flashed out of sight, flames of purple and rose, of foam-white and pink.

The gloaming came, silverly. The dew glistened on the fronds of the ferns, in the cups of the moss. From glade to glade the cuckoos called. The stars emerged delicately, as the eyes of fawns shining through the green gloom of the forest. Once more the moon snowed the easter frondage of the pines and oaks.

No one came nigh. Not a sound had sighed from the oak since Mûrta had sung at the goldening of the day. At sunset Mûrta had risen, to lean, intent, against the vast bole. His keen ears caught the jar of a beetle burrowing beneath the bark. There was no other sound.

At the fall of dark the watchers heard the confused far noise of a festival. It waned as a lost wind. Dim veils of cloud obscured the moon; a low rainy darkness suspended over the earth.

Thus went the second day and the second night.

When, after the weary vigil of the hours, dawn came at last, Mûrta rose and struck the oak with a stone.

"Cathal?" he cried, "Cathal!"

There was no sound: not a stir, not a sigh.

347

"Cathal! Cathal!"

Mûrta looked at Diarmid. Then, seeing his own thought in the eyes of his friend, he returned to his side.

"The Blind One has been here," said Diarmid in a low voice.

At noon there was thunder, and great heat. The noise of rustling wings filled the underwood.

Diarmid fell into a deep sleep. When the thunder had travelled into the hills, and a soft rain fell, Mûrta climbed into the branches of the oak. He stared down into the hollow, but could see nothing save a green dusk that became brown shadow, and brown shadow that grew into a blackness.

Cathal!" he whispered.

Not a breath of sound ascended like smoke.

"Cathal! Cathal!"

The slow drip of the rain slipped and pattered among the leaves. The cry of a sea-bird flying inland came mournfully across the woods. A distant clang, as of a stricken anvil, iterated from the barren mountain beyond the forest.

"Cathal! Cathal!"

Mûrta broke a straight branch, stripped it of the leaves, and, forcing the thicker end downward, let it fall sheer.

It struck with a dull, soft thud. He listened : there was not a sound.

"A quiet sleep to you, monk," he whispered, and slipped down through the boughs, and was beside Diarmid again.

At dusk the rain ceased. A cool green freshness came into the air. The stars were as wind-whirled fruit blown upward from the tree-tops. The moon, full-orbed and with a pulse of flame, led a tide of soft light across the brown shores of the world.

The vigils of the watchers were over. Mûrta and Diarmid rose. Without a word they moved across the glade : the faint rustle of their feet stirred the bracken : then they left the undergrowth, and were among the pines. Their shadows lapsed into the obscure wilderness. A doe, heavy with fawn, lay down among the dewy fern, and was at peace there.

III

At midnight, when the whole isle lay in the full flood of the moon, Cathal stirred.

For three days and three nights he had been in that dark hollow, erect, wedged as a spear imbedded in the jaws of a dead beast. He had died thrice : with hunger, with thirst, with

weariness. Then when hunger was slain in its
own pain, and thirst perished of its own
agony, and weariness could no more endure,
he stirred with the death-throe.

"I die," he moaned.

"Die not, O white one," came a floating
whisper, he knew not whence, though it was
to him as though the crushing walls of oak
breathed the sound.

"I die," he gasped, and the froth bubbled
upon his nether lip. With that his last
strength went. No more could he hold his
head above his shoulder, nor would his feet
sustain him. Like a stricken deer he sank. So
thin was he, so worn, that he slipt into a narrow crevice where dead leaves had been, and
lay there, drowning in the dark.

Was that death, or a cold air about his feet,
he wondered? With a dull pain he moved
them: they came against no tree-wood—the
coolness about them was of dewy moss. A
wild hope flashed into his mind. With feeble
hands he strove to sink farther into the crevice.

"I die," he gasped, "I die now at the last."

"Die not, O white one," breathed the same
low sweet whisper, like leaves stirred by a nest-
ing bird.

"Save, O save," muttered the monk, hoarse
with the death-dew.

Then a blackness came down upon him from a great height, and he swung in that blank gulf as a feather swirled this way and that in the void of an abyss.

When the darkness lifted again, Cathal was on his back, and breathing slow, but without pain. A sweet wonderful coolness and ease, that he knew now! Where was he? he wondered. Was he in that Pàras that Colum and Molios had spoken of? Was he in Hy Bràsil, of which he had heard Aodh the Harper sing? Was he in Tir-na'n-Og, where all men and women are young for evermore, and there is joy in the heart and peace in the mind and gladness by day and by night?

Why was his mouth so cool, that had burned dry as ash? Why were his lips moist, with a bitter-sweet flavour, as though the juice of fruit was there still?

He pondered, with closed eyes. At last he opened them, and stared upward. The profound black-blue dome of the sky held group after group of stars that he knew: was not that sword and belt yonder the sword-gear of Fionn? Yon shimmering cluster, were they not the dust of the feet of Alldai? That leaping green and blue planet, what could it be but the harp of Brigit, where she sang to the gods?

351

A shadow crossed his vision. The next moment a cool hand was upon his eyes. It brought rest, and healing. He felt the blood move in his veins : his heart beat : a throbbing was in his throat.

Then he knew that he had strength to rise. With a great effort he put his weariness from off him, and staggered to his feet.

Cathal gave a low sob. A fair beautiful woman stood by him.

"Ardanna !" he cried, though even as the word leaped from his lips he knew that he looked upon no Pictish woman.

She smiled. All his heart was glad because of that. The light in her eyes was like the fire of the moon, bright and wonderful. The delicate body of her was pale green, and luminous as a leaf, with soft earth-brown hair falling down her shoulders and over the swelling breast ; even as the small green mounds over the dead the two breasts were. She was clad only in her own lovliness, though the moonshine was about her as a garment.

" Like a green leaf : like a green leaf," Cathal muttered over and over below his breath.

"Are you a dream?" he asked simply, having no words for his wonder.

" No, Cathal, I am no dream. I am a woman. '

352

"A woman? But . . . but . . . you have nobody as other women have: and I see the moonbeam that is on your breast shining upon the moss behind you!"

"Is it thinking you are, poor Cathal, that there are no women and no men in the world except those who are in thick flesh, and move about in the suntide?"

Cathal stared wonderingly.

"I am of the green people, Cathal. We are of the woods. I am a woman of the woods."

"Hast thou a name, fair woman?"

"I am called Deòin." [1]

"That is well. Truly 'Green Breath' is a good name for thee. Are there others of thy kin in this place?"

"Look!" and at that she stooped, lifted the dew of a white flower in the moonshine, and put it upon his eyes.

Cathal looked about him. Everywhere he saw tall, fair pale-green lives moving to and fro: some passing out of trees, swift and silent as rain out of a cloud: some passing into trees, silent and swift as shadows. All were fair to look upon. tall, lithe, graceful, moving this way and that in the moonshine, pale green as the leaves of the lime, soft shining, with radiant eyes, and delicate earth-brown hair.

[1] *Deo-uaine.*

353

"Who are these, Deòin ?" Cathal asked in a low whisper of awe.

"They are my people : the folk of the woods : the green people."

"But they come out of trees : they come and they go like bees in and out of a hive."

"Trees ? That is your name for us of the woods. *We* are the trees."

" *You* the trees, Deòin ! How can that be ? "

"There is life in your body. Where does it go when the body sleeps, or when the sap rises no more to heart or brain, and there is chill in the blood, and it is like frozen water ? Is there a life in your body ? "

"Ay, so. I know it."

The flesh is *your* body ; the tree is *my* body."

"Then you are the green life of a tree ? "

"I am the green life of a tree."

"And these ? "

"They are as I am."

"I see those that are men and those that are women and their offspring too I see."

"They are as I am."

"And some are crowned with pale flowers."

"They love."

"And hast thou no crown, Deòin, who art so fair ? "

"Neither hast thou, Cathal, though thy face

354

is fair. Thy body I cannot see, because thou hast a husk about thee.

With a low laugh Cathal removed his raiment from him. The whiteness of his body was like a flower there in the moonshine.

"That shall not be against me," he said. "Truly, I am a man no longer, if thee and thine will have me as one of the wood-folk."

At that Deòin called. Many green phantoms glided out of the trees, and others, hand-in-hand, flower-crowned, crossed the glade.

"Look, green lives," Deòin cried in her sweet leaf-whisper, rising now like a wind-song among birchen boughs: "look, here is a human. His life is mine, for I saved him. I have put the moonshine dew upon his eyes. He sees as we see. He would be one of us, for all that he has no tree for his body, but flesh, white over red."

One who had moved thitherward out of an ancient oak looked at Cathal.

"Wouldst thou be of the wood-folk, man?"

"Ay, fain am I; for sure, for sure, O Druid of the trees."

"Wilt thou learn and abide by our laws, the first of which is that none may stir from his tree until the dusk has come, nor linger away from it when the dawn opens grey lips and drinks up the shadows?"

"I have no law now but the law of green life."

"Good. Thou shalt live with us. Thy home will be the hollow oak where thy kin left thee to die. Why did they do that evil deed?"

"Because I did not believe in the new gods."

"Who are thy gods, man whom this green one here calls Cathal?"

"They are the Sun, and the Moon, and the Wind, and others that I will tell you of."

"Hast thou heard of Keithoir?"

"No."

"He is the god of the green world. He dreams, and his dreams are Springtide and Summertime and Appletide. When he sleeps without dream there is winter."

"Have you no other god but this earth-god?"

"Keithoir is our god. We know no other."

"If he is thy god, he is my god."

"I see in the eyes of Deòin that she loves thee, Cathal the human. Wilt thou have her love?"

Cathal looked at the girl. His heart swam in light.

"Ay, if Deòin will give me her love, my love shall be hers."

356

The Annir-Coille moved forward and brushed softly against him as a green branch.

He put his arms around her. She had a cool, sweet body to feel. He was glad she was no moonshine phantom. The beating of her heart against his made a music that filled his ears.

Deòin stooped and plucked white, dewy flowers. Of these she wove a wreath for Cathal. He, likewise, plucked the white blooms, and made a coronal of foam for the brown wave of her hair.

Then, hand in hand, they fared slowly forth across the moonlit glade. None crossed their path, though everywhere delicate green lives flitted from tree to tree. They heard a wonderful sweet singing, aerial, with a ripple as of leaves lipping a windy shore of light. A green glamour was in the eyes of Cathal. The green fire of life flamed in his veins.

IV

Molios, the saint of Christ, that lived in the sea-cave of the Isle of the Peak, so that even in his own day it was called the Holy Isle, endured to a great age.

Some say of him that before his hair was

357

N

bleached white as the bog-cotton, he was slain
by the heathen Picts, or by the fierce summer-
sailors out of Lochlin. But that is an idle
tale. His end was not thus. A culdee, who
had the soul of a bat, feared the truth, though
that gave glory to God, and wrote both in ogham and lambskin the truthless tale that
Molios went forth with the cross and was slain
in a north isle.

On a day of the days every year, Molios
fared to the Hollow Oak that was in the hill-
forest beyond the rath of Ecta MacEcta.
There he spake long upon the youth that had
been his friend, and upon how the Evil One
had prevailed with Cathal, and how the islander
had been done to death there in the oak. Then
he and all his company sang the hymns of
peace, and great joy there was over the doom
of Cathal the monk, and many would have
cleft the great tree or burned it, so that the
dust of the sinner might be scattered to the
four winds : only this was banned by Molios.

It was well for Cathal, who slept there
through the hours of light ! Deep slumber
was his, for never once did he hear the moon-
tide voices, nor ever in his ears was the long
rise and fall of the holy hymns.

But when, in the twentieth year after Cathal
had been thrust into the hollow oak, Molios

came at sundown, being weary with the heat, the saint heard a low, faint laughter issuing from the tree, like fragrance from a flower.

None other heard it. He saw that with gladness. Quietly he went with the islanders.

When the moon was over the pines, and all in the rath slept, Molios arose and went silently back into the forest.

When he came to the Doom-Tree he listened long, with his ear against the bark. There was no sound.

His voice was old and quavering, but fresh and young in the courts of heaven, when it reached there like a fluttering bird tired from long flight. He sang a holy hymn.

He listened. There was no laughter. He was glad of that. All had been a dream, for sure.

Then it was that he heard once again the low, mocking laughter. He started back, trembling.

"Cathal!" he cried, with his voice like a wuthering wind.

"I am here, O Molios," said a voice behind him.

The old Culdee turned, as though arrow-nipped. Before him, white in the moonshine. stood a man, naked.

At first, Molios knew him not. He was so

359

tall and strong, so fair and wonderful. Long
locks of ruddy hair hung upon his white
shoulders : his eyes were lustrous, and had the
lovely, soft light of the deer. When he moved,
it was swiftly and silently. No stag upon the
hills was more fair to see.

Then, slowly, Cathal the monk swam into
Cathal of the Woods. Molios saw him whom
he knew of old, as a blue flame is visible within
the flame of yellow.

" I am here, O Molios."

Strange was the voice : faint and far the tone
of it : yet it was that of a living man.

" Is it a spirit you are, Cathal ? "

" I am no spirit. I am Cathal the monk
that was, Cathal the man now."

" How came you out of hell, you that are
dead, and the dust of whose crumbling bones
is in the hollow of this oak ? "

" There is no hell, Culdee."

" No hell ! " Molios the Saint stared at the
woodman in blank amaze.

" No hell," he said again ; "and is there no
heaven ? "

" A hell there is, and a heaven there is : but
not what Colum taught, and you taught."

" Doth Christ live ? "

" I know not."

" And Mary ? "

"I know not."

"And God the Father?"

"I know not."

"It is a lie that you have upon your lips. Sure, Cathal, you shall be dead indeed soon, to the glory of God. For I shall have thy dust scattered to the four winds, and thy bones consumed in flame, and a stake be driven through the place where thou wast."

Once more Cathal laughed.

"Go back to thy sea-cave, Molios. Thou hast much to learn. Brood there upon the ways of thy God before thou judgest if He knoweth no more than thou dost. And see, I will show you a wonder. Only, first, tell me this one thing. What of Ardanna whom I loved?"

She was accursed. She would not believe. When Ecta took the child from her, that was born in sin, to have the water put upon it with the sign of the Cross, she went north beyond the Hill of the Pinnacles. There she saw the young king of the Picts of Argyll, and he loved her, and she went to his dùn. He took her to his rath in the north, and she was his queen. He, and she, and the two sons she bore to him are all under the hill-moss now: and their souls are in hell."

Cathal laughed, low and mocking,

"It is a good hell that, I am thinking, Molios. But come . . . I will show you a wonder."

With that he stooped, and took the moonshine dew out of a white flower, and put it upon the eyes of the old man.

Then Molios saw.

And what he saw was a strangeness and a terror to him. For everywhere were green lives, fair and comely, gentle-eyed, lovely, of a soft shining. From tree to tree they flitted, or passed to and fro from the tree-boles, as wild bees from their hives.

Beside Cathal stood a woman. Beautiful she was, with eyes like stars in the gloaming. All of green flame she seemed, though the old monk saw her breast rise and fall, and the light lift of her earth-brown hair by a wind-breath eddying there, and the hand of her clasped in that of Cathal. Beyond her were fair and beautiful beings, lovely shapes like unto men and women, but soulless, though loving life and hating death, which, of a truth, is all that the vain human clan does.

"Who is this woman, Cathal?" asked the saint, trembling.

"It is Deòin, whom I love, and who has given me life."

"And these . . . that are neither green

362

phantoms out of trees, nor yet men as we
are ? "

" These are the offspring of our love."

Molios drew back in horror.

But Cathal threw up his arms, and with glad
eyes cried :

" O green flame of life, pulse of the world !
O Love ! O Youth ! O Dream of Dreams ! "

" O bitter grief," Molios cried, " O bitter
grief, that I did not slay thee utterly on that
day of the days ! Flame to thy flesh, and a
stake through thy belly—that is the doom thou
shouldst have had ! My ban upon thee Cathal,
that was a monk, and now art a wild man of
the woods : upon thee, and thy Annir-Coille,
and all thy brood, I put the ban of fear and
dread and sorrow, a curse by day and a curse
by night ! "

But with that a great dizziness swam into the
brain of the saint, and he fell forward, and lay
his length upon the moss, and there was no
sight to his eyes, or hearing to his ears, or
knowledge upon him at all until the rising of
the sun.

When the yellow light was upon his face he
rose. There was no face to see anywhere.
Looking in the dew for the myriad feet that
had been there, he saw none.

The old man knelt and prayed.

363

At the first praying God filled his heart with peace. At the second praying God filled his heart with wonder. At the third praying God whispered mysteriously, and he knew. Humble in his new knowledge, he rose. The tears were in his old eyes. He went up to the Hollow Oak, and blessed it, and the wild man that slept within it, and the Annir-Coille that Cathal loved, and the offspring of their love. He took the curse away, and he blessed all that God had made.

All the long weary way to the shore he went as one in a dream. Wonder and mystery were in his eyes.

At the shore he entered the little coracle that brought him daily from the Holy Isle, a triple arrow-flight seaward.

A child sat in it, playing with pebbles. It was Ardan, the son of Ardanna.

"Ardan mac Cathal," began the saint, weary now, but glad with a strange new gladness.

"Who is Cathal?" said the boy.

"He that was thy father. Tell me, Ardan, hast thou ever seen aught moving in the woods —green lives out of the trees?"

I have seen a green shine come out of the trees."

Molios bowed his head.

"Thou shalt be as my son, Ardan; and when

364

thou art a man thou shalt choose thy own way, and let no man hinder thee."

That night Molios could not sleep. Hearing the loud wash of the sea, he went to the mouth of the cave. For a long while he watched the seals splashing in the silver radiance of the moonshine. Then he called them.

"O seals of the sea, come hither!"

At that all the furred swimmers drew neaɪ

"Is it for the curse you give us every year of the years, O holy Molios?" moaned a great black seal.

"O Ròn dubh, it is no curse I have for thee or thine, but a blessing and peace. I have learned a wonder of God, because of an Annir-Coille in the forest that is upon the hill. But now I will be telling you the white story of Christ."

So there, in the moonshine, with the flowing tide stealing from his feet to his knees, the old saint preached the gospel of love. The seals crouched upon the rocks, with their great brown eyes filled with glad tears.

When Molios ceased, each slipped again into the shadowy sea. All that night, while he brooded upon the mystery of Cathal and the Annir-Coille, with deep knowledge of hidden things, and a heart filled with the wonder and mystery of the world, he heard them splashing to and fro in the moon-dazzle, and calling, one to the other, "We, too, are the sons of God."

At dawn a shadow came into the cave. A white frost grew upon the face of Molios. Still was he, and cold, when Ardan, the child, awoke. Only the white lips moved. A ray of the sun slanted across the sea, from the great disc of whirling golden flame new risen. It fell softly upon the moving lips. They were still then, and Ardan kissed them because of the smile that was there.

SEANACHAS

———

Seanachas

THE SONG OF THE SWORD

These are of the Seanachas [1] told me by Ian
Mòr, before the flaming peats, at a hill-shealing,
in a season when the premature snows found
the bracken still golden, and the ptarmigan with
their autumn browns no more than flecked and
mottled with grey.

He has himself now a quieter sleep than the
sound of that falling snow, and it is three
years since his face became as white and as
cold.

He had pleasure in telling *sguel* after *sguel*
of the ancient days. Far more readily at all
times would he repeat stories of this dim past
he loved so well than the more intimate tales
which had his own pulse beating in them, that
I have given elsewhere. Often he would look
up from where he held his face in his hands as
he brooded into the dull, steadfast flame that
consumed the core of the peats; and without

---

[1] The word "Seanachas" means either traditionary
lore or the "telling of tales of olden time," and it is in
this sense that it is used here.

preamble, and with words in no apparent way linked to those last spoken, would narrate some brief episode, and always as one who had witnessed the event. Sometimes, indeed, these brief tales were like waves ; one saw them rise, congregate, and expand in a dark billow—and the next moment there was a vanishing puff of spray, and the billow had lapsed.

I cannot recall many of these fugitive tales—seanachas, as he spoke of them collectively, for each *sgeul* was of the past, and had its roots in legendary lore—but of those that remained with me, here are four. All came upon me as birds flying in the dark : I knew not whence they came, or upon what wind they had steered their mysterious course. They were there, that was all. Ancient things come again in Ian's brain, or recovered out of the dim days, and seen anew through the wonder-lens of his imagination.

It was in a white June, as they call it, in the third year after the pirates of Lochlin had fed the corbies of the Hebrid Isles, that the summer-sailors once more came down the Minch of Skye.

An east wind blew afresh from the mountains, though between dawn and sunrise it veered till it chilled itself upon the granite peaks of the Cuchullins, and then leaped north-westward with the white foam of its feet caught from behind by the sun-glint.

The vikings on board the *Svart-Alf* laughed at that. The spray flew from the curved black prow of the great valley, and the wake danced in the dazzle—the sea-cream that they loved to see.

Tall men they were, and comely. Their locks of yellow or golden or ruddy hair, sometimes braided, sometimes all acurl like a chestnut tree bud-breaking in April, sometimes tangled like sea-wrack caught in a whirl of wind and tide, streamed upon their shoulders. In their blue eyes was a shining as though there were torches of white flame behind them, and that shining was mild or fierce as home or blood filled their brain.

The *Svart-Alf* was the storm-bird of a fleet of thirty galleys which had set forth from Lochlin under the raven-banner of Olaus the White. The vikings had joyed in a good faring. Singing south winds had blown them to the Faroe Isles, where from Magnus Cleft-Hand they had good cheer, and the hire of three men who knew the Western Isles, and had been with the sea-kings who had harried them here and there again and again.

From Magnus-stead they went forth swelled
with mead and ale and cow-beef; and they
laughed because of what they would give in
payment on their way back with golden torques
and bracelets and other treasure, young slaves,
women dark and fair, and the jewel-hilted
weapons of the island-lords.

Cold black winds out of the north-east drove
them straight upon the Ord of Sutherland.
They sang with joy the noon when they
rounded Cape Wrath and came under the
shadow of the hills. The dawn that followed
was red not only in the sky but on the sheen
of the sword-blades. It was the Song of the
Sword that day, and there is no song like that
for the flaming of the blood. The dark men
of Torridon were caught unawares. For seven
days thereafter the corbies and ravens glutted
themselves drinking at red pools beside the
stripped bodies which lay stark and stiff upon
the heather. The firing of a score of homesteads smouldered till the rains came, a day
and two nights after the old women who had
been driven to the moors stole back wailing.
The maids and wives were carried off in the
galleys; and for nine days, at a haven in the
lone coast opposite the Summer Isles, their
tears, their laughter, their sullen anger, their
wild gaiety, their passionate despair gave joy

to the yellow-haired men. On the ninth day
they were carried southward on the summer-
sailing. At a place called Craig-Feeach,
Raven's Crag, in the north of Skye, where a
Norse Erl had a great dûn that he had taken
from the son of a king from Eireann whose
sea-nest it had been, Olaus the White rested
awhile. The women were left there as a free
spoil ; save three who were so fair that Olaus
kept one, and Haco and Sweno, his chief cap-
tains took the others.

Then, on an evening when the wind was
from the north, Olaus and ten galleys went
down the Sound. Sweno the Hammerer was
to strike across the west for the great island
that is called the Lews; Haco the Laugher was
to steer for the island that is called Harris ;
and Olaus himself was to reach the haven
called Ljotr-wick in the Isle of the Thousand
Waters that is Benbecula.

On the eve of the day following that sailing
a wild wind sprang up, blowing straight
against the north. All of the south-faring galleys save one made for haven, though it was a
savage coast which lay along the south of Skye,
In the darkness of the storm Olaus thought
that the other nine wavesteeds were following
him, and he drove before the gale with his men
crouching under the lee of the bulwarks, and

with Finnleikr the Harper singing a wild song
of sea-foam and flowing blood and the whirling
of swords.

The gale was spent nigh three hours after
dawn; but the green seas were like snow-
crowned hillocks that roll in earth-drunkenness
when the flames surge from shaken mountains. Olaus knew that no boat could
live in that sea except it went before the wind.
So, though not a galley was in sight, he fared
steadily, north-westward.

By sundown the wind had swung out of
the south into the east; and by midnight the
stars were shining clear. In the blue-dark
could be seen the white wings of the fulmars,
seaward-drifting once again from the rocks
whither they had fled.

Then came the dawn, when the sun-rain
streamed gladly, and a fresh east wind blew
across the minch, and the *Svart-Alf*, that had
been driven far northward, came leaping
south-westwardly, with laughter and fierce
shining of sky-blue eyes, where the vikings
toiled at the oars, or burnished their brine-
stained swords and javelins.

All day they fared joyously thus. Behind
them they could see the blue line of the mainland and the dark-blue mountain crests of
Skye; southward was a long green film, where

Coll caught the waves ere they drove upon
Tiree ; south-eastward, the grey-blue peaks of
Halival and Haskival rose out of the Isle of
Terror, as Rùm was then called. Before them,
as far as they could see to north or south, the
purple-grey lines that rose out of the west
were the contours of the Hebrides.

"Dost thou see yonder blue splatch,
Morna ?" cried Olaus the White to the woman
who lay indolently by his side, and watched the
sun-gold redden the mass of ruddy hair which
she had sprayed upon the boards, a net wherein
to mesh the eyes of the vikings : " Do you see
that blue splatch ? I know what it is. It is the
headland that Olaf the Furious called Skipness.
Behind it is a long fjord in two forks.
At the end of the south fork is a place of the
white-robes whom the islanders call Culdees.
Midway on the eastern bend of the north fork
is a town of a hundred families. Over both
rules Maoliosa, a warrior-priest ; and under
him, at the town, is a greybeard called Ramon
mac Coag. All this I have learned from Anlaf
the Swarthy, who came with us out of Faroe."

Morna glanced at him under her drooped
eyelids. Sure, he was fair to see, for all that
his long hair was white. White it had gone
with the terror of a night on an ice-floe, whereon a man who hated the young Erl had set him

adrift with seven wolves. He had slain three, and drowned three, and one had leaped into the sea ; and then he had lain on the ice, with snow for a pillow, and in the dawn his hair was the same as the snow. This was but ten years ago, when he was a youth.

She looked at him, and when she spoke it was in the slow, lazy speech that in his ears was drowsy-sweet as the hum of the hives in the steading where his home was.

"It will be a red sleep the men of that town will be having soon, I am thinking, Olaus. And the women will not be carding wool when the moon rises to-morrow night. And——"

The fair woman stopped suddenly. Olaus saw her eyes darken.

" Olaus ! "

" I listen."

" If there is a woman there that you desire more than me I will give her a gift."

Olaus laughed.

" Keep your knife in your girdle, Morna. Who knows but you may need it soon to save yourself from a Culdee ! '!

" Bah ! These white-robed men-women have nought to do with us. I fear no man, Olaus ; but I have a blade for any woman that will dazzle your eyes."

376

" Have no fear, white wolf. The sea-wolf knows his mate when he has found her."

An hour after sun-setting a mist came up. The wind freshened. Olaus made silence throughout the war-galley. The vikings had muffled their oars, for the noise of the waves on the shore could now be heard. Hour after hour went by. When at last the moonlight tore a rift in the häar, and suddenly the vapour was licked up by a wind moving out of the north, they saw that they were close upon the land, and right eastward of the headland of Skipness.

Anlaf the Swarthy went to the prow. Blackly he loomed in the moonlight as he stood there, poising his long spear, and sounding the depths while the vessel slowly forged shore-ward. By the time a haven was found, and the vikings stood silent upon the rocks, the night was yellow with moonshine, and the brown earth overlaid with a soft white sheen wherein the long shadows lay palely blue.

There was deep peace in the island-town. The kye were in the sea-pastures near, and even the dogs slept. There had been no ill for long, and Ramon mac Coag was an old man, and dreamed overmuch about his soul. This was because of the teaching of the Culdees. Before he had known he had a soul he was a man, and would not have been taken unawares, and he over-lord of a sea-town like Bail'-tiorail.

Olaus the White made a wide circuit with his men. Then, slowly, the circle narrowed.

A bull lowed, where it stood among the sea-grass, stamping uneasily, and ever and again sniffing the air. Suddenly one hiefer, then another, then all the kye, began a strange lowing. The dogs rose, with bristling felts, and crawled sidelong, snarling, with red eyes gleaming savagely.

Bethoc, the young third wife of Ramon, was awake, dreaming of a man out of Eireann who had that day given her a strange pleasure with his harp and his dusky eyes. She knew that lowing. It was the *langanaich an aghaidh am allamharach*, the continued lowing against the stranger. She rose lightly, and unfastened the leather flap, and looked down from the Grianan where she was. A man stood there in the shadow. She thought it was the harper. With a low sigh she leaned downward to kiss him, and to whisper a word in his ear.

Her long hair fell over her eyes and face and blinded her. She felt it grasped, and put out her hand. It was seized, and before she knew what was come upon her she was dragged prone upon the man.

Then, in a flash, she saw he had yellow hair, and was clad as a Norseman. She gasped. If the sea-rovers were come, it was death for all there. The man whispered something in a tongue that was strange to her. She understood better when he put his arm about her, and placed a hand upon her mouth.

Bethoc stood silent. Why did no one hear that lowing of the kine, that snarling of the dogs which had now grown into a loud continuous baying? The man by her side thought she was cowed, or had accepted the change of fate. He left her, and put his foot on a cleft; then, sword under his chin, he began to climb stealthily.

He had thrown his spear upon the ground. Soundlessly Bethoc stepped forward, lifted it, and moved forward like a shadow.

A wild cry rang through the night. There was a gurgling and spurting sound as of damned water adrip. Ramon sprang from his couch and stared out of the aperture. Beneath he saw a man, speared through the back, and pinned to the soft wood. His hands claspt the frayed deerskins, and his head lay upon his shoulder. He was laughing horribly. A bubbling of foam frothed continuously out of his mouth.

The next moment Ramon saw Bethoc. He

had not time to call to her before a man slipped
out of the shadow, and plunged a sword
through her till the point dripped red drops
upon the grass beyond where she stood. She
gave no cry, but fell as a gannet falls. A black
shadow darted across the gloom. A crash, a
scream, and Ramon sank inert, with an arrow
fixed midway in his head through the brows.

Then there was a fierce tumult everywhere.
From the pastures the kye ran lowing and
bellowing in a wild stampede. The neighing
of horses broke into screams. Here and there
red flames burst forth, and leaped from hut
to hut. Soon the whole rath was aflame.
Round the dûn of Ramon a wall of swords
flashed.

All had taken refuge in the dûn, all who
had escaped the first slaying. If any leaped
forth, it was upon viking spear, or if the face
of any was seen it was the target for a swift-
sure arrow.

A long, penetrating wail went up. The Culdees on the farther loch heard it, and ran from
their cells. The loud laughter of the sea-
rovers was more dreadful to them than the
whirling flames and the wild screaming lament
of the dying and the doomed.

None came forth alive out of that dûn, save
three men, and seven women that were young.

Two of the men were made to tell all that Olaus the White wanted to know. Then they were blinded, and put into a boat, and set in the tide-eddy that would take them to where the Culdees were. And for the Culdees they had a message from Olaus.

Of the seven women none were so fair that Morna had any heed. But seven men had them as spoil. Their wild keening had died away into a silence of blank despair long before the dawn. When the light came, they were huddled in a white group near the ashes of their homes. Everywhere the dead sprawled.

At sunrise the vikings held an ale-feast. When Olaus the White had drunken and eaten, he left his men and went down to the shore to look upon the fortified place where Maoliosa the Culdee and his white-robes lived. As he fared thither through what had been Bail'-tio-rail, there was not a male left alive, save the one prisoner who had been kept. Aongas the Bowmaker, as he was called ; none save Aongas, and a strayed child among the salt grasses near the shore, a little boy, naked, and with blue eyes and laughing sunny smile.

THE FLIGHT OF THE CULDEES

On the wane of noon, on the day following
the ruin of Bail'-tio-rail, sails were descried far
east of Skipness.

Olaus called his men together. The boats
coming before the wind were doubtless the
galleys of his own fleet which he had lost sight
of when the south-gale had blown them against
Skye; but no man can know when and how
the gods may smile grimly, and let the swords
that whirl to be broken, or the spears that are
flat become a hedge of death.

An hour later, a startled word went from
viking to viking. The galleys in the offing were
the fleet of Sweno the Hammerer. Why had
he come so far southward, and why were oars
so swift and with the sails strained to the utmost
before the wind?

They were soon to know.

Sweno himself was the first to land. A
great man he was, broad and burly, with a
sword-slash across his face that brought his
brows together in a frown which made a

perpetual shadow above his savage blood-shot eyes.

In a few words he told how he had met a galley, with only half its crew, and of these many who were wounded. It was the last of the fleet of Haco the Laughter. A fleet of fifteen war-birlinns had set out from the Long Island, and had given battle. Haco had gone into the strife, laughing loud as was his wont, and he and all his men had the berserk rage, and fought with joy and foam at the mouth. Never had the Sword sung a sweeter song.

"Well," said Olaus the White, grimly, "well, how did the Raven fly?"

"When Haco laughed for the last time, with waving sword out of the death wherein he sank, there was only one galley left. Of all that company of vikings there were no more than nine to tell the tale. These nine we took out of their boat, which was below waves soon. Haco and his men are all fighting the sea-shadows by now."

A loud snarling went from man to man. This became a wild cry of rage. Then savage shouts filled the air. Swords were lifted up against the sky, and the fierce glitter of the blue eyes and the bristling of the tawny beards were fair to see, thought the captive women, though their hearts beat against their ribs like eaglets against the bars of a cage.

Sweno the Hammerer frowned a deep frown when he heard that Olaus was there with only the *Svart-Alf* out of the galleys which had gone the southward way.

"If the islanders come upon us now with their birlinns we shall have to make a running fight," he said.

Olaus laughed.

"Ay, but the running shall be after the birlinns, Sweno."

"I hear that there are fifty and nine men of these Culdees yonder under the sword-priest, Maoliosa?"

"It is a true word. But to-night, after the moon is up, there shall be none."

At that, all who heard laughed, and were less heavy in their hearts because of the slaying and drowning of Haco the Laughter and all his crew.

"Where is the woman Brenda that you took?" Olaus asked, as he stared at Sweno's boat and saw no woman there.

"She is in the sea."

Olaus the White looked. It was his eyes that asked.

"I flung her into the sea because she laughed when she heard of how the birlinns of Som-

hairle the Renegade drove in upon our ships,
and how Haco laughed no more, and how the
sea was red with Lochlin blood."

"She was a woman, Sweno—and none
more fair in the isles, after Morna that is
mine."

"Woman or no woman, I flung her into the
sea. The Gael call us the *Gall:* then I will let
no Gael laugh at the Gall. It is enough. She
is drowned. There are always women : one
here, one there—it is but a wave blown this
way or that."

At this moment a viking came running
across the ruined town with tidings. Maoliosa
and his Culdees were crowding into a great
birlinn. Perhaps they were coming to give
battle : mayhap they were for sailing away
from that place.

Olaus and Sweno stared across the fjord.
At first they knew not what to think. If
Maoliosa thought of battle surely he would not
choose that hour and place. Or was it that he
knew the Gael were coming in force, and that
the vikings were caught in a trap ?

At last it was clear. Sweno gave a great
laugh.

"By the blood of Odin," he cried, "they
come to sue for peace ! "

Slowly across the loch the birlinn, filled with

385

white-robed Culdees, drew near. At the prow
stood a tall old man, with streaming hair and
beard, white as sea-foam. In his right hand he
grasped a great Cross, whereon was Christ
crucified.

The vikings drew close one to the other.

"Hail them in their own tongue, Sweno,"
said Olaus.

The Hammerer moved to the water-edge, as
the birlinn stopped, a short arrow-flight away.

"Ho, there, druids of the Christ-faith!"

"What would you, viking-lord?" It was
Maoliosa himself that spoke.

"Why do you come over here to us, you that
are Maoliosa?"

"To win you and yours to God, Pagan."

"Is it madness that is upon you, old man?
We have swords and spears here, if we lack
hymns and prayers."

All this time Olaus kept a wary watch inland
and seaward, for he feared that Maoliosa came
because of an ambush.

Truly the old monk was mad. He had
told his Culdees that God would prevail, and
that the Pagans would melt away before the
Cross.

The ebb-tide was running swift. Even
while Sweno spoke, the birlinn touched a low
sea-hidden ledge of rock.

A cry of consternation came from the white-robes. Loud laughter went up from the vikings.

" Arrows ! " cried Olaus.

With that, three-score men took their bows. There was a hail of death-shafts. Many fell into the water, but some were in the brains and hearts of the Culdees.

Maoliosa himself stood in death, transfixed to the mast.

With a despairing cry the monks swept their oars backward. Then they leaped to their feet, and changed their place, and rowed for life or death.

The summer-sailors sprang into their galley that they had pulled through the narrow strait. Sweno the Hammerer was at the bow. The foam curled and hissed.

The birlinn grided upon the opposite shore at the self-same moment when Sweno brought down his battle-axe upon the monk who steered. The man was cleft to the shoulder. Sweno swayed with the blow, stumbled, and fell headlong into the sea. A Culdee thrust at him with an oar, and pinned him among the sea-tangle. Thus died Sweno the Hammerer.

Then all the white-robes leaped upon the shore. Yet Olaus was quicker than they.

387

With a score of vikings he raced to the Church
of the Cells, and gained the sanctuary. The
monks uttered a cry of despair, and, turning
fled across the moor. Olaus counted them
There were now forty in all.

" Let forty men follow," he cried.

Like white birds, the monks fled this way
and that. Olaus, and those who watched,
laughed at them as they stumbled, because of
their robes. One by one fell, sword-cleft or
spear-thrust.

At the last there were less than a score—
twelve only—ten !

" Bring them back ! " Olaus shouted.

When the ten fugitives were captured and
brought back, Olaus took the crucifix that
Maoliosa had raised, and held it before each in
turn.

" Smite," he said to the first monk. But the
man would not.

" Smite ! " he said to the second ; but he
would not. And so it was to the tenth.

" Good," said Olaus the White, " they shall
witness to their god."

With that he bade his vikings break up the
birlinn, and drive the planks into the ground,
and shore them up with logs.

When this was done he crucified each Culdee. With nails and with ropes he did unto

each what their god had suffered. Then all
were left there by the water-side.

That night, when Olaus the White and the
laughing Morna left the great bonfire where
the vikings sang and drank horn after horn
of strong ale, they stood and looked across
the loch. In the moonlight, upon the dim
verge of the farther shore, they could discern
ten crosses. On each was a motionless white
splatch.

MIRCATH [1]

When Haco the Laugher saw the islanders coming out of the west in their birlinns, he called to his vikings, "Now of a truth we shall hear the Song of the Sword!"

The ten galleys of the summer-sailors spread out into two lines of five boats, each boat an arrow-flight from that on either side.

The birlinns came on against the noon. In the sun-dazzle they loomed black as a shoal of pollack. There were fifteen in all, and from the largest, midway among them, flew a banner. On this banner was a disc of gold.

"It is the Banner of the Sunbeam!" shouted Olaf the Red, who with Torquil the One-Armed was hero-man to Haco. "I know it well. The Gael who fight under that are warriors indeed."

"Is there a saga-man here?" cried Haco. At that a great shout went up from the vikings: "Harald the Smith!"

[1] The Mire Chath was the name given to the war-frenzy that often preceded and accompanied battle.

A man rose among the bow-men in Olaf's
boat. It was Harald. He took a small square
harp, and he struck the strings. This was the
song he sang:

> Let loose the hounds of war,
>   The whirling swords !
> Send them leaping afar,
> Red in their thirst for war;
> Odin laughs in his car
>   At the screaming of the swords !
>
> Far let the white ones fly,
>   The whirling swords !
> Afar off the ravens spy
> Death-shadows cloud the sky.
> Let the wolves of the Gael die
>   'Neath the screaming swords !
>
> The Shining Ones yonder
>   High in Valhalla
> Shout now, with thunder,
> *Drive the Gaels under*,
> *Cleave them asunder*,—
>   *Swords of Valhalla!*

A shiver passed over every viking. Strong
men shook as a child when lightning plays.
Then the trembling passed. The mircath, the
war-frenzy came on them. Loud laughter
went from boat to boat. Many tossed the
great oars, and swung them down upon the

sea, splashing the sun-dazzle into a yeast of foam. Others sprang up and whirled their javelins on high, catching them with bloody mouths: others made sword-play, and stammered thick words through a surf of froth upon their lips. Olaf the Red towered high on the steering-plank of the *Calling Raven*, swirling round and round a mighty battle-axe: on the *Sea-Wolf*, Torquil One-Arm shaded his eyes, and screamed hoarsely wild words that no one knew the meaning of. Only Haco was still for a time. Then he, too, knew the mircath; and he stood up in the *Red-Dragon* and laughed loud and long. And when Haco the Laugher laughed, there was ever blood and to spare.

The birlinns of the islanders drove swiftly on. They swayed out into a curve, a black crescent there in the gold - sprent blue meads of the sea. From the great birlinn that carried the Sunbeam came a chanting voice:

O, 'tis a good song the sea makes when blood is on
    the wave,
And a good song the wave makes when its crest of
    foam is red!
For the rovers out of Lochlin the sea is a good grave,
And the bards will sing to-night to the sea-moan of
    the dead!

Yo-ho-a-h'eily-a-yo, eily, ayah, a yo !
Sword and spear and Battle-axe sing the Song of
Woe !

    Ayah, eily, a yo !
    Eily, ayah, a yo !

Then there was a swirling and dashing of
foam. Clouds of spray filled the air from the
thresh of the oars.

No man knew aught of the last moments
ere the birlinns bore down upon the viking-
galleys. Crash and roar and scream, and a
wild surging ; the slashing of swords, the
whistle of arrows, the fierce hiss of whirled
spears, the rending crash of battle-axe and
splintering of the javelins ; wild cries, oaths,
screams, shouts of victors, and yells of the
dying ; shrill taunts from the spillers of life,
and savage choking cries from those drowning
in the bloody yeast that bubbled and foamed in
the maelstrom where the war-boats swung and
reeled this way and that ; and, over all, the loud
death-music of Haco the Laugher.

Olaf the Red went into the sea, red indeed,
for the blood streamed from head and shoulders, and fell about him as a scarlet robe.
Torquil One-Arm fought, blind and arrow-
sprent, till a spear went through his neck, and
he sank among the dead. Louder and louder
grew the fierce shouts of the Gael ; fewer the

savage screaming cries of the vikings. Thus it was till two galleys only held living men. The *Calling Raven* turned and fled, with the nine men who were not wounded to the death. But, on the *Red-Dragon*, Haco the Laugher still laughed. Seven men were about him These fought in silence.

Then Toscar mac Aonghas, that was leader of the Gael, took his bow. None was arrow-better than Toscar of the Nine Battles. He laid down his sword and took his bow, and an arrow went through the right eye of Haco the Laugher. He laughed no more. The seven died in silence. Swaran Swiftfoot was the last. When he fell, he wiped away the blood that streamed over his face.

"*Skoal!*" he cried to the hero of the Gael, and with that he whirled his battle-axe at Toscar mac Aonghas ; and the soul of Toscar met his, in the dark mist, and upon the ears of both fell at one and the same time the glad laughter of the gods in Valhalla.

THE SAD QUEEN

"There was darkness over Eiré: they adored things of Faerie." **The Fiacc Hymn.**

Two men lay bound in the stone fold behind the great wall of Dun Scaith in the Isle of Mist.

One was Ulric the Skald; the other was Connla the Harper. Only they two lived when the galleys went down in the Minch, and the Gael and the Gall sank in the reddened waves.

For a long hour they were swung on the waves and on the same spar—the mast of the *Death-Raven*, which Svén of the Long Hair had sailed in from the north isles, with a score galleys of a score men in each. Farcha the Silent had met him with two score galleys of ten men in each.

They had fought since the sun was in the south till it hung above the west. Then there were only the *Death-Raven* and the *Foam-Sweeper*. Ulric sat by Svén and sang the death-song and the song of the swords; Connla sat by Farcha and sang the high song of victory.

When the galleys met through the bloody tangle in the seas, where spears rose and fell like boughs and branches of a wood in storm, and where men's hair clung black and limp past wild eyes and faces red with blood, Svén leaped into the *Foam-Sweeper*, and clove the head from a spearman who thrust at him, so that it fell into the sea, and the headless man shook with a palsy and waveringly mowed an idle spear.

But in that doing he staggered, and Farcha thrust his spear through him. The spear fixed Svén to the mast. Then an arrow from the sea struck him across the eyes, and he saw no more; and when the *Foam-Sweeper* sank and dragged the *Death-Raven* with it, the two kings met : but Farcha was now like a heavy fish swung this way and that, and Svén thought the body was the body of Gunhild whom he loved, and strove to kiss it, but could not because of the spear and seven arrows which nailed him to the mast.

When the moon rose, the waters were in a white calm. Mid-sea, a great shadow passed northward : the travelling myriad of the herring-host.

When Ulric the Skald sank from the mast,

Connla the Harper held him by the hair, and gave him breath, so that he lived.

Thus when two spears drifted near, neither snatched at them. Later, Connla spoke. "One pulls me by the feet," he said ; "it is one of your dead men who is drowning me," But at that Ulric drew a long breath, and strengthened his heart : then, seizing one of the spears, he thrust it downward, and struck the dead man whose hair tangled the feet of Connla, so that the dead man sank.

When they heard cries, they thought the galleys had come again, or others of Svén's host, or of Farcha's : but when they were dragged out of the sea, and lay staring at the stars, they knew no more, for sounds swam into their ears, and mist came into their eyes, and it was as though they sank through the boat, and through the sea, and through the infinite blank void below the sea, and were as two feathers there, blown idly under dim stars.

When they woke it was day, and a woman stood looking darkly at them.

She was tall, and of great strength ; taller than Connla, stronger than Ulric. Long black hair fell upon her shoulders, which, with her breast and thighs, were covered with pale bronze. A red and green cloak was over the right shoulder, and was held by a great brooch of gold. A yellow torque of gold was round her neck. A three-pointed torque of gold was on her head. Her legs were swathed with deerskin thongs, and her feet were in coverings of cowskin stained red.

Her face was pale as wax, and of a strange and terrible beauty. They could not look long in her eyes, which were black as darkness, with a red flame wandering in it. Her lips were curled delicately, and were like thin sudden lines of blood in the whiteness of her face.

"I am Scathach," she said, when she had looked long at them. Each knew that name, and the heart of each was like a bird before the slinger. If they were with Scathach,[1] the queen of the warrior-women of the Isle of Mist, it would have been better to die in water. The grey stones of Dun Scaith were russet with old blood of slain captives.

"I am Scathach," she said. "Do I look upon Svén of Lochlann and Farcha of the Middle Isles?"

"I am Ulric the Skald," answered the northman.

---

[1] Scathach (pronounced *Ska'ah*, or *Skiah*): the name of the island of Skye is by some said to be derived from the famous Amazonian queen who lived there, and taught Cuchullin the arts of war.

"I am Connla the Harper," answered the Gael.

"You die to-night," and with that Scathach stood silent again, and looked darkly upon them for a long while.

At noon a woman brought them milk and roasted elk meat. She was fair to see, though a scar ran across her face. They sent word by her to Scathach with a prayer for life; they would be helots, and put birth upon women. For they knew the wont. But the woman returned with the same word.

"It is because she loved Cuchullin," the woman said, "and he was a poet, and sang songs, and made music as you do. He was fairer than you, man with the yellow hair, man with the long, dark hair; and you have put memories into the mind of Scathach. But she will listen to you harping and singing before you die."

When the darkness came, and the dew fell, Ulric spoke to Connla. "The horse Rimemane is moving among the stars, for the foam is falling from his mouth."

Connla felt the falling of the dew.

"It was thus on the night I loved," he said below his breath.

Ulric could not see Connla's face because of the shadows. But he heard low sobs, and

knew that Connla's face was wet with tears.
" I too loved," he said ; I have had many
women for my love."

" There is but one love," answered Connla
in a low voice ; " it is of that I am thinking and
have remembrance."

" Of that I do not know," said Ulric. " I
loved one woman well so long as she was
young and fair. But one day a king's son
desired her, and I came upon them in a wood
on a cliff by the sea. I put my arms about her
and leaped down the cliff. She was drowned.
I paid no eric."

" There is no age upon the love of my love,"
said Connla softly : " she was more beautiful
than the stars." And because of that great
beauty he forgot death and his bonds.

When the warrior-women led them out to
the shore, Scathach looked at them from where
she sat by the great fire that blazed upon the
sands.

She had been told that which they said one
to the other.

"Sing the song of your love," she said to
Ulric.

"What heed have I of any woman in the
hour of my death ? " he answered sullenly.

"Sing the song of your love," she said to
Connla.

Connla looked at her, and at the great fire
round which the fierce-eyed women stood and
looked at him, and at the still, breathless stars.
The dew fell upon him.

Then he sang—

Is it time to let the hour rise and go forth, as a hound
    loosed from the battle-cars?
Is it time to let the hour go forth, as the White Hound
    with the eyes of flame?
For if it be not time, I would have this hour that is
    left to me under the stars,
Wherein I may dream my dream again, and at the last
    whisper one name.

It is the name of one who was more fair than youth
    to the old, than life to the young;
She was more fair than the first love of Angus the
    Beautiful, and though I were blind
And deaf for a hundred ages I would see her, more
    fair than any poet has sung,
And hear her voice like mounted songs crying on the
    wind.

There was silence. Scathach sat with her
face between her hands, staring into the flame.

She did not lift her face when she
spoke.

"Take Ulric the Skald," she said at last, but
with eyes that stared still into the flame,
"and give him to what woman wants him, for
he knows nothing of love. If no woman

wants him, put a spear through his heart, so that he die easily.

" But take Connla the Harper, because he has known all things, knowing that one thing, and has no more to know, and is beyond us, and lay him upon the sand with his face to the stars, and put red brands of fire upon his naked breast, till his heart bursts and he dies."

So Connla the Harper died in silence, where he lay on the moonlit sand, with red embers and flaming brands on his naked breast, and his face white and still as the stars that shone upon him.

THE LAUGHTER OF SCATHACH THE QUEEN.

In the year when Cuchullin left the Isle of Skye, where Scathach the warrior-queeu ruled with the shadow of death in the palm of her sword-hand, there was sorrow because of his beauty. He had fared back to Eiré, at the summons of Concobar mac Nessa, Ard-Righ of Ulster. For the Clan of the Red Branch was wading in blood, and there were seers who beheld that bitter tide rising and spreading.

Cuchullin was only a youth in years; but he had come to Skye a boy, and he had left it a man. None fairer had ever been seen of Scathach or of any woman. He was tall and lithe as a young pine; his skin was as white as a woman's breast; his eyes were of a fierce bright blue, with a white light in them as of the sun. When bent, and with arrow half-way drawn, he stood on the heather, listening against the belling of the deer; or when he leaned against a tree, dreaming not of eagle-chase or wolf-hunt, but of the woman whom he had never met; or, when by the dûn, he

played at sword-whirl or spear-thrust, or raced
the war-chariot across the machar—then, and
ever there were eyes upon his beauty, and
there were some who held him to be Angus
Òg himself. For there was a light about
him, such as the hills have in sun-glow an
hour before set. His hair was the hair of
Angus and of the fair gods, earth-brown
shot with gold next his head, ruddy as
flame midway, and, where it sprayed into a
golden mist of fire, yellow as windy sunshine.

But Cuchullin loved no woman upon Skye,
and none dared openly to love Cuchullin, for
Scathach's heart yearned for him, and to cross
the Queen was to put the shroud upon oneself.
Scathach kept an open face for the son of Lerg.
There was no dark frown above the storm in
her eyes when she looked at his sunbright
face. Gladly she slew a woman because
Cuchullin had lightly reproved the maid for
some idle thing; and once, when the youth
looked in grave silence at three viking captives
whom she had spared because of their comely
manhood, she put her sword through the heart
of each, and sent him the blade, dripping red,
as the flower of love.

But Cuchullin was a dreamer, and he loved
what he dreamed of, and that woman was not

Scathach, nor any of her warrior-women who made the Isle of Mist a place of terror for those cast upon the wild shores, or stranded there in the ebb of inglorious battle.

Scathach brooded deep upon her vain desire. Once, in a windless, shadowy gloaming, she asked him if he loved any woman.

"Yes," he said. "Etáin."

Her breath came quick and hard. It was for pleasure to her then to think of Cuchullin lying white at her feet, with the red blood spilling from the whiteness of his breast. But she bit her under lip, and said quietly:

"Who is Etáin?"

"She is the wife of Mídir."

And with that the youth turned and moved haughtily away. She did not know that the Etáin of whom Cuchullin dreamed was no woman that he had seen in Eiré, but the wife of Mídir, the King of Faerie, who was so passing fair that Mac Greine, the beautiful god, had made for her a Grianan all of shining glass, where she lives in a dream, and in that sun-bower is fed at dawn upon the bloom of flowers and at dusk upon their fragrance. *O ogham mhic Gréine, tha e boidheach,*[1] she

---

[1] "O beauty of my love the Sun-lord" (*lit.* "O youth, son of the Sun, how fair he is!").

sighs for ever in her sleep ; and that sigh is in all sighs of love for ever and ever.

Scathach watched him till he was lost behind the flare of the camp fires of the rath. For long she stood there, brooding deep, till the sickle of the new moon, which had been like a brown feather over the sun as it sank stood out in silver-shine against the blue-black sky, now like a wake in the sea because of the star-dazzle that was there. And what the Queen brooded upon was this : Whether to send emissaries to Eirèann, under bond to seek in that land till they found Mídir and Etáin, and to slay Mídir and to bring to her the corpse, for a gift from her to lay before Cuchullin ; or to bring Etáin to Skye, where the Queen might see her lose her beauty and wane into death. Neither way might win the heart of Cuchullin. The dark tarn of the woman's mind grew blacker with the shadow of that thought.

Slowly she moved dûn-ward through the night.

"As the moon sometimes is seen rising out of the east," she muttered, "and sometimes, as now, is first seen in the west, so is the heart of love. And if I go west, lo, the moon may rise along the sunway ; and if I go east, lo, the moon may be a white light over the setting sun. And who that knoweth the heart of man or woman can tell when the moon of love is to appear full-orbed in the east, or sickle-wise in the west ? "

It was on the day following that tidings came out of Eirèann. An Ultonian brought a sword to Cuchullin from Concobar the Ard-Righ.

" The sword has ill upon it, and will die unless you save it, Cuculain, son of Lerg," said the man.

" And what is that ill, Ultonian ? " asked the youth.

" It is thirst."

Then Cuchullin understood.

On the night of his going none looked at Scathach. She had a flame in her eyes.

At moonrise she came back into the rath. No one meeting her looked in her face. Death lay there, like the levin behind a cloud. But Maev, her chief captain, sought her, for she had glad news.

" I would slay you for that glad news, Maev," said the dark Queen to the warrior-woman, " for there is no glad news unless it be that Cuchullin is come again ; only ; I spare, for you saved my life that day the summer-sailors burned my rath in the south."

Nevertheless Scathach had gladness because
of the tidings. Three viking galleys had been
driven into Loch Scavaig, and been dashed to
death there by the whirling wind and the narrow, furious seas. Of the ninety men who had
sailed in them, only a score had reached the
rocks, and these were now lying bound at the
dûn, awaiting death.

"Call out my warriors," said Scathach, "and
bid all meet at the oak near the Ancient
Stones. And bring thither the twenty men
that lie bound in the dûn."

There was a scattering of fire and a clashing
of swords and spears when the word went
from Maev. Soon all were at the Stones
beneath the great oak.

"Cut the bonds from the feet of the sea-
rovers, and let them stand." Thus commanded
the Queen.

The tall, fair men out of Lochlin stood with
their hands bound behind them. In their eyes
burned wrath and shame, because that they
were the sport of women. A bitter death
theirs, with no sword-song for music. "Take
each by his long yellow hair," said Scathach,
"and tie the hair of each to a down-caught
bough of the oak."

In silence this thing was done. A shadow
was in the paleness of each viking face.

" Let the boughs go," said Scathach.

The five score warrior women who held the great boughs downward sprang back. Up swept the branches, and from each swung a living man, swaying in the wind by his long yellow hair.

Great men they were, strong warriors ; but stronger was the yellow hair of each, and stronger than the hair the bough wherefrom each swung, and stronger than the boughs the wind that swayed them idly like drooping fruit, with the stars silvering their hair and the torch-flares reddening the white soles of their dancing feet.

Then Scathach the Queen laughed loud and long. There was no other sound at all there, for none ever uttered sound when Scathach laughed that laugh, for then her madness was upon her.

But at the last, Mael strode forward and struck a small clarsach that she carried, and to the wild notes of it sang the death-song of the vikings :

O arone, a-ree, eily arone, arone!
'Tis a good thing to be sailing across the sea !
How the women smile and the children are laughing
    glad
When the galleys go out into the blue sea—arone !
    O eily arone, arone !

But the children may laugh less when the wolves
    come,
And the women may smile less in the winter-cold;
For the Summer-sailors will not come again, arone!
        O arone a-ree, eily arone, arone!

I am thinking they will not sail back again, O no!
The yellow-haired men that came sailing across the
    sea:
For 'tis wild apples they would be, and swing on green
    branches,
And sway in the wind for the corbies to preen their
    eyne,
        O eily arone, eily a-ree:

And it is pleasure for Scathach the Queen to see this
To see the good fruit that grows upon the Tree of the
    Stones.
Long, speckled fruit it is, wind-swayed by its yellow
    roots,
And like men they are with their feet dancing in the
    void air!
        O, O, arone, a-ree, eily arone!

When she ceased, all there swung swords
and spears, and flung flaring torches into the
night, and cried out:

    O arone a-ree, eily arone, arone,
    O, O, arone, a-ree, eily arone!

Scathach laughed no more. She was weary
now. Of what avail any joy of death against

the pain she had in her heart, the pain that was
called Cuchullin?

Soon all was dark in the rath. Flame after
flame died out. Then there was but one red
glare in the night, the watch-fire by the dûn.
Deep peace was upon all. Not a heifer lowed,
not a dog bayed against the moon. The wind
fell into a breath, scarce enough to lift the
fragrance from flower to flower. Upon the
branches of a great oak swung motionless a
strange fruit, limp and grey as the hemlock that
hangs from ancient pines.

AHÈZ THE PALE

The moon sent her lances through the forest
of Broceliande, among giant thickets of oak
and beech. Under their boles the fire-flies
trailed green fires. At long intervals a night-
jar intermittently churred his passionate note
to his mate, she swaying silent on a near
branch. But the cry of the night-jar, the faint
rustle of a wolf's foot among the acorn-garths,
or of a doe uneasy amid the fern, the innumerable whisper of the green leafy world—what
were these but breaths of sound upon the sea
of silence.

The nightingales had been still for a moon-
quarter or more. For three farings of sun
and moon the wind had scarcely reached
Broceliande from the sea, or had reached it
only to lapse where the fronds of the bracken
were motionless as the pines. Through the
long days sullen thunders had prevailed.
Sometimes their hollow booming came inland,
and the sea moaned among oak-glades round
whose roots no wave had ever lapped, whose
green lips had never felt the foam-salt which

in tempests whitens leagues of the mainland.
Sometimes their prolonged reverberations
came out of the south, and the void echoes of
the Black Mountain travelled the green way
of the oak summits beyond where the dunes
fringe the extreme of the forest. But north
or south, east or west, the thunders had not
lapsed for days. Ubiquitous, they were a perpetual menace : yet though lightnings flashed
continually along their livid flanks, these
scimitars and dreadful spears were not let
loose. Save by night, when the obscure dome
unveiled, there was no cessation of that hollow
minatory voice, a sullen monotone : the skiey
fires darted and flickered their adder-tongue,
but flamed no solitary oak into a sudden blaze,
blasted no homestead, charred no fugitive life.

In the profound silence of this night, a long
wailing chant ascended from the shadow of
the forest.

After the first interval, a figure stirred
stealthily amid the fern, in a glade near the
westward margin of Broceliande, and moved
swiftly to where the chant rose and fell, a thin,
solitary cadence in that remote and consecrate
region.

For in those days the forest of Broceliande
was the holy of holies of the Druids, who,
within its solitudes, maintained their most

secret rites and mysteries. Beyond the reach
of their spells, not only the wolf and the bear,
but the korrigan and the nain, the pool-sprite
and the swamp-demon, the were-wolf and the
soulless ghoul that was like a woman, made
the greenglooms a terror by day—a living
death by night.

It was no druid, however, who tracked furtively the chanting voice, for the moonlight
glistered on an iron breastplate and on a
plumed and strangely-shaped bronze helmet.
The man who thus dared secret death
made no effort to escape into the recesses of
the forest. Stealthily he drew closer to where
the priest of Teutatês sang. When, at last, he
was so near the fane, a single tall stone, that
he was within a javelin-flight of the solitary
white-robed chanter, he crouched, and waited.

The priest was a youth, and fair. As, in
his slow, circling walk he came nigh the spot
where the interloper lay amid the fern, he
stopped and stared dreamily at the moon,
which swung goldenly in the green dusk
between two lofty oaks. In his eyes there was
a light that was not lit there by Teutatês. He
smiled and drew farther into the wood, so that
he could look at the yellow globe as a fair face
set far above him.

There was silence now. The druid had

ceased his chant, had forgotten his god. But
the gods never slumber, nor do they forgive.
The youth moved a step or two forward into a
thick garth of fern. Slowly he raised his
arms.

"To thee, O Goddess, I pray!" he cried,
softly. "To thee I pray! Grant me that
which is the sweetest and surest thing in the
world!"

He stared upward, his lips parted, his eyes
shining.

"She loves me," he murmured again: "she
loves me, O Goddess! Grant me that which
is the sweetest and surest thing in the world!"

Astorêt must have heard the prayer, or did
Teutatês frown upon her and have his own
dark will? For, even as Arân the Druid
spoke, a sword sprang from the gloom and
passed through his back and into his heart
and out beyond his breast, so that he died in
that moment and soundlessly, save for the
bubbling of a red foam upon his lips.

Swiftly the slayer dragged the body a score
of yards deeper into the wood. Then, with
famished haste, he denuded the druid, and,
having taken off his own raiment and armour,
put it upon the silent one, in exchange for the
white priestly garment wherewith he had
already clothed himself.

415

Of his weapons he kept none save a long, broad-bladed dagger, which he secured to the belt beneath the robe he now wore. But first with it he slashed the face of the dead man, so that none might know him.

" Lie there," he muttered with savage irony : "lie there, Jud Mael ! At dawn the druids will come, and will find thee here, and will throw thy sacrilegious body on the altar-flame, as a peace-offering to Teutatês. For now *I* am Arân the Druid, who has departed no man knows where."

He turned at that, and passed swiftly into the forest, moving eastward.

He walked till dawn. Because of the smile in his eyes, he saw neither korrigan nor ghoul : because of the triumph in his heart he feared neither the tusk of the wild boar nor the fang of the wolf. Once, at sunrise, he laughed. That was because, from the summit of a granite scaur, he saw a dark colum of smoke rising from the Circle of Stones where he had slain Arân the Druid.

" So that is the end of Jud Mael," he muttered: "and now . . . Ahèz may grind her teeth that she has missed the killing of her own prey, though her heart will leap because of that slaying and burning there in the forest."

Again, before he left that place, he muttered; and with clenched fist thrust his arm menacingly against that vague west wherein his death slipped stealthily after him from tree to tree. By noon he was within three miles of the Altar of Teutatês, for all that he had walked a score since midnight. He had wandered in a circle, but knew it not; for he was in a dream. When he came to note the sun it was high overhead. Later, he slept. It was a sweet sleep that he had, amid a garth of bracken beset with brambles. All through his dream he heard the deep execration of Ahèz, daughter of Môrgwyn, the lord of Gwenêd: the low moaning of the dead man, Arân the Druid: and the sound of his own laughter.

He woke suddenly at the sun-down howl of a wolf. For a moment the sweat broke out upon his white face. It was not because of the howl of the wandering beast, but because his fear translated that savage sound into the cry of Ahèz. A glance at his white robe reassured him. He smiled. What was Arân now? The Druids, at the two great festivals of the year, spoke of the strange faring of the soul. It came, they said, as a flying bird: it slipped away, according as were a man's deeds, as a bird, as a wolf, as a snake, or as a toad. His skin grew cold for a moment as he thought he

might meet Arân in some such guise : would
the dead man recognise him ?

He had the instinct of the wanderer against
sleeping twice in the same place. Moreover,
hunger now began to torment him. He crept
slowly from his lair, and wandered this way
and that in search of wild fruits and palatable
herbs. Suddenly his gaze was arrested by a
glint of flame. Sinking to the ground, he
watched eagerly; fearful lest what he had seen
was the torch of a pursuer. In a brief while,
however, he discerned that the light was that
of a fire.

With tread as stealthy as that of a wolf near
a fold he stole out of the wood, and from whin
to whin till he was close upon the fire. Beside
it sat an old man. Jud Mael looked long at
the woodlander. His instinct was to kill him,
for the sake of the roasted hedgehog which the
old man was about to devour : but the risk
was too great, for even if the woodlander were
unknown to the druids his dead body might
afford a fatal clue. So, at the last, he decided
to speak.

So quietly did he draw near that he was at
the old man's side unheard.

The peasant stumbled to his feet, startled :
but when he saw the white robe of a druid he
looked reassured, and made an obeisance.

"What do you do here, in the sacred wood, you who are clad in skins?"

"I am not within the precincts, holy one. This glade is open ground. Surely you know it, who are Arân the Chanter."
Jud Mael started. A hunted look came into his wolfish eyes. He knew there was no resemblance between Arân and himself. How then did this old man take him for the druid whom he had slain.

"How know you that I am Arân the Druid, old man?"

"Am I wrong, holy one? I took you to be Arân, for I heard that he had wandered in the forest, and had been seen of no man since yester moonrise."

"Even so, I am Arân. And why are you here?"

"I was told to wait on the outskirts of the wood, and to light a great fire, so that the flame of it should be seen of the wanderer. But as darkness was not yet come, and I was weak with hunger and had slain this beast, I made a small fire that I might eat."

"I too am hungered, I have tasted no food for a night and a day."

"Eat, then, holy one."

"But you?"

"Oh, I can find roots beneath these oaks. It

419

is not fit that I should eat when Arân the Druid is weary with hunger. Eat!"

Jud Mael ate. As he devoured the white sweet meat his courage rose. By the time he had finished, the woodlander brought him some ground-berries wherewith to slake his thirst.

"Tell me, old man," Jud Mael said at last, having placed himself so that he could see any white-robe coming out of the darkness from the forest : "tell me what was said concerning me."

"Nought that I know of, save that you had wandered."

"And thou hast heard nought else to-day?"

"Surely. All who dwell by the wood have heard of the death of one who ventured into the holy precincts. He was a warrior. He died with blood. The druids burned his accursed body at sunrise. Some say that he was slain by Arân—and, as it is an evil thing for a druid to take life, that he, you, O holy one, went into the deep forest to do penance."

"Did you hear the man's name?"

"Yes. It was Jud Mael."

"How was that known?"

"There was a sword upon him that was

the sword given to the lord Jud Mael by Môrgwyn the King, because of what he did in some great battle—I know not what, nor what battle. There was a rune carved on it. Moreover, his helmet had the dragon of the Lords of Mael."

"I do not know the man. What of him?"

"It is not for me to speak."

"Speak, man. I command you."

"They say he was a fugitive."

"A fugitive? . . . from the King?"

"No."

"From whom then?"

"From the King's sister, the lady Ahèz."

"The lady Ahèz?"

"Yes: Ahèz the Pale they call her, because she is so cream-white and fair."

"Why should Jud Mael fly from her?"

"They say he did her a great wrong."

"What wrong?"

"How do I know, holy one? I can but repeat idle gossip."

"Tell me what you have heard."

"Idle tongues have it that Jud Mael promised marriage to Ahèz the Pale: but that when she bade him fulfil his vows, as she was with child to him, he laughed and said he could wed no woman, not even the King's sister, because that in his own place beyond the Black

P

Mountains he had already a wife and children."

"What else did you hear?"

"Nothing, holy one."

"Did not Ahèz the Pale speak to the King?"

"They say she did, but who knows?"

"What else do they say about that, they who say she did?"

"That King Môrgwyn let his riding-whip fall across her shoulder, and bade her begone and not enter his presence again till she rode into the castle-wynd either with Jud Mael by her side as her wedded lord or with Jud Mael's head as the price of her honour."

"Well——?"

"That is all."

"Have you not heard whither Jud Mael fled?"

"No."

"Nor if Ahèz the Pale has been seen, on that hopeless quest of hers?"

"No."

"Old man, wouldst thou earn some gold?"

"Gladly, holy one."

"Then go at dawn—nay, go at once, for now that I am found there is no need for you to wait here—and seek out the lady Ahèz. Tell her what you know concerning that which

422

happened in this forest. Tell her that you nave spoken with Arân the Druid, and that it was he who slew Jud Mael, and that he knew the man—so that she may know for a surety that he who wronged her is no longer among the living."

There was no response from the woodlander. Jud Mael leaned forward and looked closely at him. He saw that the old man's eyes were intently staring.

"What is it, old man, what do you see, that you stare like that?"

"Yonder . . . in the oak-glade yonder . . on a white horse . . . yes, yes, it is Ahèz the Pale . . ."

With a stifled cry the druid sprang to his feet.

Yes, the woodlander was right. A woman, with long yellow hair, rode on a great white war-horse. She was chanting low to herself, with her eyes turned upon the moon. She had not yet seen those who had descried her.

With the silent swiftness of a beast of prey he slid back behind a mass of gorse, then glided from whin to whin till he was under the oaks again.

The old man stood, with gaping mouth and rapt eyes, as the night-rider drew nigh.

Ah, she was fair indeed, he thought; just

like moonlight she was, fair and white and wonderful.

As the white war-horse trampled the bracken the words Ahèz chanted became audible.

But this was in the old, old, far-off days,
But this was in the old, old, far-off days.

Guenn took up his sword, and she felt its shining
blade,
And she laughed and vowed it fitted ill for the handling
of a maid.

He looked at her, and darkly smiled, and said she
was a queen:
For she could swing the white sword high and love
its dazzling sheen.

They rode beneath the ancient boughs, and as they
rode she sang,
But at the last both silent were: only the horse-hoofs
rang.

She lifted up the great white sword and swung it
'neath his head—
"Ah, you may smile, my lord, now you may smile,"
she said.

For this was in the old, old, far-off days,
For this was in the old, old, far-off days.

Suddenly Ahèz reined in the great white stallion she rode. She had caught sight of the woodlander. At that moment she saw a white-robed figure glide into the darkness of the forest.

"Tell me, forester," she asked—and the old woodlander wondered in his heart whether the beauty of her face excelled that of her voice—"tell me if the lord Jud Mael passed this way?"

"The lord Jud Mael is dead, great lady. He was slain overnight. Only this moment there was one with me here who slew him— yea, and knew him to be Jud Mael."

"And what will the name of that man be, and where may I find him?"

"He is called Arân the Chanter. He is a druid. He may be found at the Sacred Castle. But this moment he went yonder, to the eastward."

"Then I will seek Arân the Chanter," she said : and, so saying, Ahèz the Pale rode onward in the moonlight.

It was only then that the woodlander noticed she carried a white babe in the fold of her left arm. He knelt, and prayed to his gods.

Once more, as she rode, she caught sight of a white-robed figure flitting rapidly before her.

"Ah, Arân the Chanter," she murmured, " I would fain have word of you ! "

At the first mile she passed the Well of Death—a deep fount in the forest where the nains were wont to meet. And as she rode she heard the nains chanting.

She had the old ancient wisdom. She knew the wood-speech. And the song the nains sang was of blood, and of the red footsteps in the wood.

And when Ahèz passed the Well a nain appeared. She was like a woman, but was all of green flame. She sang:

And this was in the old, old, far-off days,
And this was in the old, old, far-off days,

Whereat Ahèz the fearless chanted back:

O Nain, what was in the old, old, far-off days?

And the nain laughed, and sang:

O Blind One, who followest a dead man that is alive?

And having chanted this she vanished. But Ahèz knew what the nain meant, and the blood-flame rose in her.

So, she followed a dead man who was alive! Who could this be but Jud Mael. Ah, the white-robed druid!

She took a long dagger from her girdle, and

426

pricked the flank of the white stallion till the
blood trickled red.

As the steed sprang onward through the
moonshine, the nains chanted. She heard their
wild mocking laughter, and wondered if to
Arân, the flying druid, that was Jud Mael, the
fugitive from death, their voices rang with wild
terror.

Once, from an oak-glade, she saw him look
back over his shoulder.

The eyes of the gods were in the Wood of
Broceliande that night. Whether Jud Mael
turned to the right or to the left, or fled onward
with stumbling feet, seeking for dark places
and briery thickets and the conduits of damp
caverns, the moonbeams tracked him like
hounds.

While still afar off, Ahèz the Pale saw this
thing, and she smiled.

Once he stopped for a few panting moments
He heard her chanting :

For this was in the old, old, far-off days,
For this was in the old, old, far-off days.

Then, blind with fear, he stumbled on.

For a brief while thereafter he had hope.
The sound of the following hoofs grew fainter.
Thrice, on furtively looking back, he could

discern no white rider, no white horse. Once, in a rearward glade, he saw two leverets playing in the moonshine. He drew a long breath. It was well, he thought; for he had now a wide glade to cross, a vast glade horribly white with the moonflood, with but a single isle of refuge midway, a solitary lightning-blasted oak.

Jud Mael hesitated to traverse this terrifying void, yet dared not skirt it lest the woman on the white horse should cut him off. At last he fell on his hands and knees, and slowly crawled through the dewy fern.

He had gone half-way, when suddenly his heart leaped against his throat.

A great white stallion was trampling down the bracken at the edge of the glade. A woman, with long moonlit hair, rode it; and as she rode in silence he heard the crying of a child.

With gasping haste he crawled close to the oak. There, among its cavernous roots, he hoped to escape unseen.

Ahèz the Pale rode straight for the solitary tree. When the great stallion trampled among the far-spreading roots, she drew rein.

"Come forth, Jud Mael," she cried.

Jud Mael shivered. At last the man within

him wrestled with the coward, and he rose to his feet, and stepped out into the moonlight.

"Art thou Arân the Druid, O thou who wearest a white robe, or art thou Jud Mael?"

"I am Jud Mael, O Ahèz, whom I have loved."

"And it was thou who slew the priest?"

"He came to his death."

"As thou to thine. But first, lest I slay thee where thou standest, take this child that is your child. He is no child of mine, though I bore him. I am of the royal line, that never bore a coward, and what could this child be but a coward and a traitor? The boy must die."

"I cannot slay the little one, Ahèz."

"I have not tracked thee down to bandy words. Take thou the child."

Slowly Jud Mael advanced. On his white face the sweat glittered like dew.

He put out his arms, and enfolded the child. Then, with steadfast eyes, he looked up at Ahèz.

"She stared at him unflinchingly, but made no sigh.

"Ahez!"

"Hast thou not heard me, dog?"

Jud Mael flushed a deep red.

"Beware, woman! After all, it is but a

woman you are, and you are alone here, and
I can slay you as easily as I could a fawn of
the forest."

"Thou liest."

The man looked at her defiantly; then,
sullenly, his eyes fell.

"What wouldst thou, Ahèz?"

"Slay this child."

With a sudden savage gesture the man took
the broad knife from the belt that was below
his white robe. He hesitated a moment, then
abruptly plunged the iron blade into the child's
breast. There was a long gasping sound, a
clinching of little fingers, a spasmodic twitching
of little hands and feet. A thin jet of blood
spurted up in the face of Jud Mael. He stood,
shaking, trembling like a leaf.

"Why hast thou made me do this thing,
Ahèz?"

"Thou wert a liar, and betrayed me. Thinkest
thou I shall bear the seed of a traitor?"

"But to what end?"

"To what end? . . . That thy soul may
pass into some evil thing, and die and utterly
perish. For now thou hast slain thine own
blood. Bring me the child. Alive, it was
thine; slain, it is mine."

Jud Mael slowly drew near. He lifted the
inert small body. Ahèz leaned sideways as

430

though to take it in her arms. As she gripped
the child with her left hand, she raised her
right arm. The next moment a dagger flashed
in the moonlight, and with a scraping, gurgling
sound, sank in between the shoulders of Jud
Mael.

The man staggered, reeled, and would have
fallen but for the heaving flank of the stallion.

Ahèz leaned back, and with a wrench pulled
away the dagger. Then before the stricken
man would recover she thrust the blade into
his neck.

Jud Mael gave a hoarse cry. As he fell, he
slashed at the thigh of Ahèz, but the weapon
missed and made a deep cut in the belly of the
stallion. Snorting and rearing, the great beast
swung round and trampled upon the fallen
man, neighing savagely the while.

When he lay quite still, Ahèz dismounted.
She took the body of the child and piled loose
stones above it, to keep it sacred against wild
beasts and birds of prey.

Thereafter, with Jud's knife, she severed the
man's head, and by its long black hair slung it
to the tangled mane of the stallion.

Then she mounted, and rode slowly back by
the way she had come.

431

THE KING OF YS AND
DAHUT THE RED

The King of Ys and Dahut the Red

(Proem)

In the days when Gradlon was Conan of Arvor, or High-King of the Armorican races who peopled Brittany, there was no name greater than his. From the sand-dunes of the Jutes and Angles to where the dark-skinned Basque fishermen caught fish with nets, the name of Gradlon was a sound for silence. Arvor was become so great a land that Franks were called wolves there, and like wolves were hunted down. The wild cry that survives to this day in the forests of Dualt and Huelgoet, in the granite heart of Cornovailles, *A'hr bleiz! A'hr bleiz!* was heard often then : but no wolf ever so dreaded the cry as the haggard Frankish fugitives.

Gradlon, Conan of Arvor, was in the midway of life when for once he staunched the thirst of his sword. This was when he went over into the lands of the Kymry, the elder

435

brothers of his Armorican race, and there fought with them against Saxon hordes, till the red tide ebbed. Thereafter he had gone far northward till the Oeban Gaels hated the singing of Breton shafts, and till the mountain-tribes of the Picts paid tribute. Thence, at last, he returned. When he came to his own land, he brought with him two treasures which he held chief among all treasures he had won : a black stallion, and a woman, white as cream, with eyes like blue lochs and with long great masses of hair red as the bronze red berry of the wild ash. The name of the horse was Morvark : the name of the woman, Malgven. When men spoke of the Tameless One they meant Morvark : and after a time they seldom said Malgven, but "the Queen," because Gradlon made her the Terror of Arvor, or "the White Queen," because of her foam white beauty, or the "Red Queen," because of her masses of ruddy hair, which, when unfastened, was as a stream of blood falling over a white cliff.

None knew whence Morvark came, nor whence Malgven. What passed from lip to lip was this : that the great, black, tameless stallion was foaled of no earthly mare, but of some strange and terrible sea-beast. It had come out of the North, on a day of tempest.

Amid the screaming of the gale in the haven where Gradlon and the men of Arvor were, a more wild, a more savage screaming had been heard. Gradlon went forth alone, and at dawn he was seen riding on a huge black stallion, which neighed with a cry like the cry of the sea-wind, and whose hoofs trampled the wet sands with a sound like the clashing of waves. The hair of Gradlon was streaming out on the wind like yellow seaweed on a rushing ebb; his laughter was like the hallala leaping of billows: his eyes were wild as falling stars.

It was when far in the Alban northlands that the Breton king and Malgven were first seen together. She was not a conquest of the sword. The rumour by the fires had it that she was the queen of a great prince among the Gaels; that she was wife to the King of the Picts: that she was of the fair, perilous people of Lochlin, who were even then seizing for their own the Alban isles and western lands. But one saying was common with all: that she was a woman of dark powers. One and all dreaded her sorceries. Gradlon laughed at these, when she was not by, but swore that there had never been since the first woman so great a sorceress over the heart of man.

For many months they were together in

Alba, nor did once Malgven sigh for the place
or the man she had left, nor did ever any
herald come to Gradlon calling upon him to
give up the woman. When she had learned
the Armorican tongue she spoke to some of the
Breton chiefs, but she had eyes for one man
only. She loved Gradlon as he loved her.
When they asked her concerning her people,
she looked at them till they were troubled :
then she answered, I was born of the Wind
and the Sea : and, troubled more, they asked
no further.

It was when they were upon the sea, off the
Cymric coasts, that the child of Malgven was
born.

For three days before that birthing, strange
voices were heard rising from the depths. In
the hollow of following waves the long-dead
were seen. In the moonshine the flying foam
was woven into white robes, wherefrom shining
eyes, calm and august, or filled with communicating terror, looked upon the trembling
seamen.

On the third day white calms prevailed. At
sundown the web of dusk was woven out of
the sea, till it rose in purple darkness and hung
from the Silver Apples, the Great Galley, the
Hounds, the Star of the North, and the Evening
Star. At the rising of the moon, a sudden

froth ran along the black lips of the sea. A
Voice moaned beneath the travelling feet of
the waves, and trembled against the stars. Men,
staring into the moving gulfs beneath them,
beheld vast irresolute hands, as of a Swimmer
who carried Ocean upon his unfathomable
brows; others, staring upward into the dust of
the Milky Way, discerned eyebrows terrible
as comets, and beneath them pale orbs as of
forgotten moons, with long wind-uplifted hair
blowing from old worlds idly swinging in the
abyss, far back into the starless inlands of the
Silent King.

And as that Breath arose, the knees of the
seafarers were as reeds in a shaken water.
An old druid of the Gaels whispered *Mananann! O Mananann!*

Gradlon the king lay upon the fells of she-
wolves, and bit his lips, and muttered that if
a man spoke he would take his heart from
him and throw it to the filmy beasts of the
sea.

It was then that Malgven's labour was
done. Her belly opened, and a woman-child
came forth, and at the first cry of the child
the Voice that was a Breath ceased. And when
there was no more any moaning of the un-
numbered, cries and laughters came from the
deeps; and like a flash of wings meteors fled

439

by ; and beyond the unsteady masts were sudden
green and blue flames, plumes worn by demons
whose meeting pinions were made of shadow,
and beyond these the dancing of the little
stars. And by these portents Cradlon was
troubled. But Malgven smiled and said :
" Let the girl be called Dahut, Wonder, for
truly her beauty shall be the wonder of all who
come after us. She is but a little foam-white
human child : but the sea is in her veins, and
her eyes are two fallen stars. Her voice will
be the mysterious voice of the sea : her eyes
will be the mysterious light within the sea :
therefore let her be called Dahut. She shall
be the little torch at the end, for me, Malgven :
she shall be the Star of Death for the multitude whom she will slay with love : she shall
be the doom of thee and thine and thy people
and the kingdom that is thine, O Gradlon,
Conan of Arvor : therefore let her be called
Dahut, Wonder ; Dahut, the sweet evil singing
of the sea ; Dahut, Blind Love ; Dahut, the
Laugher ; Dahut, Death. Yea, let her be
called Dahut, O Gradlon, she to whom I have
given more than other women give to those
whom they bear : for I am of those children
of Danù of whom you have heard strange
tales, of those Tuath-De-Danann whose lances
made of moonshine can pierce granite walls

and whose wisdom is more old than the ancient forgotten cromlechs in your land and in mine, and whose pleasure it is to dwell where are the palaces of the Sidhe, that are wherever green hills grow dim and pale and blue as the smoke above woods.

Thus was it that the sea-born child of Gradlon of Arvor and Malgven the Dannite was called Dahut.

When the Armoricans returned to their own land, the brother of Gradlon, whom he had made Tarist or vice-Regent welcomed Gradlon for their father, the old King of Cornouailles still lived, though blind from the Gaulish arrow which had crossed his face slantwise in a great battle on the banks of the Loire. It was not till the seventh year thereafter that Gradlon again fared far. For three years he was among the Kymry, the Alban Gaels, the Picts, the Islesmen, the Gaels, of Erie, the Gaels of Enona : then when he was in that land which is now called Anglesey, a deep craving and weariness came upon him to see Malgven again, though less than a year back had she gone from him, to rule in Arvor in his place, for Arz his brother had been slain in a Frankish foray.

Her beauty was so great that he wore the days in sorrow because of it. When he arose

at dawn it flashed against his eyes out of the
rising sun : when he looked at the sea, it
moved from wave to wave, and beckoned to
him : when he stared at the cloud-shadowed
hills he saw it lying there adream : when he
fared forth at the rising of the moon it took
him subtly, now with a birch branch that
caught his hair as often it had tangled with
Malgven's long curling locks, now with the
brushing of tall fern that was a sound like the
rustling of her white robe, now because of
two stars shining low above dewy grass,
which were as her shining eyes.

There was no woman in the world so beautiful, he knew : and yet both men and women
prophesied that Dahut would be more beautiful still—Dahut the Red as the girl was already
called because of her ruddy bronze-hued hair,
wonderful in mass and colour as was that
of her mother : more wonderful far, said
Malgven, smiling proudly, who knew Dahut
to be of the Tuath-De-Danann even as her
mother was, and that she would be a torch
to light many flames and mayhap fires vast
and incalculable.

So one day Gradlon arose and said " For
Dahut," and broke his sword : and said " For
Arvor," and broke his spear : and said, " For
Malgven," and bade every prisoner be set

442

free, and the ships be filled with treasure and provision.

When he saw the black rocky coasts of Finistère once more he swore a vow that he would never again leave his land, or Malgven.

Everywhere as he journeyed to Kempêr he heard the rumour of the Red Queen's greatness, of her terrible beauty, of Dahut the Beautiful, Dahut the perilous, Dahut the Sorceress. And he laughed to think that the girl of ten summers was already so like the woman who bore her : and his heart yearned for both, as his ears longed to be void of the ceaseless moan of the sea. His first joy was when he rode through the forest of Huelgoet and heard no sound but the croodlin of wild doves and the soft, sleepy purring of the south wind lapping the green leaves. When he reached the great town, as Kempêr was then called, he saw black banners falling from the low walls of the Fort. He rode onward alone, and found Malgven lying on a high couch with her golden diadem on her head, and her long hair clasped with golden rings, and her snow white arms alongside her breastplate of curiously carven mail, which she wore above a white robe. Beside her sat the old blind King.

From that day Gradlon never smiled. For five years from that day he strove against the

bitter hours and in all unkingly ways, but
without avail. He could not forget the beauty
of Malgven. For one year he strove furiously
in war. For a second year he hunted wild
beasts, from forest to forest, from the domains
of the north to the domains of the south and
from the domains of the east to the domains
west. For the third year he loved women by
day, and cursed them through sleepless remembering nights. For the fourth year he drank
deep. For the fifth year the evil of his life
was so great that men murmured against him:
and many muttered "Better the old blind
King, Arz-Dall, or the young sorceress Dahut
herself."

During all these years Gradlon had no sight
of Dahut. Because that she was her mother's
self, and because that her beauty was so like
yet greater than that of Malgven, the King
had sent her to Razmôr, his great fort in the
north, where are the wildest seas and the
wildest shores of Armorica. And in all these
years Gradlon had but one joy, and that was
when he mounted the great black stallion,
Morvark, and rode for hours, and for leagues
upon leagues, by the falling surf of the seas. For
when he rode the great horse, the sea-beast as
the Armoricans called it in their dread, he
dreamed he heard voices he heard at no other

time, and often, often, the long cry of Malgven
that he had first listened to with shuddering
awe among the Gaelic hills.

It was at the end of the fifth year that he
came suddenly upon Dahut, when he was
riding on Morvark by the wild coast of Razmôr.
When his gaze drank in her great beauty, he
reined in his furious stallion, and his heart
beat, for it was surely Malgven come again, in
immortal Dannite youth. Then, remembering
that Morvark would let no mortal mount
him, save only Gradlon and Malgven that was
gone, he flung himself to the ground, and lay
there as though dead—whereat with a loud
neighing, terrible as the storm blast, Morvark
raced with streaming mane toward Dahut.
And when he was come to her, the girl laughed
and held out her arms, and the black stallion
whinnied with red nostrils against her cream-
white breasts, and his great eyes were like
dark billows that have sunken rocks beneath
them, and when he bent low his head and
Dahut's ruddy hair streamed over her white
shoulders, like blood falling over a white cliff,
it was as though beneath this sunlit white
cliff brooded the terror and mystery of noc-
turnal seas. Then Dahut mounted Morvark,
and rode back toward the King her father.
As she rode, the moan of Ocean broke across

the sands. Waves lifted themselves out of windless calms, and made a hollow noise as of travelling thunders. On the unfurrowed flowing plains, billows, like vast cattle with shaggy manes, rose and coursed hither and thither, with long, low, deliberate roar upon roar. Among the rocks and caverns a myriad wave relinquished clinging hands, only to spring forward again and seize the dripping rocks and swirl far in and long watery fingers so swift and fluent yet with salt grip terrible and sure.

Gradlon looked at Dahut, and at the snorting stallion Morvark, and at the suddenly awakened and uplifted sea.

"*Avel, avelon, holl avel!*" he cried: "wind, wind, all is but wind! vain as the wind, void as the wind!"

For he had seen that the woman, whose beauty was so great that his heart beat for fear of its strangeness, was no other than Dahut his daughter: and by that passing loveliness and that terrible beauty, and by the bending to her of the Tameless Morvark, and by the portents of the Sea which loved her, he knew that this was the daughter of Malgven, who was of the ancient and deathless children of Danù.

When Gradlon rode back to Kempêr with

446

Dahut before him upon Morvark, all who saw them fell on their knees. So great was the beauty of Dahut, and so strange was already the public rumour of the Sorceress, of this Daughter of the Sea. Her skin was white as new milk, as the breasts of doves : her hair was long and thick and wonderful, and of the hue of rowan berries in sunlight, of bronze in fire-light, of newly spilled blood trickling down a white cliff : her eyes were changeful as the sea, and, as the sea, were filled with unfathomable desires, and with shining light full of terror and beauty.

But because Dahut could not live far from the wild seas she loved, she bade Gradlon make a new great town, and to build it by Razmôr, where the square-walled castle was, on the wave-swept promontory.

And thus was the town of Ys built by Gradlon, Conan of Arvor, for the mystery and the delight and the wonder and the terror that was called Dahut the Red.

BIBLIOGRAPHICAL NOTE

By Mrs. William Sharp

The publication of *Pharais* (1894) and *The Mountain Lovers* (1895) by William Sharp, under the pseudonym of "Fiona Macleod," was followed by that of two volumes of Tales: *The Sin-Eater and Other Tales* in 1895, and *The Washer of the Ford and Other Legendary Moralities* in 1896, published by P. Geddes and Colleagues, to which firm William Sharp was literary adviser. In 1897 the contents of the two books were rearranged and published in a three-volumed paper-covered edition entitled *Barbaric Tales*, *Dramatic Tales*, *Spiritual Romances*, and to each volume a new tale was added. In 1900 the five volumes were reissued by Mr. David Nutt.

In America *The Washer of the Ford* and *The Sin-Eater* were brought out by Messrs. Stone & Kimball (Chicago) in 1895 and 1896; and in 1906 were reissued by Messrs. Duffield & Co.

For the purposes of the present edition various alterations have been made in the arrangement of the two original volumes; inasmuch as the major portion of their contents now form one volume. From *The Sin-Eater* the tales concerning the Achana Brothers are grouped together, with others of the same series under the sub-title of "Under the Dark Star," in *The Dominion of Dreams* (Vol. III), whereto "The Birdeen" has been transferred, and also "The Daughter of the

448

Sun" in an altered form and entitled " A Memory."
" Tragic Landscapes " now forms part of Volume VI.

The alterations in the contents of *The Washer of the
Ford* are as follows: " Ula and Urla " is now included
in *The Sin-Eater* section of this volume, because that
tale is the sequel to " The Silk o' the Kine " and was
written subsequently to the publication of *The Sin-
Eater*. Two tales from " The Shadow-Seers " will be
found in Vol. III, and two in Vol. IV. " The Woman
with the Net" and " The Sad Queen " have been
added to *The Washer of the Ford* section from *The
Dominion of Dreams*, and " Ahèz the Pale" from
Barbaric Tales. " Dahut the Red," written in 1905, is
herein reprinted from *The Pall-Mall Magazine*, where
it appeared posthumously in 1906.

The slight revision of the text, and the substitution
of the English titles of " St. Bride of the Isles " for
" Muime Chriosd," and " Cathal of the Woods " for
" The Annir Choille," are in accordance with instruc-
tions left by the author.